STOP HOUSE BLUES

MAGGIE HEMINGWAY

HAMISH HAMILTON · LONDON

HAMISH HAMILTON LTD

Penguin Books Ltd, 27 Wrights Lane, London W8 5TZ (Publishing & Editorial)
and Harmondsworth, Middlesex, England (Distribution & Warehouse)
Viking Penguin Inc., 40 West 23rd Street, New York, New York 10010, U.S.A.
Penguin Books Australia Ltd, Ringwood, Victoria, Australia
Penguin Books Canada Limited, 2801 John Street, Markham, Ontario, Canada L3R 1B4
Penguin Books (N.Z.) Ltd, 182–190 Wairau Road, Auckland 10, New Zealand

First published in Great Britain 1988 by
Hamish Hamilton

British Library Cataloguing-in-Publication Data:

Hemingway, Maggie
Stop house blues.
I. Title
823'.914[F]   PR6058.E491

ISBN 0-241-12266-X

Typeset in 11/13pt Plantin by Butler & Tanner Ltd
Printed & bound in Great Britain by
Butler & Tanner Ltd, Frome and London

121171

I

Journeying south that summer, the train seemed to travel through an infinity of wheat. The whole of that part of the country appeared to be one vast wheatfield, an endless rustling plain of bleached corn merging into the pale heat of the sky. There was not a hill, not a village, nothing to break the monotony as the traveller stared out of the carriage window. He closed his eyes against the glare, and dozed. Some time later, a break in the rhythm of the train woke him. He peered out of the window. It felt as if they were slowing down, but there was no station in sight, just the dull, empty plains and the tail of the train curving away behind him. He lay back again, but as he did so the train, gathering speed once more, lurched forward and he was jerked from his seat and thrown against the window, catapulted as it were into a line of straggling trees, a meadow with a gaunt, grey house in it, a little wood – and then the train rushed him past and all he could see by craning his neck against the carriage window was a smudge of birch trees like smoke against the horizon.

However, the singularity of the place had struck him and as he settled himself back in his seat he saw it all again quite clearly in his mind's eye. Saw it and yet had an indefinable feeling of not seeing, of what he saw not being quite what it was. At first glimpse it had seemed like some country estate set in its park, surrounded by rich farmland. But the park had been just a patchy field of dried grass, with a cottage sunk low into the ground at one side, as if to find shade. And the wall around the house had been unnaturally high, with massive double doors set into an arch. The house itself, seeming to lean against the buzzing eddies of midday air, had jarred too upon his eye: the strange, barred windows set in tiny, sightless rows very close together, the feeling of slight malevolence that seemed to hang over everything. It was not derelict; yet it felt abandoned, cut off from the rest of humanity. The most remarkable thing, however, had been a small orchard just below the wall. Set in grass so green it had glowed for an instant like a jewel in that dried-out place, as though it was watered by some spring of its own to the exclusion of all around it.

'Who picks the fruit?' mused the traveller, understanding, finally, the nature of the place.

The child could have told him that no one picked the fruit. There had been no apples on those trees for as long as he could remember. He stood between the silver birches in the plantation, where the sunshine fell in shafts onto the pale turf, and watched the shadow of the train flicker across the boles of the trees. The violent crashing of light and shade and tree trunks and empty space making the train seem as though it was jumping the tracks, jack-knifing across the railway embankment. Carriage followed carriage with a violence and a speed that became unbearable. He shut his eyes. When he opened them again the train had gone. There was just the singing of the rails away to the right, then only the trembling of the ground and then, into the silence, the sounds of the wood reasserting themselves. It was a test he set himself: to stare at the train without flinching till the last carriage had hurtled past. But he couldn't do it. Not here, among the trees. Out in the meadow it was different. Out there the train stuck

2

firmly to its rails, little square boxes with windows joined firmly to one another. Sometimes he saw figures silhouetted in the carriages. That they were human he took for granted, but that they were real people, like himself or Joseph, he doubted absolutely. No one he knew had ever been on a train. How could they? The train never stopped. It seemed to him that the people who had once got on it were like the Wild West figures in the comic paper he had found one day stuffed behind the stove at Joseph's. Every time he pulled the comic out there they were, still riding their train for him. Trapped by the artist, dangling from a carriage window with an arrow through the heart, or running along the train roof. He would read that story over and over again, huddled in the corner near the stove, right to where the last page would have been, for the first and last pages had long ago been torn off to kindle the fire. Their loss meant little, for to him they had never been. He was content for the story to have neither beginning nor end, but to exist in a perpetual motion of winning and losing. It began where he picked it up and it ended when he put it down.

In the same way the trembling of the ground around midday gave him a subconscious sense of calm and propriety. He knew that if he looked over to the east he would see a black dot become a line, then a curve, telescope into a large dot and then burst into a shrieking, jolting mass of steel. The train had come so it was midday: it was midday, therefore the train had come. But when, in a wild rush, it was gone and the space where it had been was empty and the long wheatfields still stretched on and on behind the railway tracks unmoved, unaltered, the child felt, despite, or perhaps because of, this reconfirmation of his life, a sudden sadness. A sudden longing for all the unknown things that the passage of the train across the smallness of his life conveyed. Where it came from or where it went to were beyond his speculation. Its purpose in life was to tell

3

him that it was lunch-time. He stood for a moment longer in the wood, looking through the sunlit trees, listening in his head to the singing of the rails and then turned, beating away the silence with his stick.

He began to walk towards the small, grey house on the far side of the meadow, prodding at the turf. That was how blind men walked, jabbing at the path in front of them with a white stick to make sure there was nothing to crash into. He hunched his shoulders, bent his back like a little old man and closed his eyes. As he closed them an image of something moving over by the prison wall flashed onto his retina. It floated there behind the redness of his closed eyelids and he wondered if it was real or not. You weren't supposed to open your eyes again once you'd started being blind. He stood in ticklish indecision. He'd seen it before, just fractionally before he'd closed his eyes, so technically it didn't count. If he hadn't closed his eyes in that split-second it wouldn't have counted at all. Very slightly he lifted his eyelids, so that first a little of the field showed under them, then more, then he could see the far corner of the high wall. Then he saw them. They were standing together at the angle of the wall. They were even the colour of the wall, their tunics grey like the mortar that crumbled between the bricks, their grey heads shaven close to the stoniness of their skulls. One man had his back to the child: a huge, granite back from which his arms hung in an arc of awkward inaction, as though he taunted provocation. The other man could be seen clearly in profile: a sharp, flint-chiselled face, an overhang of brow, a thin nose. He nodded his head quickly all the time in answer to the other's words so that the sun seemed to flicker strangely over the flinty planes of his face. His power was different. It was a relentless, sharp energy. Suddenly the big man turned and the child pressed himself flat against the nearest tree, afraid that he would be seen. His father had forbidden him to go to Joseph's. If he saw

4

him among the trees he would guess where he had been. But his father didn't even look in his direction. He put his hand briefly on the other man's shoulder and then moved off towards the squat house at the edge of the meadow. He walked with slow sureness, one foot following the other in wide, ambling, parallel lines. The child, in his imagination, could hear the gravel ricochet up from his crushing boots. The other man stood for a moment, watching his colleague, beating a truncheon quickly and softly against the palm of his hand, then he, too, turned away, and disappeared into the shadow of the wall. The child slipped quickly down the length of the wood, in and out of the light and shade as invisible as a roe deer. He reached the fence in front of the railway embankment and went along it, skirting the brambles and elder bushes till he was opposite his house. From there he emerged into the field, walking slowly, hands in pockets, eyes everywhere but on the one, narrow window of the house, looking for something innocuous to hold his attention till he reached the back door. As he passed the wooden privy, he heard the chain go, ran for the back door and, hearing the bolt of the privy door grate on the rough wood, flung himself into the kitchen.

His mother stared mournfully at him across the steam. 'Wash your hands.'

It was damp in the kitchen, hot and humid. He turned on the tap. The jet of clear water that twisted out into the sink seemed so lively that for an instant he almost thought it must be dry. He held his fingers under it. It was wet after all. Cool and wet.

'Soap,' said the limp voice.

He eyed the cake of soap dissolving in a puddle of water on a corner of the porcelain sink. It was green, streaked with white, bits of grit seemed to be buried deep inside it and it smelt strongly of something funny. It was issued by the government. He didn't like using it; he never did unless

5

he was being watched. He didn't like the smell. He could smell it for hours afterwards; he could wake up in the middle of the night and still smell it all over his face. The back door opened and his father came into the kitchen. The child picked up the soap and began to rub it vigorously between his hands.

They sat on three sides of the small kitchen table, facing each other and the steamy wall. His mother ladled eel stew onto their plates from the saucepan. He had forgotten it was Friday. He gazed at the lumps of fish and the clear water round them in which one or two pieces of onion floated.

'Where you been?' asked his father, picking up his fork.

'Watching the train.'

'Oh, the train,' his father grunted, 'the midday express.' He smashed the eel into the water with his fork.

'What's an express?' asked the child, knowing the answer.

His father leaned over the table towards him, under the table his finger and thumb snapped hard against the boy's bare thigh. The child gasped.

'Mind your own business,' his father snapped and began stuffing eel into his mouth. He didn't hold with lengthy conversations at meal-times, none of this question and answer routine and how's-your-father. No one talked at meal-times at work. That was how he liked it. Quiet. Getting on with it. Just the slapping and scraping business of eating. A fragment of eel fell out of his mouth and he scooped it up quickly with his fork and shoved it back in line behind his teeth. In the silence, the child's mother leaned towards him.

'It never stops,' she said in the unconvinced voice with which she answered all his questions.

He poked about with his fork on his plate and watched the filaments of fish break off and float in the clear juice.

'Why i'nt there no bread?' he heard his father say. His

6

voice reminded the child of the pain on his thigh. He put a piece of eel in his mouth and sucked at it cautiously. Once you got over the thought of what it was, it was all right. Joseph said there were eels in the long ditch and that sometimes he caught one and had it for his supper. He stared suspiciously down at the fish on his plate and then at his mother: had she got this eel out of the ditch? He looked round the table, chewing slowly. His mother put a piece of bread on his plate and sat down again, scraping her chair slowly over the floor. His father was intent on mopping up the eel water with his bread: dunking the bread with one hand, turning his plate with the other.

'I'm going to go and see Joseph this afternoon,' the child said in his mind to the heavy, bullet-shaped head bent over its plate.

'Did you hear?' he shrieked soundlessly at the head. 'Did you hear? I don't care what you say. I'm going to see Joseph this afternoon – when you've gone.'

The head looked up. The eyes in the head looked down at the child's plate and then up to his face. The head gave a meaningful jerk. It meant: eat. The child thought of his father's fingers jerking against his leg. He didn't need telling twice. He put a piece of fish quickly in his mouth. He chewed it. It didn't seem to get any smaller. He went on chewing it. It seemed to take a long time during which no one said anything. He thought it might be politic to put another piece of fish in his mouth. His mouth was now so full it was difficult to move it at all. He thought of swallowing it whole and letting his stomach take care of it, but he couldn't bring himself to do that.

His father leaned back and belched loudly, then pushed his chair away from the table and got up, swaying slightly. He grunted at his wife and ambled through the doorway into the next room, swinging the door half-shut behind him. His mother slid out of her chair and he heard dishes being piled in the sink. Suddenly, the fish in his mouth

7

dissolved and he found he could swallow again, it went down his throat in a big, soft lump – he could feel it all the way down. He rested his fork on his plate. Behind him his mother put a kettle of water to boil on the stove. He looked at the half-closed door. It was always the same. After lunch his father went through into the other room. The child wasn't allowed to go in there; he was dozing and wasn't to be disturbed. And, while he slept, his wife washed the dishes. The child swivelled round in his chair to watch his mother, from time to time putting little fork-fuls of food in his mouth and from time to time leaning the weight of his arm on the upright fork, like a man in a café watching the world go by. He heard the bubbles begin to roll cavernously in the big iron kettle as the water became hotter. His mother began to rinse the dishes under the single cold water tap over the sink, one by one; through his eyes, half-closed against the sunlight, they seemed to be an endless swirl of blue and green and splashing water. Dancing plates to the drumbeats of almost boiling water bubbles. Dancing bowls and pans that piled themselves up neatly on the draining board till the sink was empty. Then the plug was put in, the awful green soap placed at the bottom of the sink and the hot water from the kettle poured over it, but not all the water; a magic, unquan-tifiable amount was always left. He would chew impatiently through the time it took her to wash the dishes, until, at last, she would turn from the sink and hold out one red, wet, hand towards him saying:

'Where's your plate?'

And he would look down and find that, just the second before, he had eaten the very last mouthful of food. He would get up, carry the plate over to her and watch her tip it into the sink, seeing it slide through the water as a turtle might, shuddering to rest on the porcelain bed of the sea.

He hung at his mother's elbow while she dried her hands

8

and turned up the gas under the kettle again. He watched her reach down the jar of best coffee and the filter and take a cup and saucer out of the cupboard. There was only ever one cup. She never offered coffee to the child, or made a cup for herself. She fitted the filter over the cup and shook coffee into it; the grains came to the same height in the filter every day. She took the boiling water from the stove and poured it over the coffee, tilting the kettle so that every last drop ran out. The child could hear the hollow stream of liquid running into the cup and imagined the level rising slowly inside the dark, coffee-coloured cavern. As the last drop of water sank through the filter – so that for a second there was only steam rising and from it and the bitter, wonderful smell of new, wet coffee – his mother whisked off the filter cone and the child, watching intently, saw a gleam of delight momentarily lift the corners of her eyes. She held herself like a magician and her eyes pronounced the magic word: Abracadabra. They both looked at the coffee cup, once empty, now perfectly brimming with a hot, dark liquid; one drop more and it would have spilled over the top, but it was always exact, gauged to the very last drop from the kettle. Then his mother's eyes fell into their usual blank melancholy, she picked up the cup and began to move towards the room where his father slept.

'Mind away,' she said, out of habit.

But the child had already flattened himself back against the sink, lest he should jog her arm. She disappeared through the doorway and the kitchen seemed empty and silent without her. The child slipped outside.

His father stood at the living room window holding his coffee cup in one hand and the saucer in the other, watching his son play marbles in the dirt outside.

'What's he doing playing out there? Hasn't he got any lessons to do? Rolling them marbles around.'

'He's done his lessons. Did them this morning. He

started this morning, directly you left.'

There was a pause while she readjusted the distance between the china figurines and the clock on the mantelpiece. She stared balefully at the figure of a baby leading a huge dog.

'I can't help him no more. He's past me. He's just about through all his books and they don't do no others.'

Her husband took another bite at his coffee, straining it through his teeth and gobbling it round inside his mouth before swallowing it.

'They coming this Sunday or next?'

'Next.'

'She won't say "no", not my sister.'

'You think that's best?'

His wife untwisted her hands to take the cup and saucer he held out in mid-air as he passed.

'I'm off.'

She stood in the small, square room, motionless, holding the cup, staring at the official green walls and the cheap, hard chairs. She heard her husband stride through the kitchen and out through the back door. She heard the privy door slam.

Her son heard him, too. He knelt in the dust at the side of the house, leaning his back against the wall. It was so hot out there he could feel the blood inside his head throb. He rolled one of the marbles in his fingers, waiting, eyes half-closed in the silence and brightness till he was sure of being undisturbed. No one ever came round this side of the house. Only he came, lizard-like, knowing it was the sunniest wall of the house, moving along it to find his favourite spot, flattening himself against the stones, till the warm wall against his back and the heat and silence around him dissolved the real world. He heard the privy door bang a second time and held the marble still, listening to see which way the boots would tread. There was a moment's silence and then the slow creak of gravel, like ill-fitting floorboards. The creaking became fainter, till it merged with the sound the grasshoppers were making in the dry grass. It was time to go and see Joseph. He went every day to see Joseph, drawn towards the wood as though by magic.

Walking into the wood was like walking into a room. Once you were inside it was strangely light and airy, yet confined. You could see to one side the brightness of the meadow and above you, between the interlaced twigs, the pale heat of the sky. It had dark corners, too, away to the back of the wood, on the far side, but he hardly ever went there. Mid-way through the wood and deep enough into it to be almost invisible from the meadow was a tumble-down cottage. The roof had almost entirely caved in at one end and most of the glass was missing from the windows. It seemed, to the child, to be sinking quietly back into the ground from which it had originally grown. He imagined it a hiding place for runaways and convicts and its desolation frightened him with a compulsive attraction. He made himself walk close to it every time he went there, bending low beneath its blank windows and rushing past its gaping doorway. Beside the cottage ran a stream, little more than a trickle of water in a shallow ditch. It was good for floating things in and damming with moss and barricades of twigs and leaves and earth that slipped and crumbled and washed themselves away as fast as he made them. It was good for catching black minnows in the summer, when they drifted in a haze with the current of the water over sun-splashed pebbles, and then turned sharply in a pack to scatter into safety, like splinters of silver glass under his hand. And good for breaking ice on in the winter, smashing at it with the heel of his boot, watching the dark water well up over the white ice. Eventually the stream led to Joseph's. Some days it took him a couple of hours, other days he found himself there in a matter of seconds.

'You skived off, then?'

The child moved closer, affecting unconcern. 'What you doing?'

'What's it look like?'

Joseph was in his dairy. It took up half his kitchen. Along the top of an old cupboard was an array of huge glass jars, tin canisters and one or two big china jugs. They were full of milk, goat's milk, arranged in a specific order. One day old, two days, three. Milk turning into curds, milk turning into cheese, or just milk turning. It made the whole kitchen smell funny, heavy and sweet. Joseph was fussing round the containers like a solicitous fly. Peering into one and then another. His hand alighting briefly on the rim of one jar, then darting to the next, shaking them slightly, turning them, sniffing them, changing their position in the lines. The child watched, fascinated. He wondered what Joseph did with all the milk, for the goat went on giving milk, yet the number of jars didn't seem to alter. He wondered what it tasted like. He was curious in a slightly appalled way, but Joseph had never offered him any and he had never been sufficiently tempted to try it. Well, once when he had been alone in the kitchen he had very nearly got as far as sticking his finger into one of the jars. But just as he stood there, his heart thumping, his curiosity taut and urging him on and his finger poised above the jar, he had heard Joseph coming back into the room and had leaped away from the sideboard in fright, dragging all his guilt at the end of his outstretched finger and almost knocking over two of the jars. There were rules in Joseph's house, and one of them was not touching the dairy. Another was not expecting to eat when Joseph did. Sometimes he would arrive and find Joesph seated at the table, his fingers curled around the rim of a bowl, spooning something lumpy into his mouth. There would be a lot of slurping and sucking and sometimes they would talk through it and sometimes they would just sit opposite each

12

other in a companionable way until the bowl was empty. Other times when he came, Joseph would be stirring something on the stove and poking around in the mass of things that littered the draining board, searching among the debris of food for a plate or a knife, picking them up, shaking off whatever remains still clung to them. He liked watching Joseph eat bread and cheese best. It was the only time he longed to eat with him, in exactly the same way. At home when they had bread and cheese, which wasn't very often, he would be given a slice of bread and a slice of cheese to lay on the bread to eat like a sandwich without a top. When Joseph ate bread and cheese he put the remains of a loaf and the hunk of cheese in front of him directly on the top of the table without even bothering to make a space for them. Then he would take his pointed knife out of his belt and cut first a mouth-sized piece of bread which he ate straight from the mottled blade and then a similar hunk of cheese. The child wanted to eat like that when he was a man. It was wonderful.

As the child watched Joseph, bent over his milk, he remembered how his father had come in from work one evening, his huge body bursting with rage that spilled all over the kitchen where the child sat with his mother.

'You,' he had said to the child, shaking his forefinger at him, 'you, don't go near that old man any more.' He thought of how he had crept through the wood the very next afternoon as twilight fell and had found the old man at the kitchen table, binding twine slowly round the handle of a broken knife with bent fingers that barely seemed to grasp either the twine or the knife. He had closed the door behind him, but still kept his finger in the latch, swinging against it shyly, not moving away from the door.

'My dad says I can't come and see you no more.'

'He's said that, has he?'

'He's real cross.'

'He don't like being answered back. He ain't used to it,

working in there. He gets it all his own way. They all do, the screws. And it ain't just the screws, it's all them authorities, right up to the guvnor and more than that.' The old man had looked up, sharp-eyed and defensive in a way the child hadn't seen before. He hadn't liked to go any closer, so he had stayed bumping up and down against the door.

'They come to see me. "We're afraid you must leave here," they says to me. Afraid, afraid! I'll give 'em afraid. I ain't afraid of them. "Security," they says to me, "all unauthorised personnel" ... What do they think? That an old man like me is going to lead rescue parties for all them murderers and thieves! I live here, I told 'em, and my father before me. This is my house and I ain't going nowheres else. You look in your record books and you won't find this house; this house belongs to me. I got papers. Course your dad don't like me. Course he's wild. He's Authority, ain't he? Authority says do this and every-one does it. Authority likes having prisoners and they got real prisoners in that place, they can even say to them: "Stand on your head!" and the poor sods have to do it. So when someone says "no", men like your dad get beside theirselves.'

Was that true? thought the child. Was his father mad because Joseph was innocent and they couldn't touch him? Joseph was his friend. He pictured the little kitchen suddenly full of warders with the governor in their midst, the room submerged under serge uniforms and heavy boots, leaning their hate across the table. And, on the other side, Joseph, a tiny, hunched-up figure, banging on the table-top with righteous indignation. Joseph was a hero.

The old man turned and saw the child's anxious stare; he grinned at him:

'We'll leave these a-brewing,' he said, indicating the canisters of milk. 'You want to come along of me to the back of the wood? There's a sapling rotted away and came down a couple of days ago. I'm gonna drag her back and chop her up.'

The old man walked over to the sink and delved about in it as though he was trying to catch fish with his bare hands. 'Here you are.' He put a little pile of wet leaves into the boy's hands. 'You give these to the old goat while I get my axe.'

Just outside the door was a lean-to, open at the end nearest the door. It was made of corrugated iron weighted down with huge stones from the deserted cottage and further held together with bits of twine looped through holes at the edge of the corrugated iron sheets and tied around wooden posts sunk in the ground. The floor was covered with straw and from the roof hung various tools, some tied to a convenient nail, others just slotted into crevices between the corrugations. The child thought it was a marvel that the goat hadn't yet been brained by one of the implements falling onto its head. But it hadn't. If you were brave enough to look into the shed a white face would loom towards you from the cavernous darkness, a demonic smile on its lips, and from somewhere in the dark you would hear the links of a chain rattling one against the other. He held out a leaf to the goat, who rustled forward over the straw, clinking its chain. Joseph prodded at the axe to free it from its rafter, and in the moment that the goat stretched out its neck to take the cabbage leaf the child fervently hoped the axe would fall on the goat's neck. For a second it seemed to balance perfectly on the beam, then it dropped, handle first, into Joseph's hand.

'Come on,' he said.

The goat watched them through its pale eyes: the old man striding slow and easy between the slim trees and the child, trying to match his steps with the hunter's walk, caught between the shortness of his legs and the eagerness of his friendship.

'Why are we going to get firewood now, in the middle of summer?'

'Because it's there,' said the old man. 'I want it before anyone else takes it. Besides, the summer's nearly over. In a few days they'll start cutting the corn on the plains. In a few weeks there'll be mist on the ground at dawn and in the evenings a cold thin as the point of a needle.'

'How d'you know they're going to start cutting the corn?'

'I hear the farmers come in the evening to look at the wheat; every night this week they've come. I hear that old truck of Jericho's whining its way down the edge of Long Mile, and then I hear the engine cut and the silence, and I can picture him get out and stamp around, rolling wheat grains in his fingers and looking, worrit-faced, at the moon.' The old man chuckled to himself, as though he knew the answer to a riddle that perplexed other men. 'Half an hour later, I hear that old banger of Langdat come coughing along the road on the far side of Grand Plain, next to you, and choke itself into silence. And I know he's up to the same thing.'

The child looked up at the haze of gnats dancing in the hot, clear air above their heads and at the blue sky and felt the heat prickle along his arms. It didn't seem to him that summer was about to end.

Going back along the railway embankment was much cooler than coming had been. The sky was still bright blue, but there was a softness about the heat and the colour of the sunshine on the grass was yellow, where before there had just been hot light. When he reached the house he saw his mother standing in the hen run; her head was bent and her hands clutched an empty bucket. She was watching the hens scrabbling at their feed bowl. One hen was pushed out and ran wildly round the feathered ring looking for a way in, its claws clattering on the mud-packed floor. It would dart its head at what it thought were spilled drops of mash and then continue round the clustered hens, hurling itself at possible openings and falling back again. His mother stood there like another rejected hen, a twisted scrap of faded material. She heard the child approach and looked up, her face red, wisps of hair clinging to her forehead in a wet, exhausted way. His mother would be glad when summer was over.

Joseph proved to be right. The child woke one morning a few days later to the noise of machinery and the wild barking of a dog. They were cutting the corn in Grand Plain. He spent all day hiding in the line of elms on the edge of the field, watching the men work, until the dust drove him home. He returned late in the afternoon, when the dog found him, made friends with him and lay at his feet, staring intently at the slowly diminishing square of corn into which he would dart every so often and return waving his tail, a grin on his empty mouth. The next day Jericho started his men on the field on the far side of the wood, near Joseph's, as though they were another section of an orchestra picking up a melody already begun by Langdat's workers. The cacophony met in an arc of dust and heat over the prison, and in the days that followed was augmented by harvesters picking up the refrain all over the vast plains that covered that part of the country-side. A whining and buzzing that advanced and receded, became an overwhelming staccato reverberation, snapped into silence, and then began again. The heat seemed to be trapped over the earth by the corn dust. The child lay beside the dog under the elm trees, covering his mouth and nose with the biggest leaves he could find. He watched the men crashing among the corn stalks and the wide field recede to a rectangle.

That night as he got ready for bed, the walls of his room seemed pushed out by the heat. It was so tightly packed

with air that he felt he could hardly walk through it. He
sat on the end of his bed in his shirt. Next door he could
hear his mother moving about in her room, undressing;
when her husband was out on night duty she generally
went to bed at the same time as her son. He sat there
listening till all was silent, till even the minimal presence
of his mother slipped out of the house into the dreamless
sleep of exhaustion, and he was alone. He leaned forward
and opened the window. The air outside was as thick as
the air in his room. Thick and warm like a carpet that he
could walk out onto from his window sill down into the
meadow near the orchard. Nothing moved outside. In the
dusk the outlines of trees and walls were distinct and still.
Down in the meadow he could see individual blades of
grass and then, as he stared at them, tiny, black shadows
hazed them over. Right in front of him sat the prison.
Even in the dusk it seemed to glow with heat, its windows
like black air-holes in a stone box. There were no lights
in it and no sound from it. He stared at it, picturing his
father walking all night along dark, stone corridors, the
sound of his footsteps beating against the walls like hollow,
iron fists, resounding against the footstep before and the
one before that and the one before that, till he seemed to
be dragging a ball and chain of sound shadows behind
him, shackled, like the men he guarded. The thought
frightened the child and he looked away, up into the sky
to avoid the image, and caught his breath at what he saw.
He climbed up onto the window sill and knelt there,
oblivious to the danger of falling, feeling his whole being
pulled through the window frame in an acute longing
towards a moon the size and colour of which he had never
seen before. It hung at one end of the prison, dwarfing it;
huge, blood-orange, so low he feared that if it moved it
would tear itself on the rough tiles of the roof, or the twigs
of the trees at the edge of Grand Plain. And move it would.
He felt sure that at any moment it would see him, tiny in

18

his window-frame, and float towards him between the prison and the trees to draw him up into itself, enfold him and carry him away. He knelt there, waiting, his body tense, staring at the moon. He thought how, in his books, they said that the moon was cold, inhospitable to man, billions and billions of miles away. But it was not so. It was soft and warm, glowing with intense blood-light, so near to him that he could stretch out his fingers through the branches of the trees and caress it. But it did not move. He gazed at it till gradually his body relaxed into drowsiness and he slid from the window sill onto his bed.

He was woken by men shouting in his head, a crackling, reverberating noise and a harsh rattle that rose swiftly above everything else, stopped abruptly and then began again. It was a mutiny on board ship – he could smell the smoke from the cannon and hear the muskets going off! No – it was a battle in the trenches – he could hear the screams of men. And the heat, the heat was all around him: a bomb must have exploded. He must be dying. There was a crash near his head and something rushed past him. It must be another bomb. He couldn't cry out, his mouth said nothing and his head was suddenly full of fear. There was a sob. He opened his eyes wide. It was his mother! He looked around, he was on his bed at home and there was his mother, standing at his window in a nightdress, wringing her hands and sobbing:

'Oh, God,' and then fainter, 'Oh, Lor'.'

There was still a smell of smoke and the sound of men screaming and other men shouting. He leaped from his bed towards the window, tripped over the tail of his shirt which was tangled between his legs and tumbled against his mother. As he fell past the window, he caught a glimpse of great orange streaks and tatters flaming against the night sky and dropping down the prison walls. It must be his moon, his moon had torn herself to death against the prison and everyone had gathered to see. He struggled to his feet, but there was no moon, it had gone. Instead there were orange flames leaping from one end of the building and a white light shining up onto the prison roof, moving rapidly backwards and forwards across it. There were men up there – two, three. One of them lying close to the parapet that ran around the roof, the other two standing up and waving their arms. They should get down, thought the child, they should get down and hide, like the other man. But they were caught in the centre by the white light; it pinned them like overturned ants against the pitched roof. He saw arms like feelers wave and lengthen behind the parapet, a round head and a black body swayed in the light. There was a crack like a very dry twig snapping and the body turned slowly and insolently, like a deliberate insult, turning its back on them all; turning and turning as it fell through the air.

'Oh, my God!' cried his mother and pulled him away from the window.

He tried to hold onto the sill with his fingertips:

'I want to watch, I want to watch!'

'It's over.'

He was surprised what strength she could have in her thin arms.

They sat in the living room, facing each other, not speaking. The child began to feel embarrassed in front of his mother to have nothing but a shirt on. When he looked down, he could see goose bumps prickling up all over his thigh and he suddenly shivered, right down his spine.

'You cold?'

He shook his head. His mother continued to stare beyond him, into the darkness, listening. Every so often she got up and went into the kitchen to look out of the window at the prison. The child stayed where he was on the hard chair. In the darkness he saw again the man falling from the roof, turning in the air. He couldn't make

20

the image go away. Independently of him it played itself over and over again. He could feel his heart racing to keep up with it and his mouth getting drier, too scared to move and too frightened to stay in the dark any longer. In the distance there was renewed shouting and bursts of gunfire, and then utter silence. The sudden silence was more terrifying than the noise: the child rushed from his chair to the far wall and switched on the light. The room was flooded with banality and everyday safeness for a second, then his mother stumbled in and switched it off again.

'Are you crazy!' she sobbed. 'What if some of them have escaped? What if they're out there? What if they're there and they see a light here? They'll come, won't they. They'll come and then what'll you do?'

She pushed him in front of her across the room. He could feel her whole body shaking, and the shaking pass into his own body, so that when she pushed him down into the chair again he was shivering uncontrollably and tears started up in his eyes. He looked down at the floor, so that she wouldn't see them and so that he didn't have to look at her anxious face, or the escaped convicts that might burst into the room. Through the kitchen door a V-shaped patch of light was visible, lying along the kitchen floor; the child stared into it, wondering where it came from in the dark house. Its shape grew indistinct as his eyes filled up with tears and clarified again as they flowed out onto his cheeks and wavered as his head shook with sobs. Then it went out. The child stiffened in horror. It had been the white light of the search beam that had hunted the men on the prison roof. It had been here; lying along the floor in his own house. His mother had walked across it: he had been within inches of it when he had run to turn on the living room light. It could have crept along the floor and swallowed him and his mother, like those men. Why hadn't it? Why ... it was full, that was why. It had gone because it was sated with death. It had left them, for another time.

'Did you see it?'

'I heard it. I wasn't going out to look at it, not with them fireworks going off. I went and bolted my door. I ain't bolted my door for as long as I can remember and the old bolt's got so rusty I didn't think she was going to budge.'

'My mum wouldn't let me turn on the light. She said if any of them escaped, they would make straight for us if they saw a light.'

'They'd either make straight for you or steer right clear of you. And you wouldn't know which it was going to be till it was too late.'

'My mum was so scared she was shaking all over. She just kept walking backwards and forwards.'

'Man on the run's a dangerous animal, you can't reckon with no one in that kind of state. Man like that's only got one idea in his head: he's out to survive, he don't hear nothing, feel nothing, nor reason nothing but staying alive. You get in his way, he won't notice he's gunned you down.'

There was a pause during which the child got the break-out at the prison and the pages of the comic stuffed behind Joseph's stove all mixed up in his head. The old man stretched his legs in the sun and leaned back against the doorpost.

'There's only one thing more dangerous than a man on the run and that's them authorities out looking for a man on the run,' he said, more to himself than to the child. 'I was more wary of them authorities that night than of any poor devil trying to find his freedom.'

'Did any of them get away?'

'Get away?'

'The men on the roof.' A sudden hope leapt up that the silence might not have been death.

'How many was up there? All I see from here was that searchlight and them flames. Old boy Langdat's going to be pleased, I thought, when a spark from that sets his bales ablaze.'

'There were two,' said the child slowly. 'At first there were three, then one . . .' his voice trailed away. The old man looked down at him.

'Well,' the child waved his hand dismissively, 'then my mum wouldn't let me see any more.' He blushed.

'Stupid bastards, going up. There ain't nowhere you can go from the roof, they've got you sitting pretty. They either picks you off or lets you starve.'

They fell silent for a moment. A small cloud of gnats rose and fell in the air above them like nervous eavesdroppers.

'What happened inside?' asked the old man.

'My dad got hurt.'

'Did he?'

'My mum just screamed when she saw him; he had blood all down his face. She sent me to bed, but I stood at the top of the stairs and I heard them talking. My dad said they jumped him. He was on duty on the top landing and the men in the end cell started screaming and shouting and he rushed up and saw smoke coming under their door, so he and the other guard went in and they jumped them. Then my mum started coming upstairs, so I ran back to bed. In the morning he had a bandage round his head and when I asked him what happened, he yelled at me to mind my own business.'

'You want to be careful of your dad. You want to watch he doesn't take it out on you for what them prisoners did to him. You shouldn't be here right now. He catch you here, it's you he's going to jump.'

'He won't catch me. He's gone back to work today.'

Under the hot, sullen sky the prison was silent. No more, perhaps, than usual, but to the old man and the child it seemed ominously so and each imagined an activity

23

going on inside that was all the worse for being noiseless.

'Weather's going to break,' said the old man finally.

'We're having visitors tomorrow,' replied the child.

He sat, that night, in the kitchen eating barley soup, spoonful by unwilling spoonful. The heat had become unbearable, but his mother refused to open the back door, because she was cooking a cake in the oven. Did he want such a draught to ruin the delicacy she was preparing for her sister-in-law? To have to get ready for visitors in this heat was bad enough. She clashed the dishes together in the sink in a rare display of emotion. She had overcooked the barley again and, when he chewed it, it stuck to his teeth. He tried swallowing a granule whole, it slithered, slippery and round down his throat, his stomach rose to meet it and he gagged. His mother turned and glared at him:

'And mind your manners, tomorrow.'

She bent down to the oven and opened the door a crack, a wet cake smell drifted out. He watched her sideways over the rim of his spoon. Her cakes made rare appearances in his life, but he thought he could remember them all, for they were all the same. They were nothing that a draught of air from the meadow could ever destroy – or enhance. They were solid, round and sunken in the centre and when they were cut open the currants that were supposed to be evenly distributed throughout were revealed to be clinging together in a moist lump in the middle of the cake. As the first slice was removed, this lump would slowly detach iself from the rest, keel over and, with the removal of the next slice, land with a soft thud on the plate. The person who received even one currant in his portion of cake was fortunate indeed.

'The kettle's on for your bath.'

'What bath?'

'You're having a bath tonight, soon as the kettle's boiled.'

'Why?'

'You know why. You know your father's sister's coming tomorrow and your uncle. Go up and get your pyjamas while I clean out the sink for you.'

He swung on the door handle at the threshold to the living room.

'I've finished.'

His mother had her back to him, bending over an open drawer in the sideboard. When she turned round he could see the glint of little silvery spoons in her hand. She looked furtively at him and he knew that he could have played in the water for an hour and she would not have dared to come in. She relied on his awareness of his nakedness being stronger than her embarrassment at it.

'You washed properly, have you? With soap?'

He extended a hand towards his mother and waved it in the air, curling the fingers into claws.

'Aargh,' he growled, 'aargh!'

But his mother only compressed her lips and turned away. She seemed unaware that his bath had turned him into the monster from the marsh and that green, slimy tendrils of carbolic soap hung from his fingers. He swung backwards and forwards in the doorway, watching her lay out her delicate weaponry, placing the spoons next to a pile of stiffly folded napkins, kneeling to unwrap flowered cups with gold-painted rims from their newspaper shrouds.

'Upstairs.'

It was almost a whisper, but he went, walking slowly as if there had been no command.

Inside his room it was hot. As hot and airless as it had been all these nights. He stood beside his bed, leaning against it with a kind of weariness, although he had no desire to sleep. He stood there waiting to feel one thing or another, waiting for his mind to tell him what to do. But

25

it seemed blank, held taut by a feeling of being on guard, and therefore unable to indulge in such a whim as sleep. He thought perhaps it was the heat. The heat that softened and relaxed him and then, paradoxically, would not let him sleep. He went and opened the window. As he did so all the lights in the prison went out. Could they sleep? In their stone cells were their eyes obediently closing, or was it then that they came alive? Was it then that they thought most of escape? Did they throw ladders of dreams across the darkness and climb to wherever they most wished to be? Did they gaze out, as he did, into a little rectangle of sky and lose themselves in it? Or did they lie in the dark cell, tense and sleepless with hate? He thought of the blood drying on the side of his father's face: had one of the prisoners waited day after day to strike that blow, or had it happened suddenly, by accident? He heard his mother at the foot of the stairs and he ran across the room, turned out the light and climbed into bed.

Long after it was quiet he lay there, floating on the edge of wakefulness, gazing into the shadows that filled his room. He turned and wriggled, straightened his legs and bent them again into his stomach. Each time he changed position he drifted, for a moment, into sleep, and then the limbs grew heavier and pressed disjointedly into each other and he rose again to the surface of consciousness. Behind his closed eyes the image of the prison formed. A grey shell, windowless and roofless, quite deserted, with just himself in the cottage outside its walls, breathing quietly in the darkness. Joseph was gone. His parents were gone. They no longer grew corn on the Grand Plain. The elm trees to the right of the prison were leafless and the sky was white and cold. Then, suddenly, it changed. Flames leaped out of the prison and smoke, and the thick summer leaves of the elms massed at one end were fluttering and scorching in the heat. There was no sound. Just an ominous heaviness that made him bolt up in bed with a guilt like that of a helmsman who has fallen asleep on watch and woken to find his ship drifting helplessly along a rocky shore. He knelt on the window sill, pressing his forehead against the glass and looked out to where the flames had been. There was nothing, just the darkness and the trees where they always were and the wall, parallel lines of shadow. Yet he still could not reassure himself that there was no danger.

The next day was as still as all Sundays and heavier than any he had yet known. In the kitchen his mother stood in front of a stove that hissed and spat and steamed. She fed it chopped potatoes as though they were supplicatory offerings, dropping them one by one into a pan from thin, red fingers.

'Where's Dad?'

'Gone out.' She stared at him over the steam. 'You sickening for something?'

'No,' he said defensively.

'I been up twice to wake you, but you were that pale and that sound asleep, I left you. Best place for you, stop you getting dirty over there in that wood.' She banged a lid onto the pan. 'Come here,' she put a damp hand to his forehead. 'I can't tell nothing in this heat,' she muttered. 'I kept you some milk warmed.' She reached among the pans on the top of the stove and poured the contents of one into a cup. Milk slid out from under crumpled, yellow skin that the child prayed would not follow it into the cup.

'Drink this outside, stay by the house and don't play in any dust – and come in when I call you and put on your best shirt. Your dad'll be going to fetch his sister soon from the bus.' The child went out.

'Mind you come when I call!' shouted his mother through the open window.

He didn't go to his usual spot overlooking the railway, he sat with his back against the kitchen wall, staring at the

27

hens poking around the clumps of nettles in their run. He saw his father come out of the gate in the wall, adjust a strange, felt hat on his head and walk in the direction of the road. He heard his mother count out plates with a delicate, clinking sound, as though they were gold coins. Over to the left, far beyond Joseph's wood, it seemed to him that the sky was thickening. The blueness that had been there day after day had turned grey at the very edge.

When he heard them call his name he went downstairs very slowly. He had sat on his bed and heard them talking, a hubbub of voices where usually there was silence. Today, the house, in which every line and every nail in every floorboard was familiar, had subtly changed. Today it all felt different. He opened the door to the living room and thought at first that there were four strangers in the room. Three of them sat in chairs and one stood. It was his father in a very white shirt. They all turned their heads to look at him. There was a long second of silence in which the child felt paralysed, in which he felt that there was some mistake. A mistake that he could rectify perhaps by going upstairs and coming down and opening the door again and finding the old familiar room emptied of all these people. He saw his mother in a strange dress with washed-out stripes all over it and yellow beads round her neck sitting on the edge of a chair with her hands in her lap, nursing them as if they were inanimate objects of an awkward shape that she had just picked up off the floor. She didn't smile at him, or call him to come in. Her eyes just stared at him, anxiously, as though he was a stranger. His father looked straight at him out of an expressionless face, and the child felt like a prisoner. It was the other woman who spoke, the one with small, round eyes that glittered like a snake's in a bony skull.

'So this is Robert,' she said and her voice was quick, too, and dry, like slithering over stones. 'Come here and

28

let me see you.' There was nothing else he could do, but walk towards her for she was, after all, his aunt. When he was near enough she grabbed him by the knees.

'You've grown,' she said and shook him to emphasise her words so that he was afraid that his legs were being snapped in two like birch twigs. She pushed him away. 'In them years. You really grown. Big enough to have some schoolin', I'll say.' She glanced sideways at her brother. His mother blushed and looked down as if it was a reproof intended for her. 'Growed enough to be helpful,' his aunt continued. 'I hope you bide telling, my boy.'

'Or I'll know the reason why!' his father growled.

The other man, whom he assumed to be his uncle, suddenly pulled out a handkerchief and blew his nose. He dabbed at his eyes.

'Summer cold,' he murmured into the handkerchief, as if he was apologising to it.

'Stacking and weighing, folding paper bags, ravelling string. I hope you're neat in your habits. Well?'

Robert couldn't understand what all these questions were for, or how he was to answer them, or even whether they referred to him.

'Well!' prompted his father.

He looked towards his mother for help, but it came unexpectedly from the man with the cold, who sneezed violently and distracted everyone's attention.

'You wouldn't think, would you,' hissed his aunt, darting her head towards her husband and addressing everyone else, 'in all this heat, to be snivelling. I never felt it so close as it is today.'

His mother roused herself from her embarrassed silence.

'It's going to break,' she said, leaning forward from the edge of her chair and nodding her head into the centre of the group. 'There's going to be a storm,' she continued breathlessly. And then stopped. They all looked at her, but she had no more to say. She twisted her fingers together and crept out to the kitchen.

His father made him sit next to his aunt at lunch. He had tried to sidle out into the kitchen to the comforting sight of his mother's anxious face through the steam, but his father had called him back.

'You! Over there, next to your aunt and mind your manners.'

It was strange to sit at a dining table that took up half the living room. He couldn't think where it came from, or ever having seen the white cloth before, that covered it. The plates that were shut up all year in the sideboard were spread out over it. There were glasses at every plate, old knives and forks from the kitchen drawer and others that had white handles. He picked one up and traced the pattern of a leaf in the cloth.

'Put that down,' said his father.

His uncle blew his nose again.

'Be all right with some food inside you, Walter.'

His mother came in carrying dishes in tea towels. Steam rose above the table and the smell of wet cloths filled the room. As she put down each dish on the table she seemed to bow before them. It was nothing more than the weight of the food and the awkward way she had of moving her body, but it seemed to Robert that, however many offerings she made, the gods would not be appeased. Opposite him his uncle fussed with his handkerchief round his nose and dabbed at the corners of his mouth. As each new dish was put in front of him it seemed to spark off bursts of undirected energy that flickered and died among shuffled cutlery and re-positioned plates. His father sat implacable. Under the white tablecloth, Robert knew that big, square hands rested, wrists turned inwards on wide-spread thighs, like a wrestler waiting to spring into action. But he stared over the top of the table as if none of them were present. It was his aunt who was the chief god. It was her scrutiny and her silence that made his mother so

30

obsequious. It was the way she raised her head slightly to peer into each dish as it was put onto the table and the way she lowered it again without comment. And the way his mother, lifting her gaze after each bow, sought the approval of those flickering eyes, until there was nothing else to bring in from the kitchen and she stood at her place, faltering before the feast. There was veal stew and fried potatoes and baked cabbage and mashed peas. His uncle shifted hopefully in his chair and his mother picked up a spoon and held it limply over the stew. She cleared her throat:

'Emily?'

Robert stared up at his aunt. Emily? Emily! That she should have a name at all surprised him, but that it should be something as light and tinkling as Emily astounded him. 'Emily' was for little girls with long hair and eyes that sparkled when you spoke to them. Had his aunt ever been a little girl? Had she . . .

'Oh, don't give me much. It looks very nice, but don't give me much. It's this heat, you don't want to eat in this heat. I'm sure Walter'll make up for me.'

His mother put little crestfallen piles of food onto a plate. As a spoonful of peas hovered above it, his aunt snatched the plate away.

'No peas. They give me wind.'

Some of the peas fell onto the table and little green stains spread out around them on the white cloth.

'Waste not,' murmured Walter and slid his knife deftly under the mashed peas to carry them away. He deposited them on the pile of plates in front of Robert's mother.

'Walter!' snarled his wife. 'They can't be eaten *now*.'

He looked sadly at the peas. 'I'm sure the cloth was clean,' he said mournfully.

His sister-in-law began to ladle veal stew next to the peas with restored confidence; she had to feed her downtrodden ally. Emily began to spike her fork at the fried

31

potatoes and turned to her brother:

'You had a real scare here, the other week . . .'

They began to talk about the break-out at the prison, building force and venom between them. No punishment, evidently, could quite satisfy their joint desires for the wicked of this world. Across the table, his mother handed his uncle a plate of food, leaning sideways as she did so and saying something inaudible. He bobbed his head in reply. She put a second spoonful of cabbage on the plate. They smiled shyly at each other. They were like two sparrows on a frozen lawn, finding themselves in the presence of crumbs and for a moment unmarauded by starlings. His mother took up another plate, Walter gallantly picked up a hot dish and held it close to help her serve more easily. They twittered quietly to each other. Between these two self-absorbed groups Robert felt temporarily forgotten, temporarily hidden. He didn't feel hungry. He felt like getting up and slipping silently from the room unnoticed. He felt like running through the birch trees to Joseph's house. Joseph would know what to make of the sense of unease that permeated the house, he would put up his head and sniff and say . . . what would he say? What was it, and why was he the centre of it?

'Robert.'

It was his mother, handing him a plate. He saw his uncle poised over his food, knife and fork held in the air, his long face and drooping eyes smiling shyly at him. He nodded his head:

'Well, boy, *bon appétit*,' he said awkwardly and began to fill his mouth very quickly with food.

Robert picked up a mashed pea on one of the prongs of his fork and sucked it. It tasted like soap. The adults around him had stopped talking; instead they scraped, sliced, bit and chewed at each other. Robert went on sucking at the ends of his fork, he didn't feel like eating any of the food on his plate. He marvelled that they could abandon themselves so easily and was relieved at the same time that they did, it turned their absorption into a kind of screen between himself and them, behind which he could become invisible to everything. There was still this feeling that lurked in the corner of the room, retreated temporarily into the shadows, but which had not gone away. It watched him, he felt, out of an eyeless face, sensing where he was, almost, rather than seeing him clearly, sending out an enveloping cloud of uneasiness that, as it touched him, turned to fear. It was linked somehow with the presence of his aunt, but it reminded him of something else. It gave him the same feeling of inescapable disaster as the white light that had crept along the floor the night the man had slowly fallen from the roof of the prison. Perhaps his aunt would go away as soon as she had finished eating and then the danger that he felt would go with her.

He gazed out of the window. Across the railway line heavy grey-brown clouds were massed. He stared at them surprised and bemused: there had been nothing but blue sky outside for weeks, as though the windows themselves had been painted blue. He looked around to see if anyone else had noticed, but their heads were all bent over their plates. Suddenly, into their silence broke voices, at first far off and then nearer; a shouting, then a whirring, clattering cacophony. His aunt threw down her fork:

'Oh, my lor'!' she shrieked, 'Oh, my lor'. Tom, what's that?' They turned to him, sitting solidly at the head of the table. He frowned.

'Well,' he began.

'It's not . . . ?' whispered his wife.

'It's them men!' shrieked his sister. 'It's them men breaking out again. I knew it. I said to Walter I didn't want to come here, not after that. Why can't they come to us? I said. I knew it!' She threw herself back in her chair and began waving her napkin in front of her face, like the

33

tail of a trapped snake thrashing wildly in the air. A dog started barking furiously and she sat bolt upright:

'Go and look, for God's sake. Go on!' she shook her brother's arm violently.

He got up slowly.

'It don't sound like them. There ain't no dogs round here, for a start.'

But, all the same, he went.

Robert knew what it was the minute he heard the dog, but he didn't say anything. Across the table his mother and his uncle seemed more alarmed by the hysterics of his aunt. She began to shriek again:

'I don't know how you can live here. Place like this. Gives me the creeps just to look at it. Right next to *that* – all them bars and walls, and them criminals inside just waiting to get at you! If they got out, they wouldn't stop at nothing. You wouldn't stand a chance, neither.' She began waving her napkin in her sister-in-law's direction:

'I'm not surprised you want to send that boy away. Schooling or no schooling; I wouldn't stay here myself, not one second, not one day . . .'

His father strode back into the room.

'It's the farmer on Grand Plain. Got the whole village out to help him get the bales in. There's going to be a storm tonight, the way the sky . . .'

'On a Sunday! On a Sunday – carting bales! There ain't nothing in this place but heathens and felons. I don't know how you could live here, Tom, I never known. And work in that place. It don't pay you no money, it don't give you no life, being among them men all the time. And your wife and boy dumped out here in this little poky house miles from nowhere. Look at him. Look at him! I ain't surprised you want me to take him away. Moping around all day on his own, thin and pale and nothing to say for hisself. It ain't right for a boy of his age, it ain't decent. He should be learning something useful, not here where, if he don't get murdered in his bed, he'll learn to disrespect the Sabbath.' She stood up. 'I'll take 'im and that's that, but don't expect me to come here no more, my nerves won't stand it. Walter, take me home!'

Walter reluctantly pushed his plate away from him and smoothed out the tablecloth behind it.

'Well, Emily . . .' he began hesitantly.

'I'm going, Walter.' She pushed back her chair and walked jerkily into the middle of the room.

'There's a cake to come, yet,' murmured her sister-in-law, twisting her hands. The expression on her face during Emily's outburst had been one of shame and pain. Shame, one would have thought, at the exposition of her pitiful life, and pain at the thought of the loss of her only son to this unloving woman. But perhaps her real tragedy was the plump cake that lolled, untasted, on its plate in the kitchen.

'Where's my coat?' snapped Emily.

Her brother got up slowly and fetched it from the peg behind the door and held it out to her. He watched her with the same stupefied gaze with which he had stared at her for the last five minutes. Behind him Walter had risen and was ineffectually trying to thank his hostess for the meal and at the same time to apologise for its being unfinished, which was made all the harder for him because she was ignoring him: her anguish was all directed towards his wife.

'Emily,' her brother said softly, 'there's no bus for another three hours.'

There was, after that, a very long silence, and when that was over everyone sat down again.

Up in his room, Robert leaned his head on his arms and stared over the top of the window sill into the dusk. Clouds were banked all behind the prison, with only streaks of sky showing, and a little, cold wind stirring the tops of the

35

trees. Everything else was still, with that certain waiting feeling there is just before a storm. But he saw only what was in his head and heard only his aunt's shrill voice saying ... saying things that even now he couldn't comprehend. Even after his father's embarrassed confirmation that they were sending him to stay with his aunt to go to school and after his mother's tears in the kitchen surrounded by dirty plates and uneaten food, it was only his aunt's words that he heard. She stood in a brilliantly lit space in his head and repeated them over and over again like a clockwork doll. They shocked him into a numbness that passed from humiliation to grief to a kind of white emptiness where both had been surpassed and he stood, as it were, far outside himself, hearing another child denounced and watching another child's wooden and unhappy face. The table with its fidgeting guests and its unpalatable food, the closed walls of the ugly room, and the strange, brown clouds that had begun to fill the blue window, all dissolving away because they were insignificant beside the betrayal that he suffered. He had never really considered his feelings for his parents; he thought that he felt nothing. Now he was surprised how nothing could produce out of itself such pain. And yet it was his aunt that he resolved to hate.

When the rain began to fall he didn't notice for some time. It wasn't till the light, thudding sound became heavier and more frequent, and drops of rain were blown inward by the rising wind and landed on his fingers that he realised what was happening. Then the wind dropped, the sky went suddenly black and the bellies of the clouds broke with rain that sang its way to earth in a solid sheet. It blotted out the prison and pressed down on the ends of the branches of the elms, so that they bent and swayed. He saw the hazed outline of uncollected bales huddled in one corner of the field and knew they would be ruined. Only the birch trees in Joseph's wood seemed unmoved

36

as if they were so slender that the drops of rain fell through their branches without touching them.

Long after his parents had gone to bed the storm started. It was as though it had spent the intervening hours positioning itself carefully, for the first crash of thunder was exactly over the centre of the house. And, as if the whole house had split open, Robert's room was immediately flooded with light. A cold light that traced round with thick shadow all the objects in his room and then left them in darkness again, while the thunder rolled out unchecked across the wide plain. Robert lay, as he did every night now, half awake, half asleep, till the time came for the tension, the strange feeling of watchfulness to fade and for sleep to creep up and cover him with warm oblivion.

In the days that followed, Robert woke every morning to the sound of rain. It was said that Langdat and his men had saved most of their bales – that was what came of being heathens. Jericho, on the other hand, a quiet, sour and God-fearing man, had had half his crop soaked beyond repair, not just in Long Mile, but even in the field behind his farm. Close as that, marvelled Robert, as he sat in the kitchen eating his breakfast. He woke these days long after his mother was up, leaping out of bed and struggling into his clothes, guiltily ashamed of having slept so long. But his mother said nothing to him, merely turning from whatever she was doing to pour milk into a pan to heat for him, as though her guilt over his imminent departure cancelled out his own. And so they lived in a state of unnatural tolerance which even his father didn't disturb.

It took him a week to break the news to Joseph. For several days he stayed away, hanging round the house, or playing near the foot of the railway embankment. Then one day he dawdled up the banks of the stream and on up through the trees. Joseph was sitting at the kitchen table surrounded by piles of apples and a stack of old newspapers. He was rolling apples slowly in sheets of paper. Robert stopped in the doorway, looking at the shadowy room full of the smell of apples and old news and goat's milk and dust. Low shafts of sunlight penetrated halfway across the cluttered room and stopped short of a line of shadow. The old man sat on the other side of this frontier of light, rolling apples in claw-like fingers, and tried to draw Robert into conversation on topics of mutual interest: the storm, his aunt's visit, who was offering free apples for the picking, how near ready the mushrooms were. But they all failed. He could sense the child's misery and saw that he was stuck fast behind his own frontier of inarticulateness, standing there helpless in the sunshine.

'You'm about as much company as a broody hen,' said Joseph gently.

The next day Robert went again to Joseph's. He found him cleaning out the goat's shed, struggling with forkfuls of wet straw, while the goat watched him, tied ignominiously to a stake in the ground, with a cynical look in its eye. They cleaned out the whole shed, brought in fresh straw and re-installed the goat without saying a word to each other. They stood, one on either side of the sodden heap of bedding, and tried to make it burn. Flames would spurt out from the straw under Joseph's match, running along each filament till they reached wetness and fizzling out in a curl of smoke until the whole heap was a mass of waving tendrils that straightened and drew together higher up in the quiet air. From time to time small leaves from the birch trees would drop softly to the ground.

'Day after tomorrow I'm going gathering mushrooms. I went to see 'em this morning; they were just about ready. You want to come along?'

Robert nodded.

It was over the mushrooms that he found his tongue. Perhaps it was something to do with their small, white vulnerability and the way, when he had plucked out their stalks, the soft green grass closed over the gap as if they had never been.

'I'm going away,' he said.

'You going far?' asked Joseph.

'They're sending me off to live with my aunt.'

'The one that come Sunday?'

Robert nodded.

'Ah,' said Joseph.

'You ain't never seen her! She looks like a snake. She got eyes on the end of her head that follow you all the time. She's always watching you, watching you, like this – flicker, flicker. And then she starts in on you, real mean. Anyone, not just me, her old man, even my dad she went at!'

'What you going there for, then?'

'Schooling.'

'Ah well, that figures. There ain't no school round here.'

'I don't need no school. I do my learning by myself. Did you go to school?'

'No. I never went to no school.'

'There you are.'

'I helped my dad on the land. You can't go helping your dad in there, they wouldn't let you – nor you wouldn't want to. An' if you can't do something useful, you'm better get some learning.'

'I don't want to go.'

'Once you go you'll not come back. Besides, there'll be other lads your age at that school. After no more'n a week you won't want to come back to a lonely old place like this.'

Robert kicked a puffball into dust and Joseph got up slowly from one knee to the other, pulling on a fence post as a lever.

'You bring them mushrooms then, lad.'

They walked back through the wood.

'Anyway,' said Robert, 'what'll you do when I'm gone?'
'What I always do, I reckon,' said Joseph.

II

Life in his aunt's house revolved around the shop, a large gloomy room hollowed out of the ground floor of the house, with bare floorboards and half-empty shelves. In winter it was heated by two paraffin stoves whose small, blue flames wavered, pinched and cold in the icy air. In summer the doors and windows were kept tightly shut against flies. Huge sheets of tinted cellophane were stuck to the panes, cutting off the brightness of life outside, sealing them into a shadowy, suffocating world where melting pats of butter floated in earthenware bowls beneath beaded fly nets and the bare boards cracked spontaneously in the stifling heat. It was here that his aunt spent most of her day. It was around this room that most of her thoughts revolved and all of her conversation turned.

The rest of the house was cramped and dark and shabby. To Robert it didn't feel like a house at all. If anyone had asked him he would have said that they lived in a cupboard and slept on shelves. Everything was hard and uncomfortable. There was no slow, easy passing of time; no grass and no trees to see out of the windows, just a concrete yard surrounded by a high, corrugated-iron fence. From this yard three steps went up to the back door of the house, which opened on a dark hallway stacked with cardboard boxes. To the left, steep stairs led to the bedrooms, on the right was the narrow parlour and straight ahead was the door to the shop. Tacked on to one corner of the parlour was a cubby hole with a sink, cooker and shelves for crockery. It was here in the evenings that Robert had to dry the dishes which his aunt washed. Out of the corner of her eye she would watch suspiciously his clumsy movements with the wet towel and he, in turn, would long for a soapy plate to leap out of her fingers and smash itself against the tap. The kitchen also doubled as a washroom. From her chair in the parlour, though his aunt could not see him, she could tell which sounds of washing were genuine and which were not.

The parlour itself was amost completely taken up by a table and three chairs. They sat round the table whether they were eating or not, for there was nowhere else to sit. It was covered by an imitation velvet cloth with a fringe of bobbles, which at mealtimes was rolled back to expose an oilcloth whose pattern had been obliterated by vigorous scrubbing, but whose odour seemed to taint everything that Robert ate. There was one other chair in the room, a strange, oblong easy-chair with wide, wooden arms. Robert was forbidden by his aunt to use this chair, nor, for quite some time, did he see anyone else sit in it. It stood there, its back to the rest of the room, staring out sideways through the window at the steps leading down from the back door out into the yard. Just above the chair, suspended from the ceiling, close to the window, dangled a strip of flypaper, brown and shiny, contributing its own sickly odour to the pervasive smell of oilcloth and disinfectant and boiled cabbage that seemed to hang in the room. The flypaper and its harvest of dead bodies was a source of lurid fascination for Robert. The slightest draught from the ill-fitting window made it swing gently backwards and forwards, the wings of its trophies fluttering slightly. But, when the door to the hall was opened, then the sudden turbulence of air would make the paper swing violently on its string, beating against the frame of the window. Limbs from the dessicated bodies would break off and whirl slowly down through the air: black feelers or filamented papery wings. If they missed the chair, they fell onto the floor and were buried among swirls of brown and green roses on the threadbare rug. Sometimes they fell onto the tallboy that was crammed between the window and the door. This object, also referred to at various times by Robert's aunt as The Bureau, was obviously to his aunt a possession of grim pride. It elevated her beyond the world of everyday bric à brac into the realms of the antique. It had come down, she informed him, from her mother's side. It was, it appeared, the one chink in her carapace of unfeelingness; but a chink, she made it clear, through which only rage would issue if he caused the slightest accident to it. You touch it, she warned him, you're for it! It looked as if it had been touched many times in its life. To Robert, it looked as if very much more use would make it fall to pieces entirely and he decided this must be the reason for his aunt's protectiveness towards it. Its dull brown veneer was chipped and scratched, and the catches on its cupboard door had long since gone, so that they swung open by themselves at any change in the temperature of the room, or if particular floorboards were trodden on. A low mirror ran along the top of it, supported at either end by short, twisted wooden pillars. Around the edge of the glass the silvering had been eaten away and black spots were scattered all over its face, so that its reflection of life was imperfect. Robert would stare into it from an oblique angle and feel his spirits sink at the image of the room it gave back to him: the colours dulled, the lifelessness exposed. There were only two games worth playing in that room: standing on the floorboards that made the cupboards open, or trying to catch bits of dead flies as they floated to the floor. But for the first few months in his aunt's house he

43

was never allowed to be alone in the parlour for very long and even when he was alone he felt his aunt's eyes on him continuously, her presence and her distrust hovering constantly around him. Even when he was having his bath.

Once a week a tin bath was set on spread-out newspapers before the fireplace and half-filled with hot water. His uncle and aunt would leave the room, their faces primly set, their eyes averted as though something unpleasant had been brought into the parlour.

'Five minutes!' his aunt would snap as she shut the door behind her. But Robert never really believed she went away. Gingerly, he would undress, crackle across the sheets of newspaper and unwillingly lower himself into the tin bath. It was always cold. It was cold in the early autumn evenings before the fire was allowed to be lit. It was even colder on winter nights in front of the mound of coke dust which sulked and wheezed and from which no warmth ever seemed to come.

It was only in his bedroom that Robert felt safe from the prying eyes of his aunt. It was to his bedroom that she sent him when she or her husband were too preoccupied to keep an eye on him. It was either 'upstairs!' or 'outside!' Outside meant the back yard: a jumble of empty cardboard boxes, crates of ginger-beer bottles and the privy. Outside meant chasing the unfriendly cats who came to scavenge from box to box. They hissed at the sticks he poked at them and arched their scrawny backs and retreated further into caverns of cardboard, pressing themselves to the ground and then springing out to scramble away with the sound of tearing claws and strange, high-pitched yowls, over the corrugated-iron fence. Or he would sit on the back steps and throw stones at the piled-up boxes to make them fall over. Or just sit and watch the melancholy twilight gather in the sky. For in those first few weeks he was not allowed beyond the fence. Upstairs meant climbing out of the box-stacked hallway into an enveloping gloom, which even at midday was dark. From the top step three doors led away abruptly, like mistrustful strangers turning sharply from one other. The first door led to Robert's room, the middle one to his aunt's bedroom and the third to the storeroom in which his uncle secreted himself for several hours a day. It was always kept locked, whether his uncle was in it or not. And it was forbidden to Robert. Sometimes his uncle would make crashing sounds inside it; sometimes he was very still.

Most of the noise in the house came from the neighbours. It took Robert a long time to get used to the idea of having neighbours pressed so close to him. He would kneel on his bed and stare out of the narrow window, down into the next-door back yard. There was always washing in it and sometimes a bantam scratching delicately at the packed earth. They grew flowers in pots: big, brash chrysanthemums and waxy gladioli that wilted at the first frost. And once the man's wife ran out in a rainstorm to gather in washing without even buttoning her chemise over her corset. It flapped open in the gusting wind and Robert saw her breasts, wet with rain. He was at first shocked, and then became furtive about his own movements in his room. What if they spied on *him*? What if they saw him through a crack in the wall when he was undressing for bed? What if they heard him through the wall, as he could hear them? At first it seemed to him that there was something almost indecent about being privy to the private noises of their lives without their knowledge. In time, however, he became fascinated and would sit cross-legged on his bed, listening excitedly as though at a play, disappointed as their incoherent shouting died away into silence. There were frequent silences in his aunt's house. Grim, brooding passages of time, which stifled even daydreams. The three of them would sit around the table in the parlour as the interminable evenings stretched listlessly ahead, and Robert would listen to the enviable spontaneity of their neighbours' outbursts. Unintelligible hurled words coming through the walls. Or great crashing sounds, as if all their pots and pans had tumbled down at once, falling into the silence of the parlour.

Robert took a dislike to the shop from the first. He would peer furtively into it through the hall door that his uncle sometimes left ajar, but he could see no magic in its gloomy cavernousness; there was nothing tempting among the tins and packets that stood in lonely groups on its shelves. It was a miserly place that had sucked the heart out of the house. It was responsible for the scrappy meals and the small, cold back room. Besides, it was his aunt's domain. At first, seeking perhaps to sharpen his desire, she refused to let him go into the shop at all. He was to leave and enter the house only by the back door. He was never to go anywhere in the house but his bedroom or the parlour. He was never to play on the stairs. Not to make a noise. She warned him: if she ever heard him from the shop she would take a strap to him. He believed her. She told him he was a disgrace. She took him by the shoulder and told him that he was lazy and stupid, that his hands were too dirty, his hair too ill-kempt. She told him that his collar was too frayed and his trousers too many sizes too big to be seen in her shop. Having thus discomforted him she dragged him in to be scrutinised by her cronies who had gathered there for the purpose. She grasped him round one of his thin wrists, her eyes darting from one woman to the next to make sure her triumph was not lost on them.

'This is him.'

And he hung from her hand like a stunned rabbit, while around him women in black, like witches, muttered and stared. They clutched shopping bags that he was sure they had come to fill with henbane and nail clippings. But he was banished to the back room before he could see them do it.

46

That night, after supper, his aunt drew an old newspaper out of a drawer in the tallboy and the envelope with the single sheet of paper inside that his mother had given him before he left home. His aunt spread the newspaper in front of him and took a pencil from among the spills in the blue jug on the mantelpiece.

'Here,' she said slapping it down beside him, 'write your letter home.'

Robert looked up at her. She stared coldly back.

'Go on. Tell her you're arrived safe.'

She sat down on the other side of the table and opened an illustrated catalogue of canned goods. Robert picked up the pencil. He stared at the blank paper and then at his aunt. She looked as if she wasn't looking. To make sure he curled his arm in front of the paper. 'Dear Mum,' he wrote and glanced over at his uncle. He was immersed in mending the clock again: a rusted alarm clock he had found in the lane at the back of the house, whose pieces he spread around him on the table each evening after supper, picking them up, staring solemnly at them, fitting one against the other and putting them down again in different positions. Robert bent over the paper. Now was his chance to escape from all this.

'I am a prisoner!' he wrote in careful, looping script. He was. He saw before him clearly his parents' house in the shadow of the prison wall and thought of all the prisoners shut inside. If they thought their son had been taken prisoner like that . . . if his father . . . his father who kept guard on prisoners every day, if his father knew . . . And his mother. If his mother found out he hadn't had a proper meal all week – all her reminding him how to hold his knife and fork proper – if she knew he'd only had broken biscuits and stuff out of tins that other people wouldn't buy, she'd come and take him away. As for his father, who had kicked his shins under the table a dozen times a day to make him mind his manners when he got to his aunt's, when *he* knew, his aunt'd really be for it. He'd probably tell the police and they'd arrest her. They'd come to the shop. With handcuffs.

He glanced up at his aunt to see if she was aware of her fate and, as if she felt his gaze, she said, without looking up:

'When you done, you give it here for me to see.'

He went suddenly cold all over. He was trapped. He drew his arm in closer to the sheet of paper. In the shadow the words seemed blacker and more solid than ever. They had taken root and were growing out of the feint blue line. He stared at them, moving his pencil ineffectually down towards them and bringing it back again. Perhaps he could change it to 'I am poorly.' No, no, that wouldn't do. 'I am probably.' There was the problem of the 'a'. He could write 'I am a probably', 'a' for clearing his throat. He cleared his throat a couple of times, wondering if his mother would understand that was what she had to do when she read the letter. His uncle looked up from his clockwork jigsaw and, without appearing to notice anything, bent his head again. There was nothing else for it. Robert covered the line of writing with his forefinger and began to draw patterns on his fingernail. His aunt put down one catalogue and picked up another.

'You finished?' she asked, licking the tip of a finger and turning pages.

'No.'

'Why not?'

'I dunno what to say.'

'What you said so far?'

'Nothing.' he muttered.

'Nothing! What you been writing then?'

Robert stared at his finger and moved it with great care a fraction of an inch.

'Dear Mum,' he read out.

'That all? That took you half-hour?'

'Dear Mum,' came an echo from the other side of the table, 'I am well and I hope you are too.'

Robert and his aunt stared in his uncle's direction. But he seemed unaware that he had spoken. He pressed a rusted spring into a socket and tried to cap it with several of the parts that lay in front of him, but none of them would fit. Undeterred by this setback he pushed the spring in and out a number of times with the tip of his finger, moving his lips silently, as though pondering the next step. His wife turned sharply again to Robert:

'We ain't going to write your letter for you.' She tapped on the table with her forefinger: 'You got ten minutes, then you give it here.'

'Dear Mum, I am a probably well,' he wrote. The 'probably' made out of 'prisoner' was difficult to decipher until you knew what was meant. Once his mother got it she would be all right. 'I have ... ' he continued and then stopped again. He wanted to write 'I have been', but he had been nowhere so far. 'I have,' he whispered under his breath, 'I have ... ' He had done nothing but wander round the house and sit on the steps in the back yard and spy on the neighbours. He thought of the woman with the bare breasts, 'I have seen inside the next-door neighbour's blouse.' He couldn't tell his mother that. 'I have hit a cat on the back leg with a pebble last night. I have caught a spider in the outside privy. In my hands.' He sighed and bent even lower over the paper. 'I have not been anywhere yet,' he wrote, 'but tomorrow I am going to school.' The pencil hovered over the feint blue line and Robert noticed a streak of shoe polish down the side of his thumb. 'I blacked my boots tonight,' he wrote proudly, 'ready.' His father, as man of the house, had cleaned the shoes at home. He looked back over what he had written. The word 'prisoner' still lurked unmistakeably behind 'probably'. A thread of fear tightened in his stomach. He traced over

49

the word, pressing his pencil hard into the paper with thick, black strokes.

'Give it here,' said his aunt, putting down her catalogue.

In the momentary silence even his uncle looked up from the broken clock.

'What's this! What's it say? "I am a" ... what?'

'I ... I ... ' Robert found he couldn't speak; his voice seemed to crack each time after the first syllable.

'What's this?' His aunt kept turning the paper this way and that in front of her eyes, like a torturer buffeting his victim. 'There's two words here written double.' She slapped the letter down onto the table and stabbed her finger at the word "prisoner". 'You tell me what that says!'

From the contortion of her mouth and the rage in her eyes, Robert saw that she already knew.

'Probably,' he whispered.

'There ain't no S in probably and there ain't no sense in "I am a probably well." Didn't your mother learn you no sense?'

Robert picked at the boot polish under his thumbnail.

'You'll learn sense here, my lad, even if you learn it off the back of my hand.'

It was worse, Robert reflected, as he undressed for bed, than being a cowboy perpetually ambushed by Indians, like the story in the comic stuffed behind Joseph's stove. It was worse, he thought, as he pulled the blankets round his head, than having to walk past the deserted house in Joseph's wood. At least once you got past it you were safe from the wanted man who he was sure lurked inside it. Here he was never safe. He and his aunt stalked each other constantly, listening, watching for some breach in the other's defences. His aunt was as dangerous as an Indian. She was wild and savage and not to be trusted. She would scalp him if she got the chance and hang his head over the mantelpiece as a trophy, in between the blue jug that had

'Present From Ostende' written on it and the calendar from the dry goods firm. It was going to be impossible to get a letter to his parents now, she would be more suspicious of him than ever. He lay in bed and watched the moon rise behind the thin stuff of the curtains, its light reflecting off the mirrored door of the wardrobe that towered at the foot of his bed like a dark cliff. Perhaps he could get a message to Joseph and Joseph could come and take him away. Joseph would be a match for his aunt, any day. He turned over onto his side and closed his eyes. It would be even better than being rescued by his parents. He could go and live at Joseph's instead. They would think he was here and his aunt would think he was there and really ... The problem was how to contact Joseph. But in the meantime there was school. A school full of children. A school full of friends. He fell asleep wondering what it would be like to have friends, picturing himself at the head of a small band of children incensed at his aunt's persecution of one of their number, marching on her shop to exact justice. Life at school would certainly be better than life in his aunt's house.

The next morning Robert and his aunt set off into a sharp cold and a clear light that seemed robbed of sleep. Though they rose no earlier than usual, everything in the house seemed to be startled awake, stunned and intimidated by his aunt's rapid footsteps and nagging voice. It irritated her to have to leave the opening of the shop to her husband, but she would not relinquish the pleasure she anticipated from parading her nephew for the first time through the town. She pushed Robert before her down the back steps, hustled him across the yard and through the door in the corrugated iron fence. Robert, dazed and sleepy, his head still buzzing from the bustle of their departure, found himself at last outside the prison walls. The air smelled of frost and chrysanthemums and the smoke of early morning fires. But his aunt, unaffected by the piercing excitement of it all, seized his hand and dragged him after her down the narrow alley between the backs of the houses. They emerged onto a side street and thence onto the lower corner of the square where it met the beginning of the High Street. Across the shabby rectangle of grass, narrow houses, shuttered and barred for the night from the incessant prying of their neighbours, were reluctantly drawing their curtains. Robert's aunt strode off down the High Street in expectation of her triumph, Robert at her heels, stumbling and trotting in a kind of lop-sided run. His aunt grasped him by the arm, pulling him after her like a thief. She looked neither to right nor left in her progress, her lips were as sourly compressed as ever and on her face could clearly be read the annoyance that this inconvenient journey caused her. But she knew that from behind every curtain, from within every dark interior of every shop she passed, she was watched; that she, at last, was seen to have a child at her side to be a trouble to her, a cross, a scourge. Her tales could rival now all tales that other women brought into her shop. Furthermore, they would surpass them; for this child, as she knew they knew, was not even *her* child, but merely that of her brother. It was for this – nephew – that she was forced to hurry through the streets at an hour when she should have been at home opening her shop. And she knew, without looking in their direction, that they nudged and pointed and commented on all these things to each other as she passed. So that, by the time she and Robert had disappeared from view under the railway arch at the bottom of the High Street, her self-esteem had swelled to such an unaccustomed size that she could not resist shaking him so that he was nearly swept off his feet and snapping 'Hurry up!' to reaffirm the power of her new acquisition.

As they approached the school, Robert tried desperately to escape from his aunt's grip. The more he struggled, the more he pulled away; the tighter she held him. The excitement of discovering the town beyond the corrugated iron fence was drained away with every step they took. She hurried him not into an intriguing new world, but into an extension of the greyness and suspicion under which he already lived. He saw it sideways, in a blurred vision: narrow houses all joined together, slithering with him down the hill to the bottom of the High Street where it ended in the mouth of a black tunnel. And everywhere eyes. Eyes in faces that stopped whatever business they were about to stare first at Robert, then at his aunt and then back to Robert. And in between the first stare and the second he felt himself labelled. He couldn't tell exactly what was on the label, but whatever it was they had got it wrong. They had looked at his aunt's face and read the label there. He couldn't see her expression, but he knew it would be as it always was. They thought of him now as she did and he was damned before he had a chance to speak.

The school had a beleaguered air about it. It was a stout grey building marooned in the centre of an asphalt yard surrounded on all sides by iron railings topped with wire netting so high that it resembled a cage. The yard was almost empty save for small black figures who clustered on the main steps, dwindled, then disappeared through the doorway. By the time Robert and his aunt reached the steps the children had vanished inside, leaving an elderly man holding a large book. To this man Robert was consigned with no exchange of words other than his aunt giving his name. The man stared solemnly at Robert as though deciding whether or not the information his aunt had given was correct, consulted the pages of his book and then, without a word, led Robert into the school. They entered a world of concrete stairs and stone corridors. They passed doors painted brown to resemble wood from behind which raucous shouting was quelled into mocking silence. And where Robert discovered that he had exchanged one kind of torment for another. What made it more perplexing was that the tormentors were not adults, but children like himself. He was unprepared for the indifference of the playground or the solidarity of the classroom, from which he was excluded. His solitary lessons at the kitchen table of the small house in the meadow had not prepared him for the noisy chanting rituals of a schoolroom. And he was lost. Everything seemed to be taught by rote: History, Geography, Arithmetic; the days of the week, the months in the year, the stars in the sky. Shouted out by forty voices that galloped names and dates and numbers, clipping and slurring the words into a patois intelligible only to themselves and their master, who beat time for them with his ruler on the parapet of his desk.

At first Robert tried to follow them. But he found himself held back not just by the alarming speed at which his classmates gabbled their lessons, but by a shyness of speaking out in such a public place. Afraid of saying the wrong word, he eventually found himself unable to say any word. To avoid detection, he made his lips move silently and stared studiously into space. It was then that he became aware of the buzzing: a low, intermittent noise that at first he could not trace. He looked around him. At the high walls of the schoolroom; at the blackboard; the master's desk perched on a wooden rostrum; the locked, glass-fronted bookcase with its half-empty shelves; the cast-iron stove in the corner near the door. The buzzing persisted. Over to his left a line of windows had been built into the wall so high up all one could see through them was sky. On one of these grimy panes a bee painstakingly scrabbled up the slippery surface, feverishly searching for a way of escape. It climbed and fell, climbed and fell. It hurled itself against the glass, unable to believe that there was anything tangible between itself and the open sky. It could feel the heat of the late autumn sun on its fur and was driven towards it by an innate fear of the paralysing cold to come.

It was the bee that was Robert's undoing. Caught up in its frantic efforts to escape, he did not notice that the rest of the class had fallen silent and had turned to stare at him.

The bee dropped suddenly out of sight. Robert waited for it to reappear, but in place of the buzzing began a rhythmic squeaking noise that grew louder. He turned quickly and saw, all together, the master, the descending cane, the leering faces of his classmates. There was a whistling sound and in the same instant he felt a kind of fire bite into his hands. He tried to pull them back across the desk, but they were pinned by the master's cane.

'Dumb?' snarled the man. 'Deaf?'

He shot out a hand and seized Robert's left ear, twisting it up to drag him to his feet.

'Kings!' he demanded.

Robert stared at him, gasping with pain. Kings? It was all incomprehensible.

'Kings!' shouted the master at the rest of the class.

'Charles . . . ' they chanted, 'Henry . . . '

'Kings!' hissed the master into Robert's face. 'Learn your kings?'

Around them the solemn liturgy rose and fell.

'No,' whispered Robert.

'No! Why not?'

'My mother . . . '

'Mother!' shrieked the man. Beads of spittle hung in the sparse hairs of his moustache. Rolling his cane off Robert's knuckles he dragged him after him down the gangway. The class around him rustled with anticipated pleasure and Robert caught glimpses of gesticulating hands and nudging elbows. He reached the front of the class.

'Up!' the master jerked his head at a boy sitting in the

front row. He leaped to his feet.

'Back!' the master stuck out his chin towards Robert's empty desk and the boy shuffled sullenly to the back of the room.

At midday they were herded out into the playground and the double doors of the school locked behind them. Uncertain of where to go or what to do Robert remained close to the door. First he leaned against the wall, then as the minutes dragged on he sat down on the front steps, huddled into a corner, as far out of sight as possible. He felt himself a target, without being able to pinpoint from where the attack might come. The other children busied themselves at first eating food which they had brought with them for lunch. Robert scuffed in the dust with his boots and tried to look as if he never ate lunch. Without food or friends he felt himself grow increasingly vulnerable to the boys who circled ever closer to him.

When he got back to his aunt's house his uncle was in the yard piling empty crates in one corner. He looked up at the creak of the corrugated-iron door and winced as it crashed shut behind the child.

'She don't like to hear that bang,' he said in a hushed tone as Robert drew level with him, and then, seeing his nephew's subdued face and bemused, abstracted eyes, asked:

'Get on all right, did you?'

The boy stared at him as though either he had not understood the question, or else the experience he had just undergone was still too painful, too recent, and too perplexing to be able to express adequately. His uncle pointed excitedly at the schoolbooks he carried under one arm:

'You got books!'

Robert looked down at them and as if the solidity of them gave him a tangible link with everyday life again he nodded, then looked up at his uncle:

'I didn't have no dinner.'

His uncle wiped his hands very slowly on the backs of his trousers, sucked his top lip and shook his head:

'She don't have no eating between meals.'

'I ain't had no meals,' persisted Robert.

'Well, we can go and see. But she won't like it.'

They walked together across the yard and up into the house. Robert's uncle cleared his throat nervously a couple of times and wiped his hands again.

'That him back?' shouted a voice from behind the shop door, a disembodied, domineering voice that came like some oracle out of the gloom of the narrow hallway, sensing their presence without needing to see them.

'Yes, Em,' replied his uncle, pushing open the door while Robert pressed himself into the darkness under the stairs. 'Says he hasn't had no dinner all day.'

'So what, I ain't no hotel.'

'You got an end of cheese or a bit of biscuit he could have? He looks done in. And he got a pile of books under his arm to study.'

'Books! What you mean – books?' She raised her voice: 'You got homework?'

Robert's muffled affirmation brought her to the hall door.

'Where is he?'

Her husband pointed to the small, shadowy figure.

'You go and put them books in your room and get downstairs and help your uncle. When you're in my house you work for me, you don't sit around reading no books till I say so.'

It wasn't until after supper was cleared away that his aunt released him at last to go and learn his lessons. He sat on the bed in his room and opened one of the books. 'Knowledge is eternal' was stamped on the first page and underneath it 'Property of the Town Council. Do not

57

deface.' What did 'deface' mean? Not to tear the cover off? He turned to the first page of all the other books and there was the same legend stamped sometimes straight, sometimes crooked, sometimes so clumsily that it blotted out the first words of the paragraph. Robert thought of the clerk stamping piles of books: knowledge is eternal ... knowledge is eternal ... He turned the pages of one of the books; dog-eared, limp, grey at the edges, they fell away from his fingers with soft, exhausted sighs, emitting a kind of waxy, cardboard odour as they did so. It was as if all the vitality of their knowledge had been drained from them by the indifference of generations of schoolchildren. The black words still stuck to the white page were like the intricate lacing of bones on a skeleton from which the flesh has been stripped.

He turned to the page of his lesson, and stared out of the window to where dusk faded slowly over the walls of successive back gardens, then over the strip of allotments which marked the boundary of the town, and plunged the open meadows beyond into darkness. From his window it seemed that with no more than a hop, skip and a jump he could clear the five or six garden walls that lay between his aunt's yard and the allotments. And be free. Stumble past the cabbage stumps and the neatly stacked bean poles and be off and running into the blackness. He would be so small no one would see him and so fast no one would catch him. Somewhere out in that darkness was his parents' house: ten, twenty, a hundred meadow-lengths away. The journey to the small town had seemed deliberately confusing. The ancient bus had trundled slowly through the afternoon, waited hours at railway crossings, lost itself in dark woods and emerged onto roads so straight among fields so flat that Robert had felt himself nodding asleep several times. He might have gone the length of the whole country, or travelled a mere ten miles.

When it was too dark even to distinguish the outlines

of the wooden huts on the allotments, Robert closed the book and went downstairs. The smell of fried potatoes from their supper still lay over everything, but the business of everyday life had been replaced by a strange calm, broken only intermittently by the click of knitting needles. Even the neighbours had been silenced. His aunt scowled at him and lowered the paper she was reading:

'Shut the door and stop creeping about.'

Robert slid into his chair. Across the table his uncle laboriously wound thin string round two knitting needles, pushing them together and pulling them apart with great concentration. Something grey and shapeless hung down between the needles. He looked up at Robert and smiled at him with almost childlike glee, waving the knitting at him: 'Dishcloths!' he whispered excitedly. Robert stared at him, horrified. He tried to imagine his father sitting in their front room, knitting. His uncle leaned over the table:

'Dishcloths!' he said louder, as though Robert was a stranger with no comprehension of the language, and nodded his head for emphasis. He dropped his voice to a stage whisper and leaned further over the table. The needles looked in danger of poking into his chest.

'We unravels string and knits it up again, that's what we do. We gets two dishcloths where anyone else would get one. Then we sells them in the shop. We sells them farthing cheaper than down the road. Real bargain they are.'

'Quiet,' snapped his wife, laying down the paper.

But his uncle prattled on:

'You knit? You can do dishcloths like me.'

'Quiet.'

'Why not?' pouted her husband. 'Why can't he knit?'

His wife ignored him.

'Come here,' she said to Robert. 'And pay attention. We're going to get some work out of you. You ain't come here to lie around.'

Unwillingly, Robert got up and went to stand by her chair. There was a pile of yellowing newspapers by her elbow. She pulled one towards her:

'See this? We make bags out of this. For the shop.'

She slid out a ruler from somewhere below the paper, ran her thumbnail down the central crease of the sheet of newsprint, then lined the ruler up against the crease.

'First thing you got to learn ... ' The hand that had been holding the paper flat at the top corner suddenly twitched, there was a screaming, ripping sound and the paper tore in two. Robert jumped back from his aunt's chair.

' ... is tearing paper. You watching?'

Robert crept back to his place. His uncle had stopped knitting, he had forgotten to sulk and was staring as at a conjuring trick.

'Go on,' he prompted, 'go on, do the next bit!'

His aunt hesitated as though unsure of whether or not she would grant this favour. Finally she picked up one of the half-sheets of paper.

'You take a piece like this, see. And you fold the top corner to the bottom. Turn it round in your hand till you got a cone. Then fold over. And tuck down.'

The squat fingers turned and twirled, plucking at the paper cone, adjusting creases and folds, her little finger held out slightly, her head on one side as if considering a work of art. Her creation complete, she tossed the bag onto the table and his uncle snatched it up, turning it in admiring hands.

'Wonderful, isn't it, eh? Clever.'

He inserted a finger into the opening of the cone. 'Quarter of sugar,' he chanted. 'Ounce of cinnamon. Two ounces of tea.' His eyes sparkled, he screwed up his face in delight and leaned towards Robert. 'Pennorth humbugs!'

His wife rarely allowed him to serve customers. He was a shadowy figure who swept and cleaned and replenished the shelves, handled the stock and did the cooking. Playing shop was as close as he ever got to it.

'Walter!'

Robert shuffled uncomfortably. If it was a kind of conjuring trick it was a trick without magic or belief. It was a cheap sleight of hand in which nothing was revealed, except the innate meanness of his aunt and the illusion of importance with which she surrounded these meaningless rituals. She had hoodwinked his uncle completely. But she would not fool him. He remembered suddenly the crumpled paper bags his mother used to fold away so carefully into the middle drawer of their sideboard: large, brown everyday ones and small ones made of thin, white paper with tiny zig-zagged edges. He twisted one foot against the other behind his aunt's chair and into their expectant silence he said:

'Why don't you use proper bags?'

The days passed, one the same as the next, each with a sense of deliberate deprivation that perplexed Robert. Life became a small concrete maze constructed of blind alleys, so that wherever he turned he came up against another brick wall. It was bounded by the narrow confines of life in his aunt's house and life at school, and he escaped from the one to seek refuge in the other only to be confronted by an identical barrenness. The people around him seemed possessed of a malignity that seethed and whispered in their blood waiting for the slightest opportunity to vent itself and against which, in his naivety and loneliness he had, initially, no defence.

He lingered in this bemused state of mind for some time, expecting each day that things would change. He could see no sense, no cause and no pleasure that anyone could possibly derive from such animosity. He expected to arrive in the schoolyard and find it had all been a game, a kind of test silently conducted, whose rigours he would be judged to have passed. He waited for some sign, too intimidated by the indifference of his schoolfellows to approach any of them himself. But he felt increasingly uneasy being alone in their midst. Like a stray traveller who finds himself encircled by a pack of dogs who pad round and round him, panting, grinning, waiting till they have exhausted his vigilance.

It had become his habit to linger in the classroom after school, not emerging into the playground until it was almost empty. As the last of the children turned out of the gates and straggled out of sight along the road, their voices echoing under the railway bridge as they passed through the tunnel into the High Street beyond, he would follow them. He would keep them in sight, but stayed always far enough behind to be unnoticed by them, and thereby he hoped to avoid the attentions of his predators. But one particular evening he realised that he had dawdled too long. The playground was deserted when he reached it and the road, bounded on either side by high, soot-blackened walls, was empty. He began to run towards the railway bridge, where the road twisted itself into an S-bend of such exaggerated proportions that the two corners of the S were invisible from each other. In the narrow street his footsteps made a light, flapping sound; as he plunged into the darkness of the tunnel they sounded slow and hollow as though they echoed up through deep water.

They were waiting for him in the corner of the last bend. They moved out of the shadows, grinning, and caught him by the coat sleeve as he tried to run past. There was a ripping, thudding sound, something pounded into his head and something else kicked away his feet. He felt himself fall into the darkness and tasted the warm, sickly sweetness of blood in his mouth. As he hit the pavement he felt all the breath knocked out of his body and then the sensation of being strangely cushioned by arms and legs that mauled at him from all sides. He bit and kicked and

62

thrashed his arms about and felt all the time as if he bit and kicked himself. However hard he fought he seemed to inflict no pain on his enemies. He heard only his own gasping, the rasp of their boots and the thud of pummelling fists which grew louder till they became a roaring in his head which drowned out everything else. The ground beneath him began to shake and he imagined the whole school had assembled to trample on him. He drew his knees into his chest, covered his head with his arms and shut his eyes tightly. But nothing happened. Instead the roaring died away, the trembling of the earth ceased and he realised that the punching had stopped some time ago. Cautiously he opened his eyes, but instead of a ring of jeering schoolboys he saw only the black arch of the railway bridge above him. He uncovered his head. A man on a bicycle whirred slowly past him and stared at him with surprise. His attackers had vanished.

He struggled to his feet and limped out into the sunshine. Everything ached. Gingerly he examined his wounds, so engrossed in his bruises that when he first heard the hollow, clip-clopping sound reverberate through the blackness of the tunnel he took it to be a carthorse negotiating the bends with a load of timber or hay. He went on with his examination; ankle to knee, knee to ribs. He stared at the bruised flesh, overwhelmed. He could never go back to school again, not after this. Meanwhile the noise grew louder, the arch of the bridge throwing it back, doubling it and holding the echo, until Robert, looking up, expected to see a four-in-hand sweep out of the darkness. Instead a boy, roughly his own age, clattered out into the sunshine, swaying and stumbling like a colt fighting some invisible rein. Robert stared at him in amazement. Even his feet were shod, one of his heavy boots built up on a kind of wooden stack. But the boy seemed to find Robert even more curious:

'Whew,' he whistled, wobbling sightly off-balance as he

63

stopped in front of him, 'your mum won't half be pleased with you when you get home. You're a real sight!'

Robert got slowly to his feet and straightened his shoulders indignantly. That this ... carthorse, swaying on strange, clog-like boots in front of him, enveloped in what looked suspiciously like a woman's washed-out jersey, should call *him* a sight.

'I'm not!' he retorted and tried to run his fingers through his hair to smooth it down in a nonchalant way. But the strands were matted together somehow and where his fingers ran against the tufts stabs of pain shot through his head.

The boy watched him, grinning: 'They really done you over, ain't they?'

Robert blushed.

'That's all right! Everyone new gets done over. They won't touch you no more.'

But Robert felt entirely crushed and near to tears. He began to brush ineffectually at the dust and dead leaves that clung to his clothes, keeping his head bent.

'Come over here,' the boy jerked his head to where, behind them, the shops began, 'you can tidy up in this window.'

He led him towards a barber's shop which had round the edge of its window a wide frame of mildewed mirror glass. Robert bent down and peered into it. The reflection that he saw was himself and yet not himself. His hair stood out in tufts around his face and it was difficult to tell which were streaks of grime and which were bruises. He licked at his finger and rubbed at the marks, but they didn't seem to go away. He brushed at the dust on his trousers and pulled at his sleeves to straighten them. With a sudden ripping sound like torn paper one of the sleeves came away in his hand. It dangled from his fingers, its loose threads waving feebly in the wind. They stared at it almost unable to believe their eyes. Robert felt the whole world stand still for a second. And then he longed fervently to be lying safe in some hospital bed, or better still dead under the railway bridge. The other boy, impressed by the drama of the situation, whistled through his teeth:

'What's your mum going to say now!'

Robert shook his head. He pulled the sleeve over his arm again, but immediately he let go it slid off and fell in the dust at their feet. His companion began to giggle, leaning against the barber's window.

Inside the shop, the barber's client, muffled to the ears in shaving soap, stared solidly before him. Suddenly, beside his own reflection, appeared that of a small boy bent double with laughter. A look of disconcertion suffused his blank features; a finger emerged from under wraps and towels and stabbed at the image in the glass. The barber strode over to the door.

'Quick!' whispered a voice in Robert's ear and an elbow nudged him in the ribs. They darted to the edge of the pavement.

'Scarper!' hissed the barber from the doorway. And his razor glinted eagerly through the soap bubbles, as though it slavered.

'What am I going to do?' Robert twisted the loose sleeve in his hands.

'Your mum be very cross?'

'It's not my mum,' confessed Robert. 'It's my aunt.'

They stared at each other solemnly: the anger of a mother was one thing, the rage of a guardian quite another.

'You that boy come to live with that woman keeps that shop up on the square?'

Robert nodded. The other boy pursed his lips and regarded him with concern:

'My gran goes in her shop sometimes. I been in there once . . . ' His voice trailed away as though the experience was beyond his powers of description. He wobbled on the kerb, looking out across the road. 'What's your name?'

65

'Robert.'

'Mine's Luke.' He whirled round on one foot and fell off the pavement into the path of a bicycle. Robert dragged him back to safety. Luke grinned at him:

'I keep telling my mum my high heels need mending, but she don't do nothing. They're going to cripple me one of these days.'

Robert looked down, embarrassed.

'Anyway, I got to go now; my mum's in bed again. See you tomorrow.' Luke launched himself into the road, weaving and hobbling among the traffic, waving his hand above his head, and limped off down a narrow street of terraced houses that faced the railway line.

Robert ran up the High Street as fast as his injuries would allow him and then paused for breath in the silent lane that led behind his aunt's house. He tried to slick back his hair and pull his socks up to hide the cuts on his legs, but the filaments of wool scratched against his skinned flesh and made him wince. Quietly he pushed open the corrugated-iron gate and slipped inside. A cat sunning itself on a pile of crates scrambled away over the fence with a sudden, rasping clatter. Nervously he put his hand up to the door, but he could not bring himself to turn the handle, instead he picked at a patch of peeling paint with his fingernail and tried to make up an excuse for his aunt. But nothing would come into his head.

He might have stood there for quite some time, thinking himself relatively safe. But from the gloomy cavern of her shop his aunt had heard the squeak of the yard gate. Now she waited for the sound of the back door opening and closing and for the loose floorboard that ran down the centre of the hall to announce the return of the child. She waited, leaning over the counter to catch the slightest tiptoeing creak. But there was nothing. The silence seemed to jeer at her. She was certain the child was there but everything was wrapped in a mist of stillness which was

66

impenetrable to her. Her patience broke:

'Keep shop!' she snapped at her husband who was arranging tins of sprats on a shelf, and marched out into the hallway. It was empty and shadowed. She strode towards the door and flung it open. Robert stood on the top step, one finger upraised in a gesture she could not understand.

'What you doing?' she demanded, grabbing him by the arm and pulling him into the hall. 'Hovering! I won't have hovering, not in my house. You come in, you come in proper. None of this loitering!'

She pushed him before her into the parlour and there the light from the window clearly illuminated his dishevelled appearance. Spreading out from the corner of one eye along his cheekbone was a black stain. A streak of dried blood flared out from one nostril across his cheek. His aunt stabbed a finger towards the bruise.

'You been fighting.'

Robert backed away from her.

'Haven't you?'

She continued to advance on him.

'Haven't you! You been . . .'

Robert stumbled back against the wall.

' . . . fighting!'

The blow landed across his head with such force that without thinking he clapped his hand to his ear to protect it. The tattered sleeve dangled in front of his aunt's eyes. She let out a roar that strangled itself into a gasp and her fists flailed in the air as though she could not make up her mind whether she was fighting Robert or the rage that paralysed her lungs.

'Ahhh,' she whispered. 'I'll . . . I'll . . . '

Her husband, listening by the bead curtain that divided the shop from the house, nervously juggled a tin of sprats from one hand to the other and wondered whether he should intervene. At that precise moment Robert's nose began to bleed. The flow of blood released the flow of air and, recovering voice, his aunt darted at him again, seized him by the hair and dragged him howling into the scullery, where she held his head under the cold water tap until both their passions were exhausted.

Later that evening, as he lay in bed, his grazes smarting from the iodine his aunt had poured over them, his bruises tender to the tips of his exploring fingers, he felt only puzzlement as to why his parents had sent him to such a place as this.

Luke was waiting for him the next morning at the bottom of the High Street.

'Thought I might have missed you,' he grinned. 'How d'you get on last night?'

Robert grimaced.

'Your eye don't look too good.'

'Yea, well, she didn't make it any better.'

'She wallop you?'

'Had a good try.'

Luke clicked his tongue in sympathy: 'Funny, isn't it, how they always make out it's your fault.'

They sauntered under the railway arch and turned in at the school gates.

'What you doing Saturday?'

'I dunno. Work for my aunt, I suppose.'

'What d'you do? Serve in the shop, an' that?'

'Well ... ' Robert thought of the crumpled newspaper bags he sat at the kitchen table trying to perfect night after night, of the knitted dishcloths and the odd lengths of used string he was made to unravel, separate into strands, knot and roll up into balls for re-use in the shop. Of the perished elastic bands he had to tie into temporary soundness:

'This and that.'

'Only I go round my uncle's Saturday afternoons, do his pigeons with him. Why don't you come too? He don't

68

like people much, not after my aunt run off with the travelling butcher. But he don't mind me and he won't mind you.'

They waited in the shuffling crowd of children to be let into the school.

'See you lunchtime,' whispered Luke as they filed in through the double doors.

Robert sat at his desk all morning, daydreaming about a jolly woman in a large hat festooned with ribbons trundling off with her lover in a painted van across the flat plains: the two of them laughing and singing, carcasses of meat swaying and jolting in the back and a cloud of dust billowing out behind them. While in the grey town her husband stroked the feathers of his racing pigeons as they shuddered and crooned, and told them endlessly the sad tale of his betrayal. Robert thought of the butcher who'd called once a week at the prison cottages. How he'd hated the sound of the musical motor horn that he played to summon the warders' wives, and the way that his mother, on hearing it, would pull her apron off, pat at her hair, snatch up her purse and go running awkwardly over the meadow towards the road. For some inexplicable reason it had made him very angry.

'Do you think it's the same one?' he asked Luke at lunch time.

'Who knows,' replied Luke. 'We never clapped eyes on them again, from that day to this.'

Luke opened up the small town to Robert as though possessed of some magic key. The blank walls of the maze did not dissolve, but he ran its alleys now in company, and the authority of their overwhelming bleakness was undermined by Luke's indifference to them. He seemed to treat it as a mere backdrop, so dull and so familiar that he accepted its presence without even noticing it. Everyone had to live somewhere. This was Life for him and it never

69

occurred to him that it could be other. Its confines were not an oppression, they were almost a comfort – like the enfolding walls of a small house. He knew every corner of it; he peopled its walls and named its streets. He could find doors in blind alleys that had been invisible hitherto to Robert, and cracks in its impenetrable walls through which he dragged him, breathless and wide-eyed, to stand proprietorial in some new lane or square, hands on hips, shaking his head with pride.

'You don't know nothing, do you?' he would exclaim.

And Robert would grin, sheepish with pleasure, and allow himself to be hustled on to new discoveries.

They kept away from the High Street where older boys hung about in groups, picking fights and watching girls. It was too prosaic and too public for their purpose. Its ugly, narrow-faced houses stared across the road at each other with eyes veiled against any intrusion. Even the small dark shops made no attempt to entice. Their windows were for the most part bare and dusty, save for a few sun-bleached placards propped against their shelves advertising brands of goods long ago gone out of fashion. They wandered instead down the side streets out to where, on the eastern flank of the town, the allotments stretched all the way to the river, separated from the outlying houses by a rickety fence. They would frequently hang over this fence, and often in the dusk of winter afternoons they would scramble through and wander among the frosted cabbages and drooping chrysanthemums, nibbling brussels sprouts, looking for a potting shed that might have been left open where they could sit out of the wind and smoke lengths of dried cow parsley stalks. Until the cold drove them back into the town again.

The town might never have existed at all had it not been for a quirk of nature that had made it the highest navigable point on the river. Below where the bridge now stood, barges and lighters, unable to go any further, tied up at wooden piers, unloaded and were loaded up again. And so the town called itself a port. But the wooden piers built out into the river, the single dockyard, the wire-fenced stockade for storing timber and crates, the dilapidated mission for seamen and the salvationist's hostel by the bridge were petty claim to such importance. Above the bridge the river had thrown up sandbanks, narrowed its channel and withdrawn itself into the pollarded calm of its upper reaches. From these sandbanks the town bathed in summer, while its children played in the shallows, netting minnows and shrieking. In periods of drought the bed of the river shrank to a narrow central channel, so that you could walk right across from one bank to the other. Cattle that were driven down to drink at it would slither on the sun-baked mud, stumble into water-holes and stretch their soft necks in fear and disbelief towards the water glimmering beyond.

Across the bridge the town petered out almost immediately, the tarmacadam ended and the white gravel of the country road began. Luke could not be persuaded to cross this dividing line. He would stand some way back on the metalled road and mournfully watch Robert scuffle his feet in the soft gravel.

'Come on!' Robert would call. But Luke would shake his head. And Robert would turn and stare at the narrowing white road in front of him, flanked by hedgerows and ditches and, in the distance, a line of trees straight and tall as the trees at home, before the road vanished round a bend, disappearing into the wide, flat fields that spread away on either side.

'Come on,' he would plead and Luke would inch a little nearer. 'You could walk for miles on this. It's soft, like grass. Look!' He bounced up and down on his heels a couple of times, but Luke was unimpressed:

'No, I couldn't. Anyway, where'd we go? We'd just get lost. And we'd have nothing to eat.'

'We could find mushrooms. And blackberries. Stuff like that.'

'Nah!' Luke screwed up his face in disgust. 'Let's go to the cattle market.'

In this no-man's land beyond the bridge a strange shanty town had grown up around the slaughter house and the logging sheds. Houses made of corrugated iron which boiled in summer and froze in winter, whose porches were festooned with washing and decked about with plants in old kerosene tins. The cattle market close by was one of their favourite haunts. It drew Robert time and time again to stand in its eerie silence, to walk between the rows of pens in the deserted yard running his hand along the iron bars, and to feel the fluttering pleasure of unidentifiable horror at the base of his spine. He and Luke would swing on the crush gates and hang over the rails, gazing at the empty auction ring.

'They don't all go for dead, you know,' remarked Luke. 'Well, p'raps the old ones. But the young ones, they got a chance. You ever seen an auction?'

Robert shook his head. Luke clambered up to the topmost rail, sat astride the bar and looked down at him.

'It's like nothing else you ever seen. All the animals is in the big ring, bleating and grunting and being poked with sticks to make them walk about. And the people buying stands all round the ring. But they don't call out what they want. They ain't allowed to. They rub their noses, or they twitches an eyebrow, or they taps on the rail in front of them with their finger. Like it's all secret. You can't tell what's happening. No one can. The animals don't know and the people don't know. There's only this one man what knows and he don't say nothing, he just writes it all down in his big book ...'

Luke's voice tailed away.

'What happens then?' prompted Robert.

72

Luke shrugged and began limping back between the pens:

'Oh, I dunno; some of them ends up in a nice field out in the country and some of them ends up round the back with their throats cut.'

His friendship with Luke enraged his aunt. She saw it as a trick, a way of evading her control. She had not counted on such a distraction as a friend occurring; she had not reckoned on his having any such support, but being entirely at her service. And she did not like it. The child had no sense of the beholdenness of his situation. He was not grateful enough. He was not abject enough. He was not ... not – she could not put her finger on it – it was as if he did not know why he was here, nor the terms of his board and lodging. It was as if they had not told him what was expected of him. She saw that even through his confusion and unhappiness, even though he obeyed her commands, he did so without believing in her dictates, without accepting the life she ordained for him as being either right or inevitable. There was no outward rebellion. There was no laughing off the privations she inflicted on him, she saw with satisfaction how they dragged him down. But never far *enough*. He managed, at the last, always to hold himself apart. He was more stubborn than she had bargained for. But she would break him in time.

It was easy for her to fill up the evenings after school and before homework with chores. It was the weekends, the hours that could be entirely hers which she was greedy for, but which she lacked the ingenuity to fill. She could have kept him prisoner in the shop. She could have tied a sacking apron round his waist and stood him in a corner to wait till help was needed with a rush of customers. But she could not bear to have anyone else serve in the shop except herself. She wanted no other hands but hers to count the money, to weigh the goods and judge, customer

73

by customer, how much short weight could be given. She disliked even having Walter there. She liked to stand by herself in the gloomy cavern knowing exactly the position of everything on the shelves and how much, down to the last grain, there was; to feel everything under her hand. She liked to stare out into the silence where the dust fell slowly through the air, till the shop door should jangle all her spider's web of nerve-ends into vigilance. Engrossed as she was by the shop, her dilemma was that she could neither bear to have Robert in it, nor out of it. When she ran short of tasks to set him to keep him in the house, she resorted to finding fault with what he did and confining him to his room for the slightest trespass. But, as he determinedly taught himself to perform his chores with greater speed, so he became more proficient and it grew harder even for her to justify these punishments.

One Saturday afternoon she cornered him as he sat re-tying a pile of perished rubber bands. His cap and scarf lay beside him, for this was the last job in a long list she had set for him. He did not look up as she stood over him, but she sensed his resistance in a barely perceptible feeling of waiting that always hung about him; a waiting till something should be over, till something should be past. Seized by irritation she flung his cap to the floor:

'Always trying to scarper, aren't you!' She rapped her knuckles on the table. 'You ain't here to play. You ain't here to spend your time hanging around with that pasty-faced cripple. You're here to work. In my shop. For good! Your parents tell you that? School holidays an' all. You ain't running home to your mum every couple of months telling tales and lounging about. You been sent off to work, you ain't been sent off to be no fancy boarder. And work you will whether you like it or not. Tell you that, did they?' She saw his fingers falter and the rubber filaments squirm out of his grasp.

'And I'll tell you something else – you don't think what

74

your dad sends *pays* for your keep, do you? "How're you going to make it up, Tom?" I says to him. "Set him to *work*," he says, "there ain't no point him coming back here." So!' She stabbed her finger at the table. 'You're in my house now, under my telling, and the sooner you behave like it the better!' And she swept out.

Robert sat for a long time staring at the rubber bands. Out in the shop, his aunt stood and listened to the silence with malicious pleasure. He hadn't known any of it. He didn't know they paid his aunt. He didn't know of his mother's tears in her steamy kitchen, or how his father swaggered in the guard room, thumbs through the thongs of his leather belt, boasting of how he'd sent his son off young, to learn a trade. He thought of his letter and knew that even if it had been posted there would never be any reply, not of the sort he wanted. His parents were in league with his aunt. The more he thought about it, the clearer it seemed to him. If he had known such things could happen, it would have been obvious to him right from the day his aunt and uncle had come for a visit. There were signs of their collusion, even then. His plans to run away back home were futile. They would only send him back here, to her. He felt himself suddenly alone in a very small lighted space completely surrounded by darkness that stretched away forever. He picked up his cap and scarf and went out.

'What kept you?' asked Luke, swinging his legs over the end of the jetty.

'Nothing,' replied Robert.

'I almost give you up! She getting worse?'

'She can't get no worse.' Robert eased himself onto the wharf steps beside Luke. 'Let's just sit here. I got to go back soon.'

For several days after that Robert felt disorientated and lost. The comforting bright image of rescue was gone,

75

leaving only the unfathomable darkness spreading out in whichever direction he looked. But, if he was not to return home, what was he to do? In the silence of his thought the answer slid across his mind like a quickly growing stain, blotting out all other colours. He was to stay here, for ever. In this dimly-lit space in which he found himself he and his aunt were to do battle. There was to be no rest from her spite, no end to the fighting; it would continue, a war of inestimable duration, of siege and perpetual, petty sniping, of minutes snatched and hours blockaded until eventually one of them was defeated. It would be a war to the death, from which the only escape would be out into the unknown darkness. Yet at first sight such an alternative seemed only to offer another kind of death fraught with terrors that could not be foreseen. The thought of escape, however impossible and dangerous it appeared to him, remained, nevertheless, in his mind. As hostilities with his aunt dragged on, he returned to it again and again, pondering over it, dreaming about it, until gradually its darkness was transformed into mysteriousness, and impossibility quickened into a tiny glow of hope. He would kneel on his bed and gaze out over the back gardens behind his aunt's house, over the bare allotments, out to where the fields stretched endless to the sky. And a little knot of trembling excitement would tighten in his stomach. Or he would sit at the table in the parlour reading in his school books of life elsewhere, of life unconfined, free of petty bickering and stale food. At first he wondered where exactly this life, that he had always unconsciously expected to exist, might be. He read everything that he could get hold of, but its exact location was never defined, it was always – somewhere else. He discussed it earnestly with Luke, but Luke was not much of a reader, nor could he imagine a life that was different from his own. But Robert persisted in his belief and came to the conclusion that such a life probably went on *every*where outside the small town.

76

Once the idea of escape became accepted it took on a small, rolling inevitability that sent shivers down Robert's spine every time he thought of it. It thrilled and frightened him and he let himself be carried away by it as if it was an already irreversible train of action. The practical preparations never entered his head. All he could feel was the fluttering thrill of almost being free. He was sure that somewhere within the small town the mechanism of escape lay hidden, waiting for him to discover it. It would be like a concealed spring that only he could press. Like a lock secretly oiled in readiness so that its key could be turned with a silence no one else in the town would hear and through which he could slip invisibly away. Like a brick ready loosened for him in a prison wall. He had no idea what he was looking for, only a conviction that he would recognise it as soon as he saw it. And so he began to roam the streets, looking for a way out.

Sometimes they would go to the disused goods yard that lay behind the square at the bottom of Station Walk, where it ended in a mass of brambles and a padlocked, five-barred gate. There was rusted barbed wire along the top of the gate and rusted tin notices tacked to the upright posts forbidding entrance and warning of fines and imprisonment. Robert and Luke would read the notices to each other, rolling the impressive words round their tongues and then, with great care not to tear their trousers, climb over the gate and jump down into the yard.

There was reputed to be a watchman on permanent duty with an alsatian dog that he deliberately kept in a state of starvation to set onto trespassers and tear them to pieces. They had seen its snarling face depicted on one of the notices. But they had never yet encountered either of them. The game was to dart from wagon to wagon across the rusted railway tracks without detection and to creep into the abandoned guard's van on the far side of the yard. Here they would crouch and listen for the snuffling of the dog, or the tramp of the watchman's boots on the cinders of the track. But all they ever heard was their own gasping breaths and the wind singing in the silent rails. Robert began to be mesmerised by these rails. Instead of running from wagon to wagon, he took to standing between them, staring in front of him to where the tracks converged into a dark line that shot straight as an arrow towards the far-distant horizon. His recklessness horrified Luke who danced and gibbered in the shadow of a wagon door, but Robert was oblivious to his wildly signalling hands. He was seized with a longing to walk out between the rusted rails till he, too, vanished into the horizon. They drew him like long beckoning fingers.

'Where do they go?' he kept asking Luke.

Luke became irritated and upset by his constant questioning.

'They don't go nowhere,' he snapped, 'nothing goes nowhere from here – it's all rusted up.'

'It must,' insisted Robert. 'It must go somewhere – all these rails.'

'Well, it don't.'

'What about the platform? I bet it says on there where they go.'

'You can't go up on there! The dog'll get you.'

'So what!' Robert flung a pebble at a perching sparrow, missed, and hit the side of one of the wagons with a dull ping that echoed round the deserted goods yard. Luke leaped to his feet:

'I ain't staying here with you. You ain't playing right. You're just going to get us caught. I tell you there ain't no trains through here. They all go on the other line.'

'What line?' Robert scrambled to his feet. Luke wished he'd held his tongue. 'Come on, let's go there!'

'We can't.'

'What d'you mean?'

'There's nothing there. It's just a line. It don't stop.

78

There ain't no station. We don't get nothing stops in this town.'

The river presented another avenue of escape to Robert. He made Luke stand on the bridge for hours all through that winter, unwillingly discussing various possibilities, while the water rushed grey as slate beneath the piers of the bridge and sucked and swirled at the river banks. When, two weeks before Christmas, the first snow fell, Luke tried to divert him with speculations on there being ice strong enough to skate on by Christmas Day. They stood, as usual, on the bridge staring at the immobilised barges tied to their moorings, tarpaulined and iced over. Logs waited in melancholy stacks on the deserted quay, covered in snow. Every so often overhanging snow from the river bank would topple into the current, dissolving almost before it hit the water, obliterated as though it had never been. Robert's heart would lurch each time a new patch fell in, and he would screw up his eyes to discern the exact moment of death – that split second between which the snow ceased to be its white self and became assimilated into the hungry stream.

'You going home for Christmas?'

'No.'

'Not at all?'

'No.'

Luke stared at him, incredulous.

'What you going to do, then?'

'I got to stay in the holidays, work for my aunt in the shop. It's some bargain or something she and my dad did. Pay for my keep – something like that.'

'They coming to see you?'

'Well, they were. Then my dad got his work roster changed 'cause they got illness. And now my mum's gone down with 'flu. So I don't know.' He shrugged his shoulders and looked away into the heart of the icy river. Watching Robert's averted face Luke felt, with a shivering of uneasiness at the back of his neck, his own complacency undermined. He thought, in sudden alarm, of the way Robert would stand in the middle of the disused railway tracks, staring down the lines, lost in a dream, and how he stared in the same way at the river and the roads leading out of the town and at the open fields beyond the allotments. And inside himself he drew back; the prospect of anything beyond his life was unimaginable and profoundly disconcerting. There was nothing beyond the small town, nothing. It was all unknown: there were just empty fields and empty sky that went on and on. No one he knew had ever left the town. Except, of course, for his aunt who'd run off with the butcher, but she'd vanished never to be heard of again – and Robert.

'You really going?' he whispered, staring anxiously at the wooden face.

The wooden face nodded, never raising its gaze from the river.

Christmas arrived as quietly as the small town could muffle it. The shopkeepers and their customers would circle the subject warily, both professing indifference, then, as the Day grew closer, assume stoical endurance in the face of inevitability. Regretfully the shopkeeper would feel compelled to get in extra stock. With much complaint his customers would buy as little as decency and custom permitted. Christmas made martyrs of them all. Only the bored shopgirls would come to life as the long-awaited permission was given to take out the box of decorations. Paperchains were hung like multi-coloured sausages in the grocer's. The shelves in the haberdashery were draped with faded Christmas paper. Two geese were suspended in the window of the butcher's shop: one for the bank manager, the other for the doctor paid for with credit accumulated on the maladies of the butcher's wife, who was sickly. A large bell, once icing-sugar white, was unfolded into concertina-ed crêpe paper perfection and fixed in the baker's window above a solitary Christmas cake wrapped in cellophane and iced with robins and snowmen. Every year this cake became the object of longing and jealousy among the children of the town, for it was common knowledge that no one ever bought it. On Christmas Day it would vanish from the window and everyone knew that the baker's children were devouring it.

'Your aunt got stuff in her window?' enquired Luke as they wandered from shop to shop up the High Street. Robert shook his head. His aunt and her customers were of the same mind about Christmas.

'Come on,' he said hastily as they reached the top of the hill, and approached her shop, 'let's go down the other side.'

He couldn't bear to be confronted with his aunt's mean-spiritedness as the days led up to Christmas. It only made him think more and more of his mother and her busy little rituals, the increasing air of gaiety she assumed until she could contain herself no longer. She would wait till they were alone in the house and then reach to the back of the kitchen cupboard, bring out an old tobacco tin and shake it so that it rattled.

'Christmas,' she would whisper.

And he would hold out his hands for it, tipping the brown-and-yellow-striped tin backwards and forwards so carefully that the Christmas inside made a sliding, slithering sound.

'What is it?' he would ask, his eyes now as bright as hers.

'Shhh!' she would say. 'Secrets. Don't tell *no one*.'

His father, however, derided the whole idea of Christmas.

'Day off, that's all.' And he would spread his legs wide under the kitchen table and open another bottle of beer.

81

He spent most of Christmas Day drinking beer out of brown bottles, sunk in a welcome abstraction from which he would occasionally rouse himself. His mother would scurry around in her best dress with food and smile encouragingly at Robert, who felt nevertheless that the day was a slight anti-climax. The present was never quite up to his expectations and no doubt because of his father, and in spite of his mother, lunch always fell rather flat. But without her guidance he could not, by himself, create Christmas. He did not know what fish it was they ate on Christmas Eve, or what else to put, besides cherries and almonds, in the white cake they had for pudding on Christmas Day. He had no money to buy meat, or nuts, or a packet of sweets to be eaten all in one go on Christmas afternoon. Or even a tin with a rusted lid.

He told Luke the best bits about Christmas at home and Luke was impressed.

'Christmas is a joke round our house. First my mum says she can't be bothered. Then, as it gets nearer, she says she ain't got no money. Well, we all know we never got no money, so we pipe down. Then my gran pitches into her, because she knows there'd be more money if my mum didn't drink it all. So we let them fight it out. Any money my mum leaves lying about my gran whips it and hides it away. But we still don't know till Christmas Day comes whether there's going to be any food, never mind any presents. Mum's supposed to come back from the pub on Christmas Eve with food and toys and things she's put money into the Christmas Club all year for. But one year she exchanged it all for drink and we didn't have nothing. My gran was so mad she threw her out. Her own daughter! Christmas morning!' Luke giggled. 'But she just went down the pub again and they took her in.'

If the small town refused to celebrate Christmas, the country people who brought the weekly market to the square outside his aunt's shop refused to ignore it. Their market fell that year the day before Christmas Eve. Instead of packing up as the daylight faded and the cold became unbearable, they stayed on till well into evening. Between the booths they strung up kerosene lanterns and flares and set out candles in stout jars along the edge of their stalls. You could smell the light in the same way that you could smell the frost on the cabbages and the scent of Christmas in the pyramids of oranges nestling in blue tissue paper. Luke was entranced. The flapping canvas awnings of the bigger stalls, the raucous cries of the market men, brown as berries even in the depths of winter, the flaring hiss of the lanterns – all had a kind of circus wildness about them. Clutching tightly to Robert's sleeve he dragged him from stall to stall, stumbling on the uneven ground:

'Here!' he would gasp. 'Here – look at *them*!'

The rest of the town seemed as awestruck as Luke; they wandered, slow as in a dream, round and round the stalls. As though they gazed at a life beyond their own and could not believe they might have a part of it.

But Robert was drawn to the back of the market. Here the smallholders sold their produce: wizened old men who stood behind orange boxes on which they had set little piles of vegetables, or herbs, or nuts, or eggs. They had a fairytale quality about them: their crinkled skin, the glint of dark eyes behind a single candle spluttering on the upturned box, and the very smallness of their offerings. It seemed to Robert as though each scrubbed turnip was in fact a magic turnip, not to be confused with the ordinary vegetables heaped up on the bigger stalls. Suddenly, behind one of these crates, he caught sight of a woman, younger than the others, wrapped in a shawl, standing before a little pile of eggs which she constantly rearranged with slow, dream-like gestures. Below the shawl a faded, flowered apron showed, of the kind his mother wore. It was as though she had just gone out from the back door of her house to feed her hens and had been whisked off, the eggs still warm in her apron pocket, by these enchanted marketeers. He tried to catch sight of her face, but she kept her head turned away from him. He stretched out a finger and gently touched one of the eggs. She looked up. And for a second they stared at each other, blankly, before Robert turned away in bitter disappointment and she bent her head again.

That winter Luke's uncle took to his bed with a succession of colds and so it fell to Luke to take care of his pigeons. Robert went along too, whenever he could. He would go without lunch on a Saturday to get to Luke's before he set off. His aunt gave up trying to stop him. Besides, it saved on food, and when she had no more work for him she wanted him out of the house. Sometimes when he arrived Luke's mother would be there having just got up, sitting at the kitchen table drinking tea and combing her hair in a tiny mirror propped against a sugar packet. While the grandmother poured stew into a white jug and tied news-paper over the top, Robert would watch Luke's mother struggling to pull a comb through her bedraggled curls. An alarming amount of hair seemed to come out in the teeth of the comb, hair of an indefinable colour, neither brown nor blonde nor grey, but seeming to be all those colours. Luke's mother saw him staring and winked at him across the table:

'Me permanent's gone.'

Robert wasn't quite sure what this meant. She wound a strand of hair round her finger and then let it drop, wrinkling her face disconsolately as the hair dangled and bounced in a limp corkscrew. Perhaps she was referring to her youth. Or her beauty. Or some other valuable possession. Robert blushed. She laughed.

'Here, Mum!' she screeched. 'Me permanent's gone!' She rocked on her chair with laughter, her whole soft body shaking, exuding a scent of cheap soap and damp linen.

'You watch your language when we got visitors.' Luke's grandmother handed him the full jug. 'Here, Luke, you hold this carefully. Make sure he has it all, and bring the jug back, love, and the string. It don't matter about the paper.' She held the door open for them. 'See if you can't chivvy him along a bit; get him out of hisself.' She peered out into the street, it had started raining again.

Luke's uncle lived at the far end of the road where it ended in the railway embankment. From the street his house looked so narrow that but for the slit of a window you would have thought it was just a wall, an extension of the embankment that curved behind it. You entered from an alley-way between two houses and were plunged into gloom even at the height of summer. There was a narrow, dark room downstairs and another upstairs. Outside, the yard was taken up completely by pigeons' cages from which there came a rolling, crooning sound. Luke's uncle was sitting downstairs in a chair wrapped in blankets when they came in, his face a strange yellowish-grey.

'Ah,' said Luke somewhat taken aback. 'You're up! You feeling better?'

'You come to do the pigeons?' his uncle gasped. 'I couldn't get out there last night. Couldn't get me breath.' He stared anxiously from one to the other. Luke searched in a cupboard for a bowl to pour the contents of the jug into.

'Their feed's in the next cupboard.' A finger wavered out of the chrysalis of blankets, like a feeler. 'Next one along,' he whispered hoarsely, 'that's it, that one.'

'I ain't looking for their feed, Uncle. I'm getting you some soup.'

His uncle became more agitated, plucking at the blankets round his shoulders, his eyes now on Luke, then, as if the sight became unbearable, on the floor, a leg of the table, the empty grate. Intermittently he would be shaken

85

by violent, jerking shudders which would almost lift him out of his chair, as though it was not some fever, but extreme anxiety propelling him towards his pigeons. Robert shifted uneasily.

'You go,' he begged Robert. 'You go. You know what to do. You know how much to give 'em.'

Luke advanced on his uncle with a bowl and spoon.

'Shall I?' asked Robert as Luke passed him.

'What?'

'Yes,' wheezed Uncle George. 'You go, you're a good boy.'

'You finish this up first,' said Luke firmly to his uncle. 'Then we'll see about them pigeons.'

Robert sidled out into the yard. The soft cooing of the pigeons to each other as he stepped outside was as soothing as the sound of water rippling endlessly over stones. It seemed to pick up all the weight of his life and float it away – his aunt, school, the small town, even the ugliness of the yard in which he stood. He walked along the line of cages. The birds dipped and swayed on their perches, stretching out their necks to him as he passed. In the last cage but one sat his favourite, Emmeline, her eyes closed, her feathers fluffed out against the cold. He called to her and clicked his tongue against his teeth. Her eyes half-opened. He undid the latch of the cage and began stroking her neck with one finger, she shivered with pleasure and a rattling, murmuring purr issued from her throat. He slid his other hand into the cage and gently picked her up. She ruffled her wings as though momentarily alarmed and opened her eyes very wide. Out in the yard she blinked at the daylight, darting her head this way and that, shaking her feathers into sleekness. She would put her head on one side and look enquiringly up at him with one bright, black eye. And he would laugh at her and nuzzle his nose into the softness of the feathers on her neck and marvel at the rapid beating of her heart and feel how he held her whole, delicate life between his hands. He took her over to the dustbin where they usually sat and let her perch in the crook of his elbow, nestled against his jersey. He talked to her and stroked her and watched the dark figures inside the house through the kitchen window. He held his arm out, and saw how the pigeon wobbled at the change of position, half-stretching her wings, fluttering the pinions to balance herself. If only he had wings like that, it would all be so simple. He could just take off and be carried far above the small town, out over the fields. He could be gone before they missed him and he need never be captured again. The pigeon, finding her equilibrium, cooed and looked up at him. Why did she stay? Why did she let herself be locked in a cage all her life? Was it that she, like Luke, had never expected any other life, never longed for any other life? He knew how his constant questioning and talk of escape unsettled Luke and made him sulky. He stared across the winter gloom of the narrow yard, into the blackened bricks of the house wall, and thought of his ceaseless search through the town for a way of escape. He had run his hands over every wall, peered into each crevice. He had explored all the alleys, hung over gates, stared down every road and combed the bank of the river. But nothing had ever revealed itself to him, the walls remained blank, the roads empty. Nothing had whispered suddenly in his ear: 'Now!' There was no leaping recognition, no sensation of a door swinging back, no answering cry from within himself, and then the magical transformation, apparent only to his eyes, of some dingy side-street into a highway to freedom. He thought of escape almost as a tangible presence that would manifest itself to him directing him, encouraging him, being there at his elbow showing him what to do. Without it he was lost in a state of not-knowing. And so he waited, with a sense of time sliding rapidly and silently past him, pacing his cage. He stretched his finger out to the bird. She never paced her

87

cage, she sat in it dozing, sleepily content. He smiled at her and tickled her under her ear; she was fed and watered and crooned at and loved; perhaps if he too had that he'd never want to escape. Looking up, he saw Luke at last leave his uncle and come towards the sink, a dish in his hand. Suddenly an idea occurred to him, he left his seat on the dustbin and entered the kitchen. Luke's uncle was pulling the blankets back round his shoulders with the limp air of one who has been forced to undergo some unpleasant operation. A few drops of soup clung to the corners of his moustache and, far from being revived by the food, he seemed more cast-down than ever. He looked up as Robert approached with a sulky, veiled expression. Then he saw the pigeon and became at once alarmed.

''Ere!' he croaked. 'Take that out again, quick!' The hand holding the blanket flapped around. 'She won't have no birds in the house. She . . .'

Robert placed Emmeline on his lap and stood back. The bird wobbled uncertainly, gripping the blanket with her claws. From beneath the blankets hands slid out and closed round the pigeon, lifting her up.

'My little old beauty.' Luke's uncle wagged his head at her. She stretched out her neck as though to peck the remains of the soup off his moustache, looked at him with her clear, black eye, and answered him with a single, rolling throaty sound that filled the kitchen and brought Luke over from the kitchen drying his hands on a dish cloth.

'What you done!'

Robert nudged him to be quiet. But nothing would have disturbed his uncle and the pigeon, they chattered and cooed to each other as if entirely alone. Finally Uncle George set Emmeline down on his lap again.

'There,' he said, smiling down at her. 'Well!'

He stretched out his legs with pleasure and leaned back in his chair. The blankets slipped from their shroud-like

88

position to form a kind of mantle round his shoulders.

He wasn't old at all, thought Robert, watching him. He couldn't be, not if he was Gran's son. And Luke's mother's eldest brother. He looked up at them with shy, defensive eyes, one arched finger stroking the pigeon's back.

'Racing season's coming on, Uncle George. You got to get better for that.'

'Ah, racing.' Uncle George smiled dreamily, his finger rested for a moment against Emmeline's wing. 'I packed in racing five year ago this August. Promised her.'

'You could now, Uncle George. You can do what you like now.'

His uncle bent his head as though examining the mother of pearl shadings on Emmeline's neck. There was an uncomfortable pause. Suddenly his head lifted and he fixed Robert with shining eyes.

'You ever seen racing?'

Robert shook his head.

'Ahhh. You never seen them, when the box is opened ...' He lifted his arm, the hand drooping down from the wrist as though disjointed. '... Take off into the sky all in a scrappy clatter of wings, getting theirselves in a line together, soaring up and up, hanging there a split second, taking their direction like, and then wheeling off in formation out across the sky.' And his inert hand suddenly jerked into life, pulled through the air, the white fingers fluttering apart, wheeling and hanging and diving. Like white pigeons in a blue sky. 'You never seen that?'

In the end it was not Uncle George who died as that winter drew to a close, but the husband of one of his aunt's customers.

'Klopps is gone,' announced his aunt between forkfuls of stewed cabbage at dinner one night.

'Ah,' replied his uncle. 'She come in your shop?'

'Course she come in my shop. Little woman, thin, got

three kids, comes in round closing time to see if anything's been knocked down.' His uncle nodded slowly and pursed his lips. Robert poked about among the bits of greasy cabbage on his plate to find another piece of sausage. But there was nothing, not even a juniper berry.

'How'd he go? Accident?'

'Heart. Drives a lorry for Wannamakers. They loaded up. He climbed in the cab. Never drove away. Pulled him out ten minutes later, dead.'

Why Mr Klopps? thought Robert. Why couldn't it have happened to his aunt? He imagined himself standing in the school playground surrounded by wide-eyed children: 'Set out the counter, opened up the shop, ten minutes later fell on the floor – dead!'

He let the words ring in his head for a moment and then laid his fork disconsolately on his plate. His aunt would never let herself be caught out by a cheap trick like that. She'd never fall to the floor. She'd thought of that already. He'd seen behind the counter where she hid a stool so tall that when you sat on it, it looked like you were still standing up. His aunt was never going to die. It was only the Mr Kloppses that died. He looked across at his aunt who was picking a piece of cabbage out of her teeth.

'She's on the list,' she said.

'Is she!' His uncle drew out the words. 'Much?'

His aunt pushed her plate away and brushed imaginary crumbs from the table:

'Enough so's I told her there and then she couldn't have no more.' She had a strange kind of glowing expression on her face. 'Enough so she'd better start thinking about repayment with no more delay.' She folded her arms and looked proudly across the table at her husband.

'Emmy, he's only just gone.'

'She'll get something from the company.'

'Not much, she won't. And she got them kids to feed.'

'I ain't feeding her kids for her.'

90

Eventually, it was Robert's father who paid part of Mrs Klopps' debt. A week after Easter, Robert was sitting in the parlour doing his homework when he heard the corrugated-iron door in the fence bang. Across the yard marched his aunt, followed by a little boy wheeling a barrow on which were piled bundles of old clothes. A black sleeve hung down one side of the barrow and trailed in the dust. He heard his aunt open the door and saw the child dig into the barrow with both arms, standing up again festooned with clothes, clutching them to him like a huge bundle of dead leaves. He looked out into the yard as if onto a stage, in an almost trance-like state. From somewhere off-stage he heard his aunt call his name and he waited, absentmindedly, for someone else to appear in the yard and answer her. Instead his aunt burst into the parlour:

'What you doing sitting there! You come when I call you. Get out in that hall and take them things from that boy.'

The child stood on the doorstep looking almost as if it had fallen asleep on its feet: its cheek lay against the mountain of clothes, its nose buried in the folds of a shirt. As Robert approached it lifted its head and as he held out his arms for the bundle an anxious expression flickered across the child's face. It gave up the clothes without a word, but Robert, looking down to see if anything had dropped in the transfer, saw one of its hands linger strangely against the material. Suddenly, he realised whose the clothes had been. That his aunt, thwarted in her demand for instant repayment of the credit she had allowed Mrs Klopps, had demanded payment in kind. Horrified, he tried to thrust them back into the child's arms, but it had already turned away.

He carried them into the parlour and stood staring contemptuously at his aunt over the bundle as if she had murdered Klopps herself.

'Put them down there.'

He dropped them into the armchair, letting them tumble out of his arms as though he could not bear to touch them. He turned to go back to his homework, but his aunt caught him by the shoulder.

'Take off your jacket.'

'What for?'

'Take it off!'

She pulled at a brown sleeve dangling over the arm of the chair, jerking it free from the rest of the pile. Limp trouser legs and empty sleeves were twined around it. They clung to it for a moment, were drawn up with it, and then, like lifeless corpses, they fell back.

'Put it on.'

Robert gasped. 'That's dead men's clothes!' he spluttered, backing away.

'Put it on!'

'No.'

He stumbled back against a chair, overturned it and crashed with it into the wall. As he fell, his aunt hurled the jacket at him and it landed over his head. Panic-stricken, he struggled to fling it off, gasped for air and took into his lungs the odour of another man's life. For a split second, in the sweat and the mustiness and the tang of machine oil, he glimpsed not only the suffocation and crushed longings of Klopps' existence, but the face of Klopps himself, as perplexed in death as it had been in life. The pale hands gestured hopelessly in the empty air and the bloodless lips moved silently, plaintively. 'How can I be dead?' the mouth whispered. 'I ain't never had no life.'

Robert went around for several days after that coughing drily to rid himself of possession by Klopps' ghost.

'What's wrong?' asked Luke.

'I got this funny taste in my mouth from them clothes she threw at me.'

The clothes themselves were now hanging in Robert's wardrobe. Luke begged daily to be allowed to come and see them, but Robert shook his head. Just the thought of them filled him with dread, a quiet, creeping dread that he could not define to himself, nor bring himself to talk about to Luke. They were the latest strategy in his aunt's battle against him, and he felt himself at last out-manoeuvred. He could only play for time, and in that time hope that escape would present itself to him. Under the weight of Klopps' clothes, under the failure of Klopps' life, he could feel his own life sinking.

'Do they go green at night?' persisted Luke.

Unable to bring himself to speak, Robert turned away and, digging clenched fists into his pocket, marched off.

'Oh, come on!' Luke hobbled after him and clutched at his arm. 'Tell me. Do wavery, green lights shine out of the wardrobe door?' Robert tried to shake him off, but Luke clung tightly to his sleeve and was dragged along beside him. 'Does it creak open in the middle of the night and there's all these clothes, glowing green on their hangers?'

'Don't be stupid,' muttered Robert.

'You wait,' said Luke breathlessly, 'till they flops off their hangers and flops onto the bed!'

'Luke, shut up!'

Luke giggled and capered unevenly about:

'All you have to do is sing: "Mr K. – go away!" over and over again. And cross yourself. They don't like that.'

They arrived at the bridge and stood in silence throwing stones at the nesting moorhens for some time.

'When are you going to wear them?' asked Luke at last.

'Never,' said Robert.

'When does she say you have to?'

'When I'm growed out of these.'

They sat down on a low wall and examined the amount of wrist and arm that hung out of Robert's jacket sleeve, the stretched seams over his shoulders and back.

'Well,' said Luke, 'that could be any day now.'

Winter dragged on into spring. A cold, late spring whose frosts killed the early buds and formed ice on the puddles long after Easter was gone.

'Summer's coming,' said Luke as they sat at the kitchen table pasting cigarette cards into his scrapbook. His mother had taken up with a bargee who was, to Luke and Robert's delight, a heavy smoker. They imagined his lust for tobacco so insatiable that the barge had to be halted at every village they passed so that he could buy more supplies.

'How else,' said Robert to Luke, 'could he get so many different pictures?'

They knew from dreary experience that you could only get one of two pictures from the cigarette packets sold in their town.

Over by the fire Luke's grandmother poked at the grate with her stick, watching the little flames that sprouted from the end of it.

'You daft brush!' she called to Luke. 'Summer won't come till after May's been and gone. You wait and see.'

She was right almost to the day. When the town despaired of ever seeing the sun again, it suddenly burst upon them and shone day after day till they longed for respite. By June the town was full of dust, the very walls of the houses reverberated heat and the High Street was littered with straw from hay lorries that rumbled through in slow procession. Robert's uncle went about the house, a handkerchief pressed to his nose, his eyes streaming.

'It's them grains,' he murmured plaintively, 'them grains, flying about.' And he would shut himself away in the storeroom. His misery infuriated his wife, who took it out on Robert. But nothing could stop the wild flowering of the meadows beyond the allotments, or the hawthorn bushes, heavy with scent, that edged the field behind the sandbanks above the bridge and dropped their petals into the water.

July slid into August and Luke took Robert swimming. At home, swimming had been something that only the eels in the ditch could do. Now, as Robert felt the water grasp his waist and thighs, he kicked and scrabbled to escape it till he had pushed himself momentarily out of his depth. Floating freely in the stream he spluttered and gasped as he felt currents, like cold fingers, pulling him this way and that as though the water was a live thing.

'Kick your legs!' yelled Luke from the sandbank. 'Do your arms!'

They would sit, later, on the river bank, drying off in the sun, laughing at the dog-fights and the duckings. The first time that Robert saw Luke's bare feet was when they went swimming. He stared at them for quite some time before he could work out what it was that was strange about them. They were perfect. They were as perfect as his own feet. The heavy stack-heeled boot lay unlaced on its side in the grass, its leather cracked and dusty, looking like a discarded instrument of torture. It was not his friend who was deformed. It was the boot that made him limp and stumble and collapse out of breath against a wall whenever he tried to run. He was about to express his indignation when Luke, who had been dozing in the sun, began to slowly stretch his legs. The white feet slid side by side through the grass. Robert held his breath as he watched them and then felt his heart give a sickening lurch of revulsion as one foot stopped short of the other and they lay disjointedly in the grass like scattered fragments of broken china.

Sometimes, as they sat there, Robert would cradle his head on his drawn-up knees, as though sleeping, and peer sideways through the bushes to where the fields stretched stubble-charred and empty.

'Now,' he would say to himself. 'Now, while no one's looking.' And in his head he felt the prickling of the stubble on his bare soles and the distance lengthening between himself and the small town. But something, some inertia, always kept him where he was.

The days passed and the inertia and fear set themselves into a kind of paralysis. Robert had never succeeded in ridding himself of the smell of Klopps' clothes. The memory of their suffocating pall dropping over his head returned to haunt him constantly. At school, wandering in the town with Luke, stacking crates in his aunt's yard, the musty, sweaty tang of death would appear from nowhere to envelop him. It would force out the clear air, till all he could breathe was its sickly odour. In panic he would feel his lungs fill with Klopps' breath. In terror he imagined himself caught and pinioned by strong arms, forced to take breath after breath. It was his aunt's doing, of this he had no doubt; she had taken Klopps' soul and turned it into a malevolent spirit with superhuman strength. In return, she had promised it Robert. As revenge for his miserable existence, Klopps could suck Robert's life out of him and force his own into Robert, until he turned into a weak, helpless shadow of the dead man. She had even got hold of Klopps' clothes, ready for the transformation. They hung on their rail in Robert's wardrobe, silent, waiting, knowledgeable and inescapable. Through them, Robert felt that Klopps had already possessed his room. As soon as he opened the bedroom door he could smell Klopps' presence and feel Klopps watching him, so that he became furtive and covert in his movements. He began to be afraid that, if he undressed and put on his pyjamas, his own clothes would vanish in the night. They became a talisman that he was terrified of losing, without them his resistance would be gone and the thing he feared most would happen – he would be made to wear Klopps' clothes. Once they fastened themselves to his back he was convinced that his self would be lost, he would become Klopps and his aunt's triumph would be complete. So he began going to bed fully dressed. He would lie there with the covers pulled up round his ears, but still he felt he could hear Klopps breathing through the shadowed dusk that filled the room. At first he would screw his eyes tight shut, afraid of what he might see, but before long his fear that Klopps might creep up on him unnoticed would force them open again. He would stare until his eyes watered at the cracks along the wardrobe door, watching for the slightest glimmer of green light. He would turn over and over in his mind all he had ever heard about ghosts, as the pale summer nights faded into blackness. How would he look? How might he speak? Would his voice be hollow like an echo, or would it be hoarse and choked with bits of earth from his grave? He would not come till it was dark, he was sure of that. And he would pray with dry, almost immobilised lips, for the moon to rise before the darkness should come, that he might not be left entirely alone. When, at last, the threatening blackness was pierced with cold, white light that trickled under the curtain and spread in a pool across the counterpane Robert would feel his courage creep back. He would dart a hand out of the bedclothes, twitch aside the curtain and flood the room with light. Looking out he would see the moon riding high in the night-blue sky and feel himself relax into the warmth of an almost forgotten peace.

It was while they sat on the river bank one afternoon, gazing mesmerised at the points of light that broke and glittered on the surface of the water that the solution to the problem of his escape hit Robert with such force that he gasped for breath. He grabbed hold of Luke:

'Tom!' he spluttered. 'Tom!'

'What?'

'Tom, your mum's friend. The bargee.'

'Where?'

'Nowhere, you idiot. Listen.' He pulled Luke close and began to whisper. 'Tom can take me away on his barge!'

Luke stared suspiciously at him. He thought that Robert had given up all hope of escape. Sullenly he jerked his arm away:

'Let go, you're hurting. What're you whispering for anyway?'

'I don't want no one to *hear*. I don't want it to get back to *her*.' Robert bounced up and down on his heels. ''Cause that's the answer.'

'What is?'

'Tom'll take me away.'

'Nah, he won't.'

'How d'you know?'

'He just won't.'

'Bet you he will.'

'Bet you he won't.'

Robert jumped to his feet. 'Let's go and ask him.'

'He won't be there.'

But he was. He was sitting on the cabin roof swinging his legs in the open hatchway, talking to a man coiling rope in a perfect circle on the deck, and smoking. Robert poked Luke with his elbow.

'Go on.'

Luke shook him off.

'I ain't doing nothing.'

'Go on. He don't ever remember my name.'

But Luke remained obstinately silent. Gripping the parapet and standing on tiptoe Robert leaned forward:

'Hello,' he called, but his voice, strangled suddenly with shyness, did not carry. He tried again. This time, at the faint sound, the man coiling rope looked up at the quay, but seeing no one bent his head again. Luke hoped that Robert was now going to give up. Instead Robert seemed almost to hurl himself off the bridge.

'Tom!' he yelled.

Both men looked up.

'Hey!' Tom's voice boomed over the water. 'Hey, Luke and Luke's friend.' He said something to his companion who laughed and shrugged his shoulders. The cigarette lodged in the corner of Tom's mouth sent out a cloud of smoke through which he waved a hand.

'Come down!'

Giggling and nudging each other they ran down on to the cobbled quay.

'There you are!' whispered Robert breathlessly as they ran.

'I wish you hadn't done this,' panted Luke.

On the wooden pier they faltered, overtaken with shyness. But Tom, smiling and nodding, waved them on. He was large and blond with eyes of such a pale blue they looked like clear water. He came from somewhere hundreds of miles away on the coast. He spoke little until he had had a couple of drinks, but he laughed and smiled and nodded at whatever anyone else said and gazed at Luke's mother as though no one else in the room could see him. Luke's grandmother called him a daft brush. But every time he came back from wherever his barge took him he would bring them sausage wrapped in silver paper, brightly coloured sweets that cut your tongue and bottles of Dutch gin, the very smell of which made Luke's and Robert's stomachs turn.

'You come to say goodbye?' he asked as they drew level.

'Goodbye?' echoed Robert.

'Tomorrow, midday, we are off.' He pointed to a tarpaulined mound on the far side of the quay. 'We load those bales tomorrow morning and then – vamoose!' He waved his hand.

'Where are you going?' asked Robert intently.

'Home.'

'Home?'

'Yes, home.' He looked at the sky. 'Winter is coming. To work in winter on a barge is not good. So I go home. When I smell the spring then I come back.' He looked shyly at Luke. 'I promise to your mother.'

Robert and Luke shuffled their feet.

'You been on a barge before?' asked the other man, throwing the end of the rope into the centre of the coiled stack.

They shook their heads.

'Take 'em over, Tom.'

Tom looked doubtful.

'He won't be back for a couple of hours. Go on, show 'em the sights.'

'You want to see?' Tom asked them solemnly.

'Yeah!'

Robert's eyes shone; it was all going so easily. He put one foot on the deck of the barge and felt it move beneath his foot as if he had stepped on to the back of some live animal. He brought his other foot on board and stood there swaying slightly while the creature below him seemed to flex its muscles against his weight and settle itself again into the water. The river raced by on either side of him, swirling, beckoning, sinuating on and on, past the pier, past the warehouse, away, far away. It pulled and gurgled at the boat's flanks, but the barge was held fast by heavy ropes. Tomorrow. Tomorrow at midday. He was shown the cabin, stood in the middle of the broad hold and was allowed to hold the tiller and feel the strong-willed river push against the submerged wooden paddle. But there had been nowhere to hide. The hold was wide open to the sky, the cabin filled with tiny cupboards and fold-away bunks without even space for a stowaway flea.

'You reckon you'd like to be a bargee, then?' grinned Tom's friend as Robert stepped back on shore. Robert turned in mid-stride:

'You need a hand? I can . . . I can do . . .' He wasn't quite sure what it was a bargee did, he waved his hand airily over the boat. '. . . anything!' Tom's friend laughed. 'I work for my aunt. In her shop. But she don't need me no more,' he added quickly, 'I can come with you tomorrow.'

'You want to work on the barge?' asked Tom.

Robert nodded.

'But you are too small!'

'No, I'm not.'

'You'd better ask Mr Aben,' grinned the other man, 'he's captain round here.'

Robert sat down on the deck.

'You can't wait here for Mr Aben!' The man lifted him up by his elbows and deposited him on the quay. 'He's out on business, could be hours. You come back tomorrow afternoon, ask for Mr Aben.'

'Tomorrow afternoon.'

'Yeah, that's right.'

They walked away from the quay and up the road past the school in silence.

'They were having you on,' said Luke as they came out from under the railway bridge and halted at the end of his street. Robert stared at him.

'Tomorrow afternoon,' repeated Luke scathingly. 'They ain't going to be there tomorrow afternoon.'

'Well,' said Robert defensively, 'I'll go in the morning.'

'You can't. It's first day of school tomorrow.'

The next morning he woke even before his aunt. He didn't care about school, or about the duplicity of Tom and his friend. He dressed and undressed several times. It wasn't going to be possible to pack a suitcase, he would have to wear everything. But even with just two of every- thing on he looked suspiciously bulky. He resigned himself to taking nothing extra save a jersey – a jersey was a seaman-like thing.

Down in the kitchen his aunt glared at him:

'What you got that old jersey on for? Where's your new jacket?'

'I'm cold,' he mumbled, bolting his bread and milk.

'That ain't got nothing to do with cold,' she snapped. 'You get upstairs and put on them new things before you leave the house.' From the shop doorway there was a sudden commotion and her husband appeared in the doorway.

'Em,' he whispered, 'the dairy's come, but I think it's wrong.'

'Can't you do nothing by yourself!'

Robert waited till he heard her voice out in the shop embroiled in argument, picked up his school books, crept into the hall and slipped out of the back door. In the lane he took to his heels, running down the High Street as though Klopps himself pursued him. There was, fortunately, no sign of Luke at the railway bridge. In the school playground children were already beginning to gather but he ducked his head below the railings and did not slow his pace. When he got close to the bridge he began to dodge from doorway to doorway; the houses had long ago been abandoned in this street, their doors boarded up. He crept towards the last of them, all the time watching the man on duty at the dock gates who sat in his corrugated-iron hut at one side of the gate staring fixedly before him at the long wooden hut on the other side of the yard. He sat so immobile, caught in such abstraction, that Robert was sure he could run below his gaze, undetected, onto the quay. From his doorway he peered past the hut to find the barge at her mooring, and at first glance could not see her. It was impossible that she should have gone – it was still hours to midday. He darted to the other side of the road and, staring through the wide mesh of the dock-yard fence, saw a tarpaulined mound where the barge had been and a little further along a small, hutch-like structure projecting above the quay. As he stared, the choking, gasping sound of an engine turning over burst into the still morning. It coughed and died, coughed again and started into life with a thin, manic hammering and a rich cloud of petrol smoke hazing the river. A man leaped onto the quay and strode along its edge. It was Tom! Then suddenly he understood – they had already loaded the barge and it had sunk low in the water under the weight of its cargo. What he could see was the top of the shrouded cargo and the wheelhouse. They were going! He could see Tom bend over something low on the quay and stand up again with a rope in his hands. Someone shouted and someone else replied. Robert ran towards the gatehouse, approaching it now from behind. The man still gazed across the yard. Robert bent double and dived past him. But it was no good. As he thought himself beyond the hut a hand grabbed at his collar, hauling him back.

'Think I don't see nothing, eh? Think I don't hear nothing?'

'They're going!' burst out Robert, struggling to free himself.

'An' you're not. Not without a pass. You got a pass?'

Above the noise of the engine Robert heard the rope that Tom had been holding clatter onto the deck of the barge.

'They're going!' Robert flung out an arm towards the barge.

'Unscheduled early departure,' sniffed the gate-keeper. He peered at a ledger. 'And it don't say nothing about no extra passenger, nor no visiting relative to be allowed onto the quay.'

Tom leaped suddenly onto the barge and simultaneously it swung out into the stream, a flurry of wash and blue smoke rising up behind it. It nosed out into the central channel and slid tantalisingly slowly out of sight beyond the town. And all the time it was leaving Robert thought: If only I ran, I could still make it. If I ran really fast . . .

103

But the gatekeeper, as though divining his thoughts, held even more tightly onto his collar.

Robert spent the rest of that day wandering the outskirts of the town like an outcast, clutching his schoolbooks under one arm, keeping well away from inhabited places. He found a patch of waste ground and sat, his back against a broken wall amid the rubble and the yellowed grass, watching ants scurry in the dust and beetles climb laboriously to the top of grass stalks. He sat and waited for the hours to pass and thought of how he'd sat in school and longed for just this freedom. Now it didn't feel like freedom at all. All it was was having nothing to do and no one to do it with. When the smell of cooking in the nearby houses became unbearable he left the waste-ground and made his way over to the allotments. He crouched behind a potting shed, looking out over the fields and tried not to think of the barge sliding away downstream. It ached at his mind but his mind was too numb with misery to counter it. The events of the morning seemed to have happened a very long time ago: happened and been swept onwards with the speed of life, leaving him floundering far behind in their wake. He stared out at the fields but he could no longer see them as exits to freedom; he stared at them with a kind of blankness and hopelessness as though blinded to them. As though he had now lost the facility to understand their meaning. Tomorrow they would make him put on Klopps' clothes and then he'd never get away.

The afternoon wore on and his greater misery began to be overlaid with the more mundane concerns of hunger, boredom and fear: fear of his truancy being discovered, fear that his aunt had found out he had gone out without Klopps' jacket. When he heard the first shouts of schoolchildren released from school, he crept back along the allotment fence and thence by side streets and intersecting alleys to his aunt's house. As he entered the hallway he could hear subdued voices from the shop; softly he closed the back door behind him and the voices fell instantly silent. His heart began to beat wildly, thumping in his chest so that his whole body shook, pounding against his ribs so loudly that he thought it must be audible all over the house. Holding on to the banisters he made himself climb the stairs as slowly as he could. He reached his room, burst through the door, tore off his jersey and flung it in the wardrobe. He was beyond detection now, safe. He sank onto his bed and felt his heartbeats subside. But his fingers still trembled as he brushed soil out of the pages of his school books and picked hayseeds off his socks. Finally, he collected his books together and went downstairs. He thought, as he hovered in the darkness on the landing, that he could hear murmuring voices, but as he trod on the first stair the sound ceased and the ominous silence began again.

Down in the parlour he laid out his books as if preparing his lessons. People came and went in the shop. In between there were long silences; long, accusatory silences during which neither his uncle nor his aunt came near him. Tendrils of fear began to wrap themselves around him until he felt paralysed. When his uncle eventually entered the parlour Robert could not bring himself to look up, he stared at the open book and the words printed on the page melted into fuzzy, black lines. He heard his uncle shuffle through to the kitchen, take a plate off the shelf and shuffle out again without a word. When some time later his aunt came into the parlour carrying a wobbling end of tripe on the plate she met his frightened glance with eyes narrowed into tiny, concentrated searchlights.

'Clear them things off.'

Supper was eaten in silence. The tripe stuck in Robert's throat; it slid down and then would go no further, it seemed to pile up mouthful by mouthful until he thought he would choke. Perhaps if he was sick his aunt would forgive him. Across the table his uncle put down his knife and fork:

'Can't manage no more, Em,' he coughed apologetically.

The tripe was very old, it had a strange brown crust all over the outside of it. Robert could remember his aunt boiling it up – days, weeks ago. He quickly laid down his own fork.

'I can't neither,' he mumbled, his mouth full.

'You get that finished!' snapped his aunt.

When supper was cleared away, his aunt went to the tallboy and from one of its drawers took out a pair of large, flat, black scissors. She laid them on the table, and they looked like sword-blades folded together. His uncle was overtaken suddenly by a fit of coughing and hastily left the room. Robert looked from the scissors to his aunt and back again. He slid his hands out of sight on to his lap and shifted uneasily on his chair.

'Get your jacket.'

He darted from the room. Up in his bedroom he automatically picked up his old jacket. Then the thought occurred to him that she was testing him to see which jacket he had worn that day. He dropped his own jacket and dragged Klopps' jacket of its hanger. It fell in folds about his fingers and above him the hanger rocked mockingly on its rail. Holding the coat as far away from him as possible he ran downstairs, entered the parlour and held out the jacket to his aunt. She snatched it away and threw it over the armchair.

'Don't play me no games! The *other* one.'

As he re-entered the parlour with his old coat his aunt picked up the scissors:

'Come here and hold it straight. Hold it out by the arms. Tight!'

The room was full of a strange, buzzing, anticipatory silence. He could scarcely bring himself to approach his aunt and when he tried to straighten out his arms towards her they remained bent at the elbow and would not move. He saw a sudden glint of steel and heard a quick rasping like a rough tongue licking dry lips. The cloth instantly tightened in his hand and there was a sudden ripping, tearing sound. As though it had come alive, the jacket leaped and twisted into the air. His hands were flung wide apart and then dropped to his sides, trailing pieces of torn cloth like dead birds. He lifted them up and turned them wonderingly, as if he could not believe what he saw: there was the lining that had been his father's shirt, there was the tear where his sleeve had caught on a branch running through the wood to see Joseph.

'Throw it in the bin.'

'You ruined it,' he whispered.

'It's rubbish. Put it in the bin!'

He gathered up the material, bunching it against his chest and pressing it together as though trying to join the broken threads, but each time he let it go it fell lifelessly apart again.

'You gone deaf?' His aunt pushed him towards the door. 'You get outside and throw that in the bin.' He stumbled before her down the hall. 'You live in my house, you do what I say. And you do it immediately. All this creeping about. All this running off. Don't think I don't know what you do . . .'

His uncle got hastily to his feet as Robert was sent hurtling past him down the steps.

'. . . don't think I don't know where you go.'

Robert had got as far as the bin and stood before it clutching his coat. His uncle coughed anxiously. Beside him his wife seized the handle of the yard broom that was leaning against the steps:

'You going to do what I say!' she shrieked, 'or do I have to take the broom to you?'

Slowly, Robert lifted off the lid of the bin. A blowfly whirled up out of the stench of decay. He peered down into the echo of its buzzing at tin cans, broken glass, packets of rotting food wrapped in newspaper whose casings had split, peelings, bones that seemed covered in soft fur sinking, as if liquefying, into the covering of ash at the bottom of the bin. Into this pit he consigned his jacket, inch by inch, watching the cloth swing slowly lower as though he himself were being forced to climb down inside the dustbin, and that at any moment his foot would touch the slimy morass and slide below it.

When, next morning, he stood before his aunt in the parlour and drew on Klopps' jacket he expected to be instantly struck dead. He expected that where the material touched his skin a violent rash would break out blistering the flesh. That the cuffs might clamp themselves around his wrists like a vice. Or that the jacket hanging down his back would become like a sack of live coals tied to his shoulders. But none of these things happened. The coat lay against his body in a heavy, skin-crawling way, and the slightest movement of his shoulders released the sweat of Klopps in a suffocating cloud about his face. Robert walked to school as stiffly as an old man, holding his arms away from his sides so that his hands should not brush against the cloth.

He sat in school feeling marked out and set apart from the others by the coat, but they took no more notice of him than usual. He spent the whole day absorbed in its smell and feel; he stared at the stains on it, the torn threads and the small, shiny patches where something had rubbed continually against the cloth. It was a map of Klopps' life, this jacket; the map of a country into which Robert now felt himself exiled. Afraid of what he might find, it took him several days before he could summon up enough courage to put his hands into its pockets. But his fingertips encountered nothing more alarming than balls of fluff and minute pieces of grit.

At night, however, he was plagued with dreams: a single

recurring nightmare in which, wearing Klopps' jacket, he would look into the mirror and see, not his own face, but the face of Klopps leering back at him. In his nightmare he would tear off the jacket but the face, wrinkled and stubbled, would remain in the mirror as though stuck forever to his head; its narrow lips would part and laugh silently at him for an unbearably long time and then slowly the mask of Klopps would slip sideways and his own young face would reappear.

Gradually he withdrew behind a carapace of indifference and stubbornness, secreting his fear deep inside himself. The possibility of escape which had suffused the small town with an almost tangible presence faded slowly, like a light being shuttered inch by inch. And the streets, to which the excitement of this possibility had given not just a third, but even a *fourth*, dimension, fell back into flatness. The town withdrew into itself, as it in fact had always been, and Robert could no longer see where he had stood and felt himself on the edge of discovery. Deprived of this conviction, he felt he had no strength left to withstand either his aunt or Klopps' ghost. He could feel himself sinking, as though through quicksand, under their combined weight. In whichever direction he turned one or other of them was always waiting to confront him. He wondered, bemused, how he had ever thought he might escape. Life as he had never known it, as he had only half-dreamt it, but which he had been instinctively certain existed, was happening elsewhere and he would never find it now.

The months passed and drew themselves out into years. Robert grew taller and began to put on more and more of Klopps' clothes until his scent and Klopps' had become mingled and almost indistinguishable. In the summers, when he went around without a jacket and rolled up his sleeves to the elbow, the collar-less working men's shirts made him look like one of the apprentices from the lumber yard. But in the winter, huddled into layers of oversized clothing, you could see more plainly that the pinched face had a closed, moody look about it within which resentment seemed to struggle with resignation. Below a suffocating weight a spark of life seemed at times to be struggling to break free of its confines and at others to be burrowing deeper to avoid detection and extinction. If life seemed to be closing round him, so too did the streets of the little town, which grew gradually smaller and offered less and less of interest to Luke and himself. With the disaffection for life proper to youth they learned to shuffle their feet and drag their heels as they walked. They stood in doorways for hours on end, water dripping all around them, their feet permanently wet, staring out at the tight-lipped town. The red-leaded doorsteps of the thin, grey houses gleamed, the windows shone with rain and the single main street was tidied clear of people, cats and bicycles. They stared, but there was never anything to see. Rain on a brick wall. The leaping, gurgling gutter that ran past their feet. The half-obliterated poster painted years ago on the side of a house where a woman held up a glass of some unidentifiable liquid and smiled a faded smile. Robert would wait patiently for a flake of paint to be washed away before his eyes: a lock of hair, a finger, the stem of a glass. But it never happened. Nor, despite the rust that dripped from it, did the screws holding the large, tin placard advertising throat lozenges on the chemist's wall ever give way with the longed-for, grating, sliding crash. Nothing ever happened. When the rain eased and the nothingness bored even Robert, they would wander reluctantly off to find another doorway. They seldom went these days even as far as the river.

'What's the point?' Robert would mutter, standing on the bridge watching the rain sink into the slow-gliding stream. 'Just more wet.'

'What d'you expect from a town like this?' Luke would remark, hunching his shoulders in imitation bravado. 'Town like this ain't never got nothing happening.' He looked contentedly around him, leaning against the parapet of the bridge and, not finding anything to engage his eye, turned his attention to spitting in the river. Spitting was Luke's current obsession. He watched the older boys perform this sophisticated feat with admiration. Undeterred by his own meagre efforts, he practised, observing to Robert:

'To get up a really good spit, you either have to have a cold all the time, or smoke. Them older boys smokes. They got money.'

To have money was Luke's ambition. Not a great deal of money. None of Luke's ambitions were particularly great. All he wanted was to have enough, after he'd given his grandmother something, for beer and cigarettes. And he longed to leave school. He longed for the day when he, too, could lounge in a gang on the corner of the square with a fag stuck in his mouth. He knew it would come, that day; it came to all the young men of the town, but nonetheless he tried to chivvy it along. He heard of every job that came free and watched with envy as one by one the older boys left school to become butcher's boy or apprentice to the local carpenter. He ached to be each one of them and consoled himself with boasting about what he would do when his turn came. He schemed about how to leave school early and how to win entrance into this place or that until he irritated even Robert's patience.

'What d'you know about work! You've never done any.'

'Course I have,' Luke would object, 'I'm always doing stuff for my gran.'

They would fall silent frequently at this point, an uneasy, truculent silence, both aware of the chasm that was increasingly widening between them.

It puzzled them and it saddened them, but neither,

III

because of his nature, could do anything to close it up again. They stared at it and turned their backs on it and waited for it to disappear of its own accord.

'Come on,' Luke would say. 'Let's go up the town.'

But Robert would shake his head and make excuses. 'I got to get back,' he would say.

'What for?'

'What d'you think *for*?'

Robert could not explain it, even to himself. He could not explain why, faced with the alternative of hanging round the edge of the square with Luke hoping to be let into the gang of youths who held court there, and stacking crates for his aunt in her back yard or unravelling and re-knotting string in the back room under the smell of last night's supper, he instinctively chose the latter. He saw how Luke was moving further and further into the confines of the small town, his feet sinking into the effortless nothingness of the place, easing himself into the comfort of complaint which boredom and narrowness of expectation offered him. No one had much of a life in the town and they knew it. Sour, envious and inert, they took reassurance from the knowledge that the deprivation was universal. But Robert could not bring himself to join them. Not of his own free will. That had to be kept apart. That had to be watching; it had to be ready just in case escape might come. It was a hope that he hardly dared believe in any more, but it hovered deep inside him at some unconscious level. If it ever happened, if ever escape presented itself – visible, tangible at last – it would occur between one second and the next. It would be something that only someone watching for such a phenomenon would notice and then they would have to drop whatever they were doing and seize the moment. It would only be one moment, thought Robert to himself, but it would mean the difference between one life and another. If he missed it, his chance would be gone. So he kept himself apart.

And then one day Luke waylaid him coming out of school, waiting for him by the steps, as he hadn't for weeks past. A Luke that cavorted unsteadily on the asphalt of the playground with all the enthusiasm of the old days:

'Here!' he yelled to Robert. 'Why's it take you longer than everybody else to come out. Listen! I got a job.'

'What!'

'Yeah, I got a job. My gran got it for me. I'm starting Monday. And not no ordinary job neither.'

'What d'you mean?'

'I'm going into business.'

Robert stared at him. 'You?'

'I told you – my gran got contacts! She knows a man who's got this business . . . Sort of . . . metal business. Well, he got several, actually. Anyway, he's taking me in with him and he told my gran that if I show promise I could buy into the business in a year's time.'

'"Buy into the business"! You ain't got no money.'

'Oh, it wouldn't take all that much, really. He says, being as how he knows my gran, we could have it at a good price. There's only just the cart – and a couple of blades.'

'What about a horse?'

'Oh, there ain't no horse. It don't need no horse.'

'*You're* going to push it!'

'Yeah.'

'That's what your job's going to be – pushing a cart?'

'No, course not. It's kind of – mending. You know, knives. Sharpening them; things like that.'

'Knife-grinding! You going into business with that old geezer goes about yelling "Knife-a-farthing"? You going to pay good money for that beat-up old pram he's got? You'll never get rich on that. I've seen him push that pram round day after day, but I've never seen no one rush out with no knives. What wages are you going to get?'

'Wages?' Luke looked at Robert with scorn. 'Don't you know nothing! You don't get no wages for no apprenticeship! I'm extremely fortunate, he told my gran, to get took on. He's had people queuing up to get their grandsons into that business. And as to getting rich, he told my gran he's had a fortune off that cart – set him up in all these other businessess what he now wants to devote his time to.' Luke dug him in the ribs. 'Not bad, eh? This time next year I'll be a partner. I'll have money, a place of my own,' he winked, 'that'll get the girls come running!'

'Luke, that old boy just wants to retire, you seen him, he's on his last legs. He's just stringing you along to get you to pay good money for nothing.'

'Don't you talk to me about stringing along! You been strung along ever since you come here, strung along of your aunt's apron strings. All you ever do is slaving.'

'And you, is that what you want to do all your life, push a pram round in the rain, sharpening knives!'

'Oh, listen! Mr High an' Mighty! You think you're sitting pretty, don't you, on auntie's shop. You always thought yourself too good for the likes of us. You're always belly-aching on about "escaping", you never want to join in anything.' Luke stuck his chin towards Robert and a belligerent light gleamed in his half-shut eyes. 'Well, why don't you go? Why don't you just clear off!' Turning sharply away from Robert, he caught sight of a boy cycling slowly towards them, the large, wire basket on the front of his bicycle loaded with boxes of provisions. 'Here, Gus!' he called. The boy stopped. 'You going up the square tonight?' Gus propped his foot against the kerb-stone.

'Might be.' He grinned.

Luke hobbled across the road towards him.

'That little blonde girl going to be there?'

'Might be.'

'See you up there, mate.' Luke thumped the handlebars of the bicycle in a display of camaraderie and hobbled off up the road. On the opposite pavement, Robert strode furiously in the same direction, making for his aunt's, determined never to speak to Luke again. A moment later, Luke turned off into his own street, without a backward glance. And Robert carried on up the hill.

He didn't see Luke again in school. During the remainder of the autumn he glimpsed him occasionally through the windows of his aunt's shop out on the square, lounging against the railings, ogling girls and laughing with the other boys, his slack-mouthed laugh. He heard his voice sometimes, floating over the corrugated-iron fence, while he stacked crates in the yard, wavering and cracking through the chrysanthemum-scented dusk: 'Knife-a-farthing, knife-a-farthing.' As the days went by, he felt a strange kind of relief not to be torn two ways anymore, to sink into a silence in which his only companion was himself. He was not as downcast as he expected to be, instead he found himself thrown into a kind of limbo in which he had a vague sense of a re-aligning, marshalling process taking place, beyond his intervention but with himself as its centre.

His parents still came into the town once a year just before Christmas. And every year it was always the same. He would be sent out to wait for their bus on the square opposite his aunt's house, standing there in the biting cold till his nose ran and his eyes watered and the lobes of his ears froze. Each year, as his parents descended from the bus they seemed to get smaller. His mother would cry. His father, ill at ease in civilian clothes, would appear anxious to leave as soon as he had arrived. His uncle would welcome them in from the yard, brew tea and repeat the conversation he had had with them the year before and the year before that. Finally, his aunt would grudgingly leave the shop, her brother would hand over the brown envelope containing the year's money and she would then retire to count out the notes and fold them away. She would reappear briefly, sullenly standing in the doorway between the shop and the hall, as, soon after, they took their leave. His mother would cease dabbing at her nose for long enough to say 'Happy Christmas, Emily'. And his aunt would stare coldly back at her as if she had committed some impropriety. Robert wondered only why his mother would not learn to keep herself out of his aunt's contempt. He wondered why they came at all. And wished that they would not.

That Christmas they came as usual, travelling for hours for a cup of sour tea, a glimpse of their son and to hand over their savings to an avaricious woman. It was as cold as always out on the square. His mother began to sob as he bent down for her to kiss his cheek. And he turned his face quickly away as he saw his father stare at the soft black hairs that now grew above the line of his lip. His uncle poured them black, stewed tea and pushed a saucer of broken biscuits across the table towards them. He set off on his hesitant tale of weather and prices and what a good boy Robert was. And his father, instead of supping his tea, grunting with boredom, and crossing and uncrossing his legs, began suddenly to question his brother-in-law on this point. Finding himself for once paid attention, and eager to gain more attention and approval, Walter enlarged on Robert's obedience and strength.

'Why,' he conjectured, waving one arm in the air, his cheeks flushed. 'I could retire! He do all the lifting now; all the carrying and fetching and stacking and I don't know what.'

'Does he serve in the shop?'

'Well, no.' Walter's face fell a little and he lowered his voice. 'Em don't like no one but herself serving. But he could, he could. He's a bright lad. Good at his figuring.' At this point his aunt appeared in the doorway:

'You've arrived,' she said without enthusiasm.

'That's right, Em,' responded her brother, turning his heavy hips in the chair, uncrossing his legs and sliding one hand into his trouser pocket. His sister moved towards him expectantly. But her brother's hand stayed inside his pocket, the knuckles showing hard through the taut cloth.

'Been hearing about all the work our Robert does in the shop.' His sister's face tightened and her eyes narrowed: 'He don't do no more than earn his keep.'

'His keep's already been paid for.'

There was a momentary silence in the parlour.

'We paying for something twice over, Em?'

His sister folded her arms, her expression twisted itself into one of contempt:

'You think what you give me keeps him – feeds him, clothes him!'

'We paid separate for them clothes,' her brother seized Robert's arm, held it briefly and then dropped it, 'and it looks like we paid dear. Come the summer he'll be leaving school.' He drew the thick brown envelope out of his pocket at last and laid it on his knee: 'Come the summer we expect him to be sending money home to us. We don't expect to be paying for him no more.' He flung the envelope on the table. 'You taking him into the shop then, Em?'

'If he come in my shop, he come in as an apprentice. And a 'prentice don't earn no more'n his keep first two years,' she almost spat the words into her brother's face. Her brother was on his feet in an instant.

'He's already served his apprenticeship; he's been fetching and carrying for you ever since he come to you as a nipper. You made that bargain – that he had to work in the shop, holidays – don't you try an' tell me now he ain't done no apprenticeship.'

'Him!' she tossed her head scornfully in Robert's direction. 'You sent him here so wet behind the ears he needed more looking after than a baby! Don't you pretend to me he were no apprentice.'

'Looking after!' drawled her brother, straddling his legs

and pushing his face down close to his sister. 'Looking after! We know what being looked after by you's like. You ain't got no little brother to bully and torment and kick around no more. He growed too big for you, didn't he? So then you got Walter. But he give in long ago. So then your little nephew come along . . .'

'What you send him here for, then?'

'We sent him,' her brother straightened up and stuck his hands self-righteously through the strap of his belt, 'and we'll take him away again. As far as I'm concerned he done his apprenticeship. He finishes this July. If you want to keep him you pay him. If not – he's leaving.'

Pushing past his sister he strode towards the door. His wife, paralysed with fright at the scene she had just witnessed, sat stock still, her gaze fluttering from Walter shuffling nervously on his chair, to Robert, to the monster of a woman with whom she had to leave him and lastly to her husband who, having reached the door, growled at her to follow him. Suppressing a sob in the damp folds of her handkerchief and clutching her handbag to her she got up and scurried after him.

They heard them cross the yard, heard the crash of the corrugated-iron gate and then the silence. Robert stared for a long time at the brown envelope that lay untouched on the table and wondered how dreadful his aunt's revenge might be. No one spoke. All of a sudden he saw her hands pounce on the back of the chair his father had sat in, raise it high in the air and drop it crashing to the floor.

'Get out,' she screamed at Robert. 'Get out, get out, get out.'

For a second the whole room quivered with the shock of her outburst. Then, bounding from his chair as though suddenly jolted awake, Robert rushed at the door, tore across the yard, through the alley, down the side street. He hurtled through the wicket gate into the allotments, pounding over cabbage stalks and through neatly-turned seed beds. He leapt the wire without even noticing it was there and found himself running across the first meadow through wet, icy grass. He could hear the blood singing in his head and it seemed to him that the gasping breaths he took were shouts of joy whose words he could not decipher. As the sky and the land spread out around him he felt as if an enormous balloon was rising above him, full of dust, full of fear, full of days and months and years, rising from his shoulders where, unseen, it had pressed down on him all this time. He was running now over a ploughed field, black frost-cut earth whose ridges crumbled beneath his boots and clung to his heels. But still he felt as if he was flying. Between the ridges pools of water lay thinly covered with ice into which his boots pounded and splashed. He heard the cracking of the ice and saw briefly the image of Klopps' face in the mirror smash into minute fragments.

He did not return to the house till it was dusk, walking back over the fields with the light fading all around him and the stillness of night settling through the freezing air. Against the horizon the small town appeared like an insignificant cluster of low huts, a dark blur rising out of the plain. He watched it with the indifference of a stranger, while all around him in the darkness he could feel currents moving, carrying him effortlessly along. They swirled about him like a protective mist within which he felt strangely calm, strangely cut off and held apart from the town which now loomed up in the darkness, took form and separated itself into walls and streets. But it no longer had the power to intimidate him; it seemed to him now a mere shell, a lifeless configuration of bricks and mortar without familiarity or association. The key had at last been turned. Somewhere a door had swung slowly open on its hinges: the process of escape had begun. Already it sang and whispered in his blood. He would re-enter the town, not in obedience to its tyranny, but to wait for the process to be completed, for the moment to come when these same currents would carry him out into the great plain far beyond the town.

As he came at last to the allotments and entered the first outlying streets, the walls seemed to shrink away from him. When he reached his aunt's house it seemed strangely subdued. There was a light on in the parlour and the curtains were drawn, but a deep silence lay over the house. He climbed the stairs to his room and found that it, too, appeared to have undergone a change, to have lost a dimension of reality. Everything looked as if it was made of cardboard: insubstantial and lifeless. Formerly it had overwhelmed him and oppressed him. Now it was as if, in his absence, a demarcation line had been drawn around its perimeter behind which its evil spirits had been contained: banished back into the walls where they hissed and writhed, imprisoned as he had once been. He pulled open the door of the wardrobe and was surprised to find solid wood beneath his fingers. Inside, Klopps' clothes drooped on their hangers, limp pieces of cloth. Quietly he closed the door. It was over. He stayed in his room all evening, perched with his knees drawn up to his chest, on the window sill, watching the moon rise over the walls and narrow yards till even the fields beyond were flooded with a whiteness of frost and moonlight. And as he gazed he saw in his mind's eye the steep roofs of a far-off city glittering silver in the white night.

III

Robert's escape, when it happened, happened all of a sudden. It came in a bundling-up of possessions, in anxiously expressed instructions in the flickering of oil lamps in a night so light he could not sleep till dawn. It rushed in urgent whispers from an uncle so aflame with the thought of escape that he could think only of the possibility that their plans might founder.

'She see you, you're done for. She look at you, she's going to change her mind.'

'She don't want me here.'

'She don't want you here – she don't want you gone. She got power over you here. Don't you go showing her your face, reminding her she's going to lose that power. You stay in your room till I get you down for that bus.'

Robert waited. And knew that in the bedroom next door his aunt waited, lying tense and watchful, eyes wide open in the curtained gloom, ears straining for each sound. So they had lived all the past weeks, waiting; watching each other, an unbearable filament of tension stretched almost to breaking point around the house, while letters fluttered backwards and forwards. Acrid lines on scraps of paper that Robert never saw. His fate was rearranged, whole constellations pushed aside and planets disregarded, new orbits planned and all without his opinion being asked once, or his wishes having been consulted. But his uncle had been there and this timid, little man had somehow achieved miracles, had engineered the escape that Robert had dreamed of ever since he had set foot in his aunt's house. He watched the morning light grow steadily brighter over the allotments and, turning, cast a last glance round his bedroom, but there was nothing to see. It had shrunk back into itself: its victim gone and nothing but dust left to gloat over. His uncle appeared in the doorway and beckoned to him. He crept out. It was now that she would get him. Here, at the head of the stairs. Her door would fly open and she would shoot out, whip-like, to seize him, her eyes glittering in her snake head. There, at the very moment of his triumph, in the darkness of the landing he would be taken prisoner, doomed forever to sweep his aunt's floors and knot twine. He rushed down the stairs, pushed past his uncle who was bending to pick up the suitcase and ran out on to the square. Over the rise, a blue and grey bus trundled slowly into sight.

'Hurry, hurry,' whispered Robert. She could still fly out of the house, she could still... The bus came to a standstill beside him, shuddered violently and then went dead. The driver stared at him uninterestedly through the closed door of the bus, then pressed a button near the steering wheel. The door wheezed open. Robert scrambled inside, followed by his uncle who paid the driver and settled the suitcase on the floor by Robert's knees.

'Well,' he said.

Robert shuffled on his seat.

'Bye,' he whispered. He wanted his uncle to be gone. He wanted to push out with both hands at this hesitating, sorrowful figure blocking the gangway of the bus, holding up his escape.

'Yes,' nodded his uncle, 'look after yourself.' And was gone. The door sighed shut, the bus rattled and coughed itself into life with a great effort and they set off. Robert

122

wrenched round in his seat, waving frantically at the disappearing image of his uncle. He was full, suddenly, of things he wanted to say to him, now that he was safe and on his way. He wanted to tell him that he would write to him. To thank him. To tell him that he was sorry he had to be left behind, alone, with her. To explain how he had to be moving on, how he'd always intended to; that there were things, things he couldn't quite put a finger on, huge important things that were missing from this small town, that he had to go away to find. But that he would come back, he would come back and tell him all about it.

The small town slid away past the windows of the bus. Then they were out on the gravelled road where the plains stretched out around them, limitless. Robert laid his head back against the head-rest of the seat and felt in his pocket for the paper with the address on it. There it was, folded and folded again into a tight little square. He did not need to take it out to look at it, he knew it by heart; it was very simple: Zak's Stores, Nile Street. Zak had a shop in the city; quite an emporium, said his uncle, sold everything. He'd written to Zak, said he had a nephew wanted a job. Zak had replied; said he was getting on, could do with a hand. So it was arranged. Zak would be nice, thought Robert, because he was his uncle's friend, if he had been his aunt's friend he would have thought twice. Because Zak was old, no doubt he would die soon, then Robert would be master of the emporium. It would, of course, be in the finest part of the city and he would put in his shop only the best things. He would grow old himself, marry and have sons and in due course they would become masters of the emporium. The sun came out from behind a cloud and shone full on his face, his eyes gradually closed, his head nodded to the swaying of the bus and he fell asleep.

The bus droned on, crossing and re-crossing the ever-widening river that ran over the plain. It stopped in hamlets and once or twice in small towns and sometimes in the middle of nowhere. And all the time people got on and off with children or baskets, or live hens that settled themselves onto the seats next to their owners, fluffed up their feathers, drew in their necks, lowered their wrinkled eyelids and dozed quite peacefully throughout the journey. At what he judged was midday, Robert ate the sandwich his uncle had stuffed into his pocket. He became thirsty, sticky, hot and restless, but still the city did not appear.

Sometime later he woke to find that they were passing through dense, grey streets that showed no signs of slipping away to reveal fields and trees. A tremor of excitement fluttered in his stomach and shivered him awake. His fingers felt for the suitcase by his knees, they trembled in his pocket to touch the small square of folded paper and the few coins his uncle had given him. Then he gave himself up to the intense thrill that flooded all through him, pressing his cheek against the window pane, drinking in all that he saw, mesmerised. It was a very curious place; everything seemed to be black: the tarred roads, the pavements, the bricks of the houses, the leaves on the trees – all black. And the pale sky which had hung above the plain all day now seemed to be covered with a grimy pall. Even the people who stood on the corners of the streets looked grey, their heads bent to the ground and a blankness where their faces should have been. At every intersection he could see roads running off at right angles into perspectives of greyness, street after street, massed and piled four-square into acres of brick. He had never imagined anything so vast could exist, that people would live pressed so tightly together for mile after mile. It horrified and thrilled him and he pressed his face even more eagerly against the glass to see what else he could be shown.

The bus shifted through an agony of gears as it found itself hemmed in by an increasing press of traffic. The houses grew taller and the streets narrower, twisting, turning, running close together and then shooting apart in a multitude of tunnel-like alleys. The buildings, many-storied as card houses, seemed to lean against each other for support: now pushed precariously out over the street, now squashed in so tightly by their neighbours that they erupted against the leaden sky in a scrabbling of chimney-stacks and stepped roofs. Clusters of brightly-lit shops glittered before his gaze and then were gone as the bus dived out of the main thoroughfare and into side streets where men in shabby clothes scurried like ants along the pavements. Where the houses huddled together in an even more wretched way, each of their stories painted over with faded signs, every window half obliterated by names now illegible with neglect. It was as though the very buildings had lost the memory of what they once had been, had long ago forgotten their life's purpose and now crouched against each other to hold at bay their utter disintegration. It was in one of these streets that the bus finally stopped. Around him the other passengers stirred, collecting their belongings and shuffling down the gangway of the bus like sleepwalkers. Outside, Robert stood on the pavement, clutching his suitcase, staring about him, letting people mill past him. He breathed in the scents and the noise and the life of the city that surged around him. He looked down at the pavement, screwed up his eyes and whispered to himself triumphantly:

'I am here!'

It proved to be surprisingly difficult to get anyone to tell him the way to Nile Street. He tried to stop various people, holding out towards them his unfolded piece of paper, but they all averted their faces, hastily crossed the road, or hurried past. Robert could not understand it. He wandered on and came to a piece of waste ground, where two or three houses appeared to have fallen in on themselves.

Smashed bricks lay everywhere, planks shored up the remains of the houses on either side whose jagged, torn-off rooms were now exposed to the mockery of wind and rain. Among the piles of rubble, stalls had been set up selling plastic buckets and gold watches and mounds of brightly-coloured sweets. Robert stared at them fascinated, turning the bevelled edge of a coin in his pocket and breathing in the overpowering aroma of sugar. He joined the small crowd that gazed longingly at the gaudy heaps, was carried round amongst them and then out again onto the roadway. There the crowd melted away before he could presume on their temporary familiarity to ask one of them for directions. He found a man sitting in a doorway, a bottle and a brown paper parcel beside him on the pavement. Robert squatted down:

'Can you tell me the way to Nile Street?'

The man nodded intently all the time Robert was speaking, his eyes wide and curious. When Robert had finished the man was motionless for a second and then, just as intently, began to shake his head, still without uttering a word.

'Leave him be!'

Robert glanced up and saw a plump woman carrying bulging shopping bags standing over him.

'Leave him be. Can't you see he's either drunk or daft?'

Robert got slowly to his feet.

'I want to get to Nile Street.'

'Oh,' her face clouded. 'Don't know that one.' She swung one of her bags out and stopped a young man who stared suspiciously across at Robert.

'Nile Street,' the woman demanded.

The young man muttered something and dodged out of range of the shopping bag.

'Canal,' explained the woman. 'Take the first road off to the right, when you get to the canal go left along it on this side and it's somewhere there.'

Robert followed her directions. Gradually the shops petered out, the houses grew smaller and the people disappeared; of the canal there was no sign. The light began to fade around him and when he turned to look back the way he had come, the city seemed like some mythical forest whose branches had parted to let him in, but had now closed round him in indistinguishable ranks. He seemed to have been walking forever in a maze of low streets; each house was identical: two windows, one door and a red-leaded doorstep. He tried to peer inside some of the windows as he hurried past but there was nothing to see. He imagined himself and his aunt and uncle shut up in one of these dark little houses, in each of these identical houses. One man, one woman, one child, like cut-out paper dolls, strings and strings of them, streets and streets of them, the same hate and tension reduplicated over and over again. At least it couldn't be here that he was going to live, he hadn't come to the canal yet. He bent his head and quickened his pace, stumbling into doorsteps and falling off kerbstones, unbalanced by the weight of his case. Head lowered, he failed to notice, above the rows of houses, that factories and warehouses were beginning to rise in solid, black towers, whose vast chimneys shot upwards, chequering the skyline in front of him like the ramparts of another city.

It was a siren shrieking from an adjacent street that first startled him. And then, in the momentary silence that followed, a pattering sound like the first raindrops before a storm. It came nearer and grew into a drumming. Round the corner burst a woman, running wildly, clattering over the cobblestones in wooden clogs, a half-unbuttoned overall flapping as she ran, strands of hair escaping from under a tightly-knotted black scarf which gave her head a strange, partly-shaved appearance. Then, hard on her heels, ran another woman. And then another and another, till a whole river of women surged round the corner of the street between the sooty walls in a stumbling, jostling mass. Above them, all around them, hooters and sirens wailed and screamed. More and more women filled the street, the drumming of their clogs reverberating in the closed space. The whole mass of them running as though each was alone, their eyes staring straight ahead, their faces blank. They terrified Robert with their running and the unknown thing from which they ran and he drew quickly back into a doorway. But the women who brushed past him in their flight hardly cast so much as a glance at him. They were so close he could feel the warmth of them and hear the slight gasp of their breath. In silence they ran, like sleepwalkers. But the staccato, panting rhythm of their breathing and the drumming of their clogs beat inside Robert's head, until he could not stay still. Blindly, he pushed out into their midst to run with them, anywhere. As he lurched from his doorway, he suddenly caught sight of men rounding the corner of the street. Not running like the women, but striding purposefully down the road as though they drove the women before them. There was no fear in these men, just a sullen heaviness. At the same moment the sirens wailed into silence and Robert halted where he was, on the edge of the pavement, ashamed of his flight in the face of these men, letting the women push past him. Then, sheepishly, he resumed his journey.

Turning the corner at the top of the street he found himself in a wide cobbled road that led straight as far as the eye could see, bounded on either side by huge brick walls. It was like stepping into a vast black canyon. The hinterland of low, mean houses was forgotten. This was a new land. A land of proportions so vast, of energies so unfathomable, it took his breath away. Keeping close to the walls, gripping tightly to his suitcase, buffeted by the crowd that swarmed down the street, he inched his way over the cobbles. At first sight, people seemed to be pouring out of crevices in the brickwork, but as he made

128

his way slowly along the street he saw that these crevices were in fact narrow gaps between buildings, alleys that twisted back from the main road in a jumble of warehouses, factories and chimneys, overhung with lofts, laced with pulleys and nets that dangled malevolently. Then, quickly as it had begun, the flood of people dwindled into twos and threes; lone stragglers hurrying after the rest. As Robert set off again he heard behind him, echoing in the cavernous street, the sound of bolts being shot, gates being slammed and locked, padlocks falling against chains. Before him a grey space opened out between the blackened walls and he found himself standing on the embankment of a wide canal, sluggish and brown, over which a bridge led into the dense barricade of warehouses lining the far bank. Suddenly, from one of the intersecting alleys close by, emerged the bent figure of a man pouncing and darting among the sheets of newspaper that blew listlessly round the corner of the street, evidently searching for something. Robert watched him waddle across the road to where waste paper had accumulated in the corner of the bridge, a woollen cap pulled low over his ears, a tattered overcoat flapping round his ankles. As he scrabbled among the litter, Robert approached him.

'Nile Street?'

The man leaped back, dancing away from him, smacking the palm of one hand against his ear repeatedly, as though to get rid of Robert's words which, insect-like, had crawled inside. With anxious backwards glances, still beating his hand against his ear, he scuttled off down the opposite alley, and disappeared.

A lane wound to the left along the backs of the ware-houses, following, he supposed, the course of the canal and he set off down it, staring up at its forbidding walls. They rose from street level, some of them entirely blank and soot-encrusted, others pierced by rows of small, arched windows, closely barred: Klemper's Manufactory,

129

Abel's Works. But his limited imagination could not envisage machinery, or factory floors. He saw only tiny cells in which men and women huddled, hammering, stitching, chiselling at small objects which lay upon their knees. He halted once as he crossed a tributary of the canal and stared, wide-eyed, over the low iron railings at water the colour of blood, along whose edges lay drifts of foam, heavy with flotsam. All was silent, the walls about him shadowed black like a ravine. The further he went, the deeper he felt himself lost and the tighter the silence seemed to grow around him. Into this silence his footsteps crashed, echoing and reverberating as though, at some distance, he was being followed. He stopped. And a second later the other footsteps stopped. He took to his heels and ran. And the echoes ran too. Suddenly the lane burst out onto a kind of square, an intersection where five narrow streets met. After the darkness of the alley, the place had a tranquil, almost peaceful air. As he looked about him, he saw that the corners of the streets had cobbles set in a circle, as though on each corner there had once been a tree. A child with matted hair, wearing only a torn shirt, trotted past him carrying a covered bowl. It darted a keen look at his suitcase and paused in mid-step as though momentarily considering the possibility of carrying off both case and bowl and then trotted on. Apart from the child, the place seemed to be deserted. Through the pall, the mellow light of early evening could be felt rather than seen by a certain softening of the outline of the buildings. Down every alley factories and warehouses wound away in a blur of brick, save one: a strange, forgotten little street of dilapidated houses which huddled into the shadows of their taller neighbours as though trying to avoid detection. On one corner Robert saw that there was a café, its plate-glass window lit either by a chance ray of evening sunlight, or by some light from within. He hurried over to it. But, as he approached, the light faded and when he got to the café he saw that it was dark. He turned away and as he did so caught sight of a small shop on the other side of the street. Almost the whole of its lower half was covered in faded advertisements painted on tin and tacked all over the door and right round the window frame leaving only the glass free, but even there names and legends had been stencilled onto the pane. He wandered across the road to take a closer look. It had the same raffish attraction as a circus poster; it mattered little that the circus had moved on, for the poster was everything one's heart could desire: the lions still roared, the tigers, snarling ferociously, still leaped through fiery hoops and the girl dancing bareback on a white pony still held out her arms to you. In the same way the ancient tin advertisements still offered the promise of a feast. Robert read them out, one by one, whispering under his breath: chocolate, coconut biscuits, blancmange powders, washing soda, Zak's Stores. Zak's Stores! He stared at the words in disbelief and read them out again. He felt his heart sink. He walked out into the middle of the road to get a better look at the shop and saw high up on the wall the street sign, Nile Street. He unfolded the scrap of paper and read it again. Slowly he went back, raised his fist and hammered on the door. The tin plates rattled, the door juddered in its frame, somewhere inside there was a feeble sound like a bell tinkling and then all was silent again. He waited a long time, during which nothing moved in the street, no one came or went and there was no sound from the darkened house before him. He pounded on the door again and as the booming and shuddering died away there was a scrabbling at the letter box from inside, a muttering and a scratching of finger nails against the metal flap. Through the half-open slit he thought he caught sight of a dark glimmer of eyes watching him and heard an uncomfortably close wheezing of breath. He cleared his throat to speak, but before he could do so a querulous female voice demanded:

131

'Where are the others?'

'What others?'

'The *others*!' rasped the voice. 'The others they sent with you.'

'There isn't anyone else, only me.'

The letterbox snapped shut in his face. Above him there was a grinding of bolts being drawn and locks being turned. The door rattled open on a length of chain. Through the narrow gap a head peered, it thrust a bristled chin towards Robert and its eyes narrowed till they were mere points of light embedded in folds of skin.

'You ain't from the Council!' it accused him.

Robert shook his head.

'Who are you?' The eyes darted to the suitcase and narrowed into even deeper suspicion. 'You selling something?'

'I come to help Mr Zak. He's expecting me.'

'Zak don't need no help no more.'

'My uncle arranged it. He sent me here.'

'Sent you, did he? Zak expecting you?'

'Is Mr Zak there?'

'Maybe.'

The old woman did not move. She had drawn her head back into the gloom of the interior from where she stared sullenly at Robert. Suddenly her eyes lit up and she darted her chin at him:

'Your uncle the devil, then? That who sent you? He sent you for Zak?'

Robert fidgeted nervously with the handle of his suitcase. This old woman was mad. The thing was to get past her to where Zak was. He stared at the ground to avoid her eyes, her lunatic's eyes that wanted to penetrate deep inside him and involve him in her madness.

'Come closer,' she wheedled. 'I can't see you proper. Can't see if you're who you say you are.'

Robert shuffled half a step forward, eyes lowered. There

was no response. Covertly he looked up. With a gloating smile she slid the chain off the hook and opened the door, shuffling back to allow him to enter. The darkness of the room after the lingering daylight blinded him temporarily. As he struggled to make out his surroundings in the gloom, he heard the bolts being thrown behind him.

He seemed to be in a wooden cave of a room: wooden floors, wooden walls, wooden shelves arched out across the murky space.

'Time to light the lamps,' said the old woman in a mocking, sing-song voice as she passed behind him. He watched her move off across the floor, wrapped from neck to ankle in a faded cotton overall. One foot dragged itself stiffly against the floorboards with a rasping sound, like a brush. She stopped half-way and turned to smile at him, a sickly sweet smile in which her eyes almost closed and her lips were pushed back over bony gums.

'Then you can see Mr Zak.'

At the far end of the room in the darkness he could make out a long counter on which various packages seemed to be piled. It was here that the old woman busied herself, striking match after match and cursing in a low voice until at last a flame threw shadows across the room making it seem more cavernous than ever. The old woman began to strike more matches and suddenly a second set of shadows danced above her head across the ceiling. Beside her on the counter the packages dissolved into a continuous line, like dark clothes heaped together.

'Come on!' she cackled.

Robert hesitated, unwilling to leave the safety of the door. When at last she heard his footsteps creak across the floorboards, she turned swiftly, so that the candles shone clear into the room.

'Come and say how-do to Mr Zak.'

But Robert could not move. He felt all the breath strangled in his throat. He could not turn and run for the door.

133

The door was bolted. He could not bring himself to turn his back. Nor could he move forward.

'Nah!' crowed the old woman. 'You ain't on no errand from no devil. If you were you'd fly over here, quick as knife. Your feet wouldn't touch the floor. You're earth-bound, like all the rest of 'em. Runnin' and runnin' till you drops. Runnin' and cryin' and moanin'. And what for? This!' and she gave the body lying on the counter a great thwack with her arm. As if in pain the corpse jerked its knee into the air. Robert jumped.

'That ain't nothin',' snapped the old woman. 'That's the rigor. Ain't you seen nothin' dead before?'

Robert tried to speak, but his voice was constricted with fright and no words would come out.

'Eh?'

Robert cleared his throat:

'I worn dead men's clothes,' he whispered.

'So what! They don't wear nothin' else round here. They're born into 'em: dead men's clothes, dead men's lives. Scurryin' round like rats. Vermin, that's what they are. Should've gone for the Pest this afternoon, when I found 'im, not the undertaker.' She began to stuff rags into an old shopping bag. 'Go on,' she jerked her head towards the corpse, 'you come all this way to see 'im. He won't bite. He never bit in life – he won't start now.'

Robert edged towards the counter. Zak looked very small, small and frail. In the calm light of the candles fixed at his head, the skin stretched across his skull seemed so thin and pale it looked transparent, the fine bones and blue-threaded veins lying exposed, as though trapped under a sheet of ice. The small flames of the candles, suddenly wavering in a strong draught, sent shadows rippling across the still face, like thoughts flitting across a mind now vacant and unable to receive them. And yet his very stillness was alarming. His arms, roughly folded across his chest, had slipped a little so that the hands were no longer piously crossed, but seemed to clutch at his throat. His knee was rigidly drawn up as though in agony. Behind him Robert could hear the old woman shuffling in the gloom. He could hear the rasp of her lame foot and the hiss of her skirt against the wooden boards as she dipped and swayed across the floor, unconcerned by Zak's presence. Unaware that at any moment his taut body was going to spring up with a terrible staggering cry – the unbearable cry of the cheated-of-life, of the done-to-death. He would see them there, alive and staring at his death and he would . . . Robert turned and stumbled for the door. But the old woman was already there, swathing herself in a large tattered shawl till she appeared even more shapeless and grotesque than ever.

'Mind you keep them candles lit. One after the other. You let the light go out, you'll have all hell in here 'fore you know what's hit you. An' he has to be sat with. Till first light.'

'I ain't staying here!'

The old woman picked up her bag:

'You got somewhere to go? You got money for 'otel, 'ave yer?' She jerked her head towards the darkening street: 'Find your way through them alleys in the dark, can yer? With this?' She kicked his suitcase and it fell over with a bang. The noise stopped him in his tracks, as if she had thrown down a barrier to prevent his escape; it drained all the impetus out of him, leaving him stranded and helpless, trapped between his fear of the streets outside and the horror of the room behind him.

'You come to stay – well 'ere you are!'

She unbolted the door, pulled the rags tighter over her shoulders and turned to peer back into the room:

'I given this place its last clean,' she screwed up her face into an even deeper expression of distaste, 'and glad to see the back on it! It were a morgue long before 'e snuffed it – not a stick of furniture, nothin' on them shelves.' She

135

picked up her bulging shopping bag and grinned slyly at Robert.

'Council'll be round in the mornin' for 'im. Oh, an' I taken me wages, 'case you was worried.' And was gone.

As the silence closed in around him, the panic in Robert's head tightened into a kind of paralysis. He found himself unable to move from the spot on which he stood, unable to lift his eyes from the floor. He stared at the dirt-engrained cracks in the floorboards, at the battered edge of his suitcase, the wavering shadows cast by the candles on the lowest panel of the door. And all the time, like independent voices in his head, chanting loudly one after the other, raced the questions 'Where shall I go?' and 'What shall I do?' blurring together and falling apart again into whispers until the noise became so unbearable that Robert, shaking with fright, pounded his fists against the empty air and suddenly screamed with them in utter despair. Instantly the light in the room dimmed. He whirled round. One of the candles had gone out. In the semi-darkness Zak looked smaller than ever, the shadows on his face deeper. Keeping close to the far wall Robert inched his way towards the counter. But the corpse did not move, it seemed locked into some deep internal struggle, some intense preoccupation compared to which the world and its remaining inhabitants were of no interest. Robert tiptoed closer and stretching out his hand drew the candles and matches towards him. As quietly as he could he struck a match, lit a candle and stuck it at the far end of the counter. If he kept the candles here he need go no nearer Zak than this. His fear had now subsided into a kind of suffocation in his throat and a light trickling of sweat down his back.

He counted the remaining candles, moving dry, cracked lips soundlessly. Fourteen. There were fourteen. Under his shaking fingers they rattled together like bones and he snatched his hand away. Was fourteen going to be enough?

Two alight at the same time. No. They wouldn't last. They would go out. He would be left. In the darkness. With ... with ... He darted a look at the corpse. It now looked hollow, vacant. Zak was somewhere else! He was in this room, somewhere else. Somewhere behind him, somewhere ... He clutched the edge of the counter to stop himself trembling, but he couldn't bear to turn round. What if he came back? Back into the corpse, now while he was standing here, next to it? What if he came back and sat in the corpse and opened its eyes and looked at him? Looked at him out of them?

Lurching away from the counter, Robert backed against the wall. He spread his arms out along its length, palms against its surface and inched his way along it, staring fixedly at the candle flame. He had to get away. He had to get as far away as possible. What if he met it? What if, as he slid his fingers along the wall, Zak was waiting for him and put out his long, bony fingers. And touched him! Robert froze, arms still outstretched, head rigidly arched back. He could not bring himself to look out into the room, instead he stared fixedly at the corpse, hypnotised by it. And all the time the candle burnt slowly down, its flame dipping and rising up again. The more he stared, the more he hated it. It had him pinned, as though to a narrow ledge on a cliff face unable to move one way or the other. It had removed him to such a plane of fear that he felt entirely at its mercy. He heard a sob echo in the room, a dry gasping sound, followed by another. He felt his body shudder and as he blinked his eyes the candle flame blurred. Enraged, humiliated, he looked down at the floor, at his immobile feet. He would go on. On along the wall, where he had been going before. He wouldn't look at Zak. Zak wasn't anywhere. He was dead. He was locked up in his dead body. He tried to push one boot stiffly against the other. At last the tense muscles gave and, groping and sliding, keeping his eyes firmly on his feet, he willed himself forward.

When at last he reached the angle of the wall, he slid down it, trembling, onto his haunches and, crouching there, surveyed the room. It lay empty and cavernous in the wavering light, his suitcase still abandoned in front of the door. Shadows lunged out across the ceiling and withdrew again into the darkness. He felt the walls firm against his back, the door very near to his right. He could see everything from here. He would not move from this corner, except to light a new candle. Only one each time, so they would last. So that he would not be . . . He stared fiercely out into the room. Looking at everything. Marking positions. Gathering in the threads of the room, so to speak; so that if anything moved, if anything untoward happened – if any thread broke in the tension of the room – he would know, instantly.

And there he sat, all night, watching.

From time to time as the candle burnt low he would force himself to creep down the length of the room, the wall always at his back, and light another. From time to time, though he struggled to keep down his fear, it broke out in waves of panic that would hold him rigid and wide-eyed for what seemed like hours at a time. All through that night he never once thought of his aunt or his uncle, or his parents. He did not think of what might become of him, nor of what, so far, his life had been. With all his resource, he held the present at bay, until sleep, sidling out of the shadows unnoticed, overcame him.

Deep inside his dreams there came a knocking. It echoed up as from a well, reverberating among the bony caverns of his mind, rousing sleep-stumbling thoughts from the shadows.

'It is Zak,' they whispered to each other. 'Zak who has been wandering the city all night long searching for Heaven, who has returned unsuccessful, broken-hearted, to re-inhabit his earth-bound body. Who knocks and knocks and cannot get back in.'

Their whispering woke Robert. He heard the knocking. He heard the tin plates rattling on the door and, for a second, he too believed it was Zak. But his eyes flew open not onto darkness, but onto a grey light seeping below the blind. In the half-dawn he could make out Zak's immobile form still lying along the counter, grey as marble, and felt sudden, dizzying relief. The cavernous terrors of the night-filled room were dissolved into banality: the shelves withdrawn into inanimate lengths of wood, the shadows that had leaped across the walls and ceiling gone, the candles burnt down to insignificant puddles of wax. He stumbled to his feet, bounded towards the door and flung it open.

A light clear as water flooded the room. Outside in the street, in the sleeping silence, the buildings were sharply defined, brick upon brick, solid, real. And on the doorstep stood a man so small that Robert had at first looked out over his head before noticing he was there. He waited till he had Robert's attention, then he swept off his cap, clutched it to his chest and said in a hoarse whisper:

'I come about Zak.'

Under the cap he was completely bald, the crown of his head as soft and shiny as the unlined face beneath it, so that his eyes peering out at Robert from lowered lids, seemed to watch him from behind a china mask.

'The undertaker?'

''is best friend.'

The mask showed no sign of outrage. The lips, when they had finished speaking, smiled quite amiably at Robert, then added:

'Mort Mortensen.'

And the small man, without giving Robert time to reply, brushed past him and scuttled into the shop. He made straight for the counter and stood looking down at the body, still and expressionless as the corpse itself. Finally, he shook his head and waddled back to Robert, who hovered by the door. He seemed to move very fast, on the tips of his toes, without giving the impression of moving at all, so that he appeared to glide rather than walk. At Robert's abandoned suitcase he stopped and with swift movements divested himself of his lantern, his knobbled stick, the tattered haversack that swung from his shoulder, and piled them all on top of the case. Then, sidling close to Robert, he began to fire a stream of questions at him in the same breathless whisper, punctuating each one by jutting out his chin, as though to impale Robert's attention, should it wander. The catechism went on and on. But Mort knew everything already. He knew about Robert, about his uncle's letter, about the vituperation of the cleaner and the summoning of the undertaker. It was very strange. It was almost as if he mocked him with his questions. But no flicker of expression creased the smoothness of his face. Robert found himself bending lower and lower to catch his words and, between the whispering and the closeness and the comfort of another person's interest in him, a feeling of confidentiality, almost of trust, arose. Yet all the while Mort's eyes, almost concealed behind their china lids, roamed round the room examining every object, ferreting in the shadows, then flickering quickly back to Robert's face.

Finally Mort stepped back, dug his hands into his pockets and smiled up at Robert: a disarming, gap-toothed smile.

'Well, old mate,' he whispered, 'what you goin' to do now? Pack up and catch the first bus 'ome? Or stay 'ere an' live on air, like Zak? He never thought 'ow 'e were goin' to keep you when you come. Nor what 'e was goin' to pay you with. New blood! 'e would say every time I tried to argue some sense into 'im. New blood! That's what 'e thought you'd be. Get this place goin' again.' Mort waved an arm at the bare room.

'But I could.'

'Nah! Look on them shelves. There ain't nothin' to sell. Couple of packets of starch. Couple of tins of custard. All them bits of string an' stuff... Nah, by the time you've 'ad all the mourners in, all the tramps an' the old women sidlin' through the door, tellin' yer 'ow they was Zak's friend an' 'ow they'll just 'ave this bar of scrubbin' soap or this packet of damp matches to remember 'im by, you won't 'ave nothin' left.' He shook his head and sighed. 'Zak put all 'is money five year ago into buyin' this place outright so that 'e never would 'ave to pay rent no more. But 'e left 'imself nothin' to buy no more stock. An' then someone opened a shop couple of streets away, all new paint an' bright lights an' bargains every week. Zak's Stores just faded away. No one come 'ere much now.' Mort's voice tailed off and he bent down to pick up his things. Panic-stricken at the thought of being left alone again, Robert bent down too, thrusting his face close to Mort's as though this might detain him.

'Isn't there anything else round here I can do? Aren't there no other jobs?'

Mortensen settled his haversack comfortably on his back.

'Well,' he pondered, 'there's things come up now an' then.'

'I don't care what I do!' burst out Robert. 'But I'm not going back. Not to *her*.'

In the china mask the dark eyes watched him, glittering, eager. 'Well, you could stay 'ere. Look around. You've 'ad invitation, like – you might as well stay. Zak didn't 'ave no relations, 'ardly no friends. There ain't no landlord to come snoopin'. But you'd best lie low; don't make no song an' dance about it, or someone'll want to know your business.' He waved his stick towards the shelves. 'Hide away what you can use. Stuff like candles, tinned food, soap. You goin' to be 'ere on your own with no money for a while. You don't want to leave it all out for Tom, Dick an' 'arry to put in their pockets. Once the undertaker's been you can shut up shop. Lock the door. Keep 'em out.' He wandered off behind the counter, passing his fingers lightly over the corpse as though to touch and commit to memory small details of his friend. He grinned across the body at Robert. 'Anything in the till?'

'I ain't looked.'

He slid out a drawer below the counter.

'Nah, cleaned out. Ah, what's this stuck at the back? Little penny?' He thrust his hand into the drawer and seemed to bob out of sight for a second as though he thrust his arm deep into Zak himself. A small coin flickered for a moment in the early morning light and then was deftly snatched out of the air. 'One for luck,' he grinned, slid it into his pocket and stumped off towards the door. 'I got to be goin'. Have me sleep. I'll put me 'ead in again on me way to work, see 'ow yer doin'.'

Late in the afternoon Robert woke, tumbling from the low bed onto the floor. Hurling himself out of confused dreams in which the shop filled with beggars and tramps, silently, relentlessly. It was as though the street outside had been tilted up and all its vagabonds poured in through the door. They milled slowly round the walls, bowing and smiling obsequiously at Robert, while behind their backs their hands scrabbled along the shelves seizing whatever objects they encountered and stuffing them into their pockets. As the wake progressed, the crowd grew denser. Their arms waved wildly, their bodies surged and pushed in the packed room. Of Zak they took no notice. Having emptied the shelves, they began unscrewing door knobs, pulling nails out of the wall and cramming them into their pockets. Fights erupted at the far end of the room, silent scuffles in which Zak's corpse was jabbed by elbows and fallen upon by skirmishers. But not a sound broke the web of silence which enmeshed the room. All Robert could hear was the rasp of his own breath and the slow thump of his heart, like some ominous approaching tread.

He tried to shoulder his way through the crowd, some of whom turned angrily on him, and then, seeing that it was their host, smiled and nodded, pushing back against their fellows to give him room. To Robert's horror the faces, as they turned, were often not human. Below muffling caps and scarves, skeletal heads would turn to him, the hinged jaws parting in toothless grins. Violently, he would back away, to lurch into some human form which, with bobbing head, would wheeze its foul breath into his face and smile at him out of sunken, rheumy eyes. The half-living and the half-dead mingled together in a grey, swirling mass, indistinguishable save that the living still had flesh on their bones. But the dead seemed to have found no grace in their death and clung still to the petty habits of their lives. Robert, trapped helplessly between the two, stared about him in panic at the scrabbling horde. At any moment Zak would be pushed to the floor and trampled on. At any moment the shelves, now completely nailless, would crash to the ground and the tense skin of silence would split into a shrieking pandemonium. Robert dived through the crowd for the door and, as he did so, felt himself fall, as if from a great height, slowly towards the floor. He felt the boards come up and hit him and the suffocating smell of dust stifle him.

He opened his eyes and sat up. He licked sleep-cracked lips, ran a finger round the collar of his shirt and listened to the warm, afternoon silence of the empty house. Tiptoeing to the head of the stairs, he started down into their narrow, curving shadows; a board creaked once and he halted, drawing back into the gloom, but there was no answering sound from below and he continued on. The back room, part storeroom, part kitchen, was overshadowed by a high wall immediately outside the window.

A large white porcelain sink glimmered in the half-light, to the left of it stretched a wooden draining board and on the adjoining wall hung the empty shelves of Zak's larder. On the floor there was a strip of coconut matting and, hidden behind a flowered plastic curtain, the tins and packets Robert had salvaged from the shop earlier that morning. Half fearing that the inhabitants of his nightmare might still crowd the front room, he pushed gently at the door to the shop. Instead of opening just a crack as he had intended, it swung wide on its hinges to reveal the whole room. Empty. He advanced a step. Entirely empty. He took another step forward, flung his arms wide and felt a deep, shivering sigh escape him. The counter where Zak had lain was as innocently bare as though there had never been anything more alarming on it than a packet of sugar. The shelves were bare. There was nothing but himself and this warm, dusty room. Absently, with an almost childish delight, he began to step in and out of the wavering bars of sunlight that lay across the floor. Moving faster and faster he began almost to dance, holding out his arms, his breath coming quicker and quicker, little croaking laughs catching in his throat. He danced till the dust he raised made him cough and then he slid to the floor. With his back against one of the walls, he drew up his knees, rested his chin on them and gazed out into the empty room, his mind contentedly blank, revelling in the warmth and silence, contemplating with awe the bravery – the ease – with which he had abandoned everything: aunt, school, the small town with its narrow, carping ways. In one fell swoop, in one day, he had just turned his back on every-thing that had dragged him down for so long. Why should turning his back – he swivelled his position on the floor to feel how simple the movement was – just turning, have taken so many years? Why had it seemed so difficult and frightening, when, as soon as you did it, you realised how easy it was? When the relief from whatever unhappiness or oppressive circumstance was so immediate, why didn't everyone do it? Was it that people didn't think they *could* turn, or was it that they didn't dare? As he sat there basking in his newly-acquired sense of peace, he imagined a great, shuffling, whispering noise as everyone all over the world turned their backs, the world's population crowded shoulder to shoulder, scuffling in the dust as they turned to face a new view of life. But what if you turned only to find yourself confronting something worse? He shivered, and tried to chase the thought away. Why should that happen to him? Maybe last night, but that was over. His aunt was miles away, out of reach, fuming and fretting in her little shop. And he was free. He could do whatever he wanted. It was all beginning. He settled back into a more comfortable position, gazing across the dusty floor. What was it that he wanted? He could feel it as a large, amorphous mass of well-being, but he couldn't pinpoint its image more exactly. It was . . . it was . . . being here! It was this room, this house, for a start: warm, silent and entirely to himself. It was Mortensen. It was the city outside, waiting for him. His daydreams were suddenly interrupted by a rap at the door. A face peered in through the lowest pane of glass and Robert recognised Mortensen. He scrambled to his feet and opened the door.

'You still 'ere, then!'

Robert grinned and shrugged his shoulders.

'Fancy coming over the road?'

They went over to the café. Walking out into the street with Mortensen scurrying by his side, Robert felt like a real man-about-town, visiting cafés and meeting friends. He hardly cared that the café was almost completely deserted. Mortensen sat him down at a table near the window. In the far corner an old man was hunched over a table trying to stick together dog-ends of cigarettes, curled, be-mittened fingers fumbled with the scraps. He caught sight of Robert staring and raised a mittened paw.

145

Over by the counter, Mortensen, a cup in one hand, a glass in the other, began a careful journey back between the rows of chairs. Behind him two faces stared with professional boredom out into the room, between water cisterns and stacks of cups. They scrutinised Robert as though he could not see them, as though he was no more animate than one of the stale biscuits in the glass case in front of them. A man, heavily built, with a long, oval face that seemed constructed to be permanently mournful, and a young woman who stared at Robert out of a lumpy, blotchy face with a simmering malice that made him shuffle uncomfortably in his chair.

'That's Lil,' said Mortensen, 'and her dad, Sol.' He slopped a cup down in front of Robert and the bitter scent of coffee swirled up into his nostrils. 'I got you something 'ot, warm you up a bit. I always 'as a little snifter, perk me up round the end of the day.' He winked, lifting the small glass swiftly to his lips, and the brown liquid made them shine ruby-red. Robert slid his hands round his cup. Coffee! He was his father's equal now, and he wished, suddenly, that they could see him here. He blew at the steam and took his first, cautious sip. The thin, acrid taste made him screw up his face and gasp; it tasted like stewed rust mixed with liquorice water.

'Bit 'ot?' whispered Mortensen hoarsely.

'Think I need some sugar.' He tilted the sugar jar and sugar rushed in an avalanche out of the metal funnel into his cup. He looked guiltily at Mortensen who watched him without expression.

'Do you good, a bit of sugar.'

Robert took another sip of his coffee; it wasn't as bad as before, now it was like sweet, stewed rust, but at least it was hot. He took another sip and then another. Opposite him Mortensen beamed and wriggled in his chair, leaning ever closer across the table, nodding encouragingly each time Robert drank.

'Found yourself a job yet?'

'Nope.'

'You got money?'

'Nope!'

'What you goin' to do, then?'

Robert stretched his legs under the table and leaned back in his chair. He wanted to do nothing but sit in cafés and wander round and do whatever he liked whenever he wanted to.

'Well . . .'

Mortensen dipped his head bird-like into his glass and came up wet-lipped, his eyes all the time never leaving Robert's face.

'Well, as Zak isn't here, I got to re-think.'

Mortensen nodded eagerly and the whole of his small body seemed to bob up and down.

'I thought I'd look around a bit and then go up the centre of town get myself a job,' he grinned, 'make my fortune!'

Mortensen exploded.

'Up there! Up there? You might as well catch the first bus back 'ome! Them up there'll take one look at you and send you packing. You got a fancy suit an' dancin' shoes, 'ave yer?' he sneered. 'You got a posh accent?'

Robert was taken aback. He picked at some grains of sugar lying on the table; he couldn't understand what he had said to enrage him.

'What's wrong with it up there?' he asked, but Mortensen ignored him.

''Ere!' he called out to Sol, who was wiping down the table where the old man had sat, 'come an' meet your new neighbour, while you got the chance. He's goin' up the posh end of town tomorrow. Make 'is fortune!' Mortensen turned away in disgust, but Sol only smiled mournfully.

'Sorry to hear about Mr Zak. Took sudden, was he?'

Robert nodded. It was all Zak's fault, if Zak had *been*

here... Soundlessly, Sol picked up Robert's empty cup and padded off. Mortensen turned back again.

'What you come 'ere for, you don't want to be 'ere?'

Robert was at a loss to know how to reply. Mortensen seemed to be offended by Robert's desire to go up to the centre of the city, by the implication that another part of the city could be better than this. But surely that was obvious; there would be a part of the city that had trees and gleaming, white buildings and smart shops and people in cars – there wasn't anything like that round here, so far as he could see. And the fact that Robert wanted to go there and make his fortune – well, that was what he had thought Mortensen would want him to say. That was what his father expected him to do, and his uncle; it was what his mother dreamed of.

'Well,' he said sullenly, 'I got to get a job.'

'You won't get no job without trainin',' snapped Mortensen. 'You got to 'ave trainin' for everything, that's my point.' Robert didn't see that it followed at all. Mortensen, a smug, self-righteous tone entering his voice, leaned over the table, stabbing at it with a chubby finger:

'Even if you go down them factories, you got to 'ave trainin'. They all want it, or they won't take you on. Whatever you reads in the back of the paper, or on them boards outside the Bureau, "Experienced" it says. Now where do you get that if you don't get took on nowhere? You got to learn it somewhere.'

But it was not a question Mortensen expected him to answer, the hoarse whisper dropped into a conversational tone and carried breathlessly on. Robert, his mind wandering for a moment, glanced out of the window. As he did so he thought he saw a shadow move behind the window of Zak's shop. He looked quickly at the upper window: there was nothing there, and then down again at the lower window and the door: they were blank and dark. But something had moved. He had seen it. Something had

148

been peering out. Little tendrils of fear began to twine themselves around him, thoughts of the night to come. He tried to push them away and looked across at Mortensen; it would be pointless to ask him if he could stay the night in his house, he seemed to have lost his friendship almost as quickly as he had made it. But a strange, sickly-sweet smile was stretching itself across Mortensen's mask-like face.

'. . . so I got idea. Why don't you come with me, as Apprentice Nightwatchman!'

The stuccoed heart of the city slid away, the carefree, sauntering dreams grew dark around the edges.

'What would I do?' Robert asked warily.

'Come with me of an evenin' down Sard's warehouse,' Mortensen jerked his thumb behind him in the direction of the canal, 'we got our own little cubby 'ole an' I'll teach you all the tricks of the trade, give you a career. Come another year's time, I reckon I'll be retirin', what with me lung an' all.' He wheezed loudly to demonstrate the truth of what he said. 'You could step right into my job.'

'And we stay there all night.'

Mortensen nodded: 'Guardin'.' He hesitated. 'Course, I couldn't pay you no wages. Sard's wouldn't give me any extra for 'avin' you there, but I could see my way to one of Sol's 'ot breakfasts every morning.'

Robert stared pensively out across the street wondering whether he really had seen Zak's ghost. If he went with Mortensen he need never find out, he need never spend another night in Zak's house. If he turned Mortensen down . . . Nightwatchman. It wasn't what he'd have chosen.

'It's a good trade to learn.' Mortensen's whisper was more unctuous than ever. He did not expect to be turned down. 'It's better than *that*!'

Robert looked round. The door of the café had just banged shut behind a dishevelled young man who muttered a few words to Sol, shambled unsteadily between the flimsy chairs to a table in the middle of the room, sunk his head on his arms and appeared to instantly fall asleep.

'You can tell 'em a mile off. Nights.'

The way Mortensen said it made it sound like some dreadful, terminal disease. 'He just woke up, I reckon.'

But Robert wasn't watching the man anymore, his attention was riveted on the activity behind the counter, to the sound of fat frying briskly in a pan, the smell of sausage crisping, the splutter of egg sliding into hot lard. It was as if a trapdoor had opened deep inside his body, so that he suddenly heard howling cries for food. In an agony of hunger he turned and twisted in his chair and when Sol appeared from behind the counter, a dishcloth flung over one arm and a plate of food in his hand, he could hardly prevent himself from leaping to his feet. Mortensen, watching his face, chuckled and nudged him playfully.

'That could be yours, old son, tomorrow mornin'! First day's wages. What d'you say?'

So it was that Robert became an apprentice nightwatchman. He soon discovered that the important trade he was to learn consisted of nothing more than sitting around in a fetid cubby-hole trying to stay awake while Mortensen dozed. At regular intervals throughout the night Mortensen would start up as though thieves had invaded his very dreams.

'We got to go round!' he would whisper anxiously to Robert. 'Just you sit there a minute.' And he would set off on a sequence of meaningless preparatory rituals, murmuring breathlessly to himself, glancing fearfully at the door. As though performing some religious ceremony for which Robert's hands were as yet unconsecrated, he would accept no help.

'That's all right, son,' he would whisper, dry-mouthed, his hands shaking so much as he filled the kettle that water slopped on the floor. 'That's all right. It's got to be done just so.'

At first Robert watched him in amazement as he scurried about the room picking up this, then that, delaying their departure by whatever means came to hand. He would stare incredulously as the old man froze at the slightest sound from beyond the closed door. Then it came to him – Mortensen was afraid of the dark! When finally their departure could be put off no longer and they set out on their patrol of the warehouse, Mortensen's whisper, so incongruous by day, now seemed entirely appropriate, his soundless, rolling gait perfectly adapted to the dark passages and steep, wooden staircases. He glided in and out of patches of moonlight which gleamed briefly on his pale, polished face turning him into an animated china doll. He would have been terrifying to encounter, had it not been that his own fear manifested itself so obviously. His hands trembled so much that the glass panes round the lantern rattled constantly, tinkling together like a small bell announcing their approach. When he opened the door to each new loft as they mounted higher and higher through the warehouse, he would involuntarily jump with fright:

'It's them pieces,' he would say, 'they move.'

They did. But not while you watched them. From one night to the next the configurations of packing cases and bales would frequently alter. The loft on Floor 7, say, which for the past two nights had been stacked from floor to ceiling with crates, might suddenly, on the third night, when you pulled open the door, be completely empty. Nothing but dust and silence. Or perhaps, on Floor 3, the curious bulks swathed in tarpaulins might one night be in one set of positions and the next night have all changed places without rhyme or reason. It was as if these mono-liths were playing some vast game of grandmother's foot-steps. Standing there in the darkness Robert quite forgot that there were such things as daylight, pulleys and chutes. The night was able to suspend logic and to put in its place an eerie sense of a private life going on behind these closed loft doors in which the huge protagonists could move at will.

It was very curious and gradually this curiosity overlaid Robert's initial fears of the vaulted darkness of the warehouse, of the boards that creaked suddenly above him, as though someone else walked there, and the occasional rush of rats' claws on the rough, wooden floors. It turned it all into a kind of make-believe, like the games of his childhood. He wanted to stalk these giants, to catch them unawares shuffling silently across the floor. He wanted to hear their muffled conversations, blurred voices coming from behind layers of sacking and slatted wooden bars.

But the dreariness of the night's routine and the stifling cubby-hole were beginning to oppress him. At first, having been shown all the mysteries of Mortensen's trade and having explored every corner of the warehouse, Robert congratulated himself on having fallen into such easy work. There was nothing to it, he thought, triumphantly stretching out in his chair till his toes touched the oil stove and he could feel the soles of his boots warm. He'd had to work harder than this at school. Harder for his aunt! They'd always talked about work like it was something difficult. They'd shaken their heads, implied it was something for grown men. He remembered his mother scurrying round, making dinners for his father, washing his shirts, and his father coming in after work, throwing himself into a chair as if he was exhausted. He probably sat around in the warders' room all day like this. Robert leaned back his head. There was nothing to it. His eye roved round the tiny room. Nothing. His gaze settled on Mortensen, sleeping heavily, his mouth lolling open. Nothing. Nothing more than this. He felt his stomach slowly turn to ice as the thoughts connected in his head.

Nothing more than Mortensen, than sitting hour after hour in this hole of a room. Forever! Nothing more to hope for than to become Mortensen. To sit and wait in the darkness for thieves all his life. To sit and *long* for thieves to come, to hear a human footfall in the passage outside, a voice however low. As silently as he could Robert slid from his chair and slipped out of the room. Closing the door behind him, he glanced at Mortensen through the glass pane. At the click of the latch the old man twitched in his sleep, his head rolling against his shoulder.

Robert made his way to the upper floors of the warehouse where he wandered between the rows of packing cases, spelling out names, ports and lading numbers, running his finger lightly against the splintered wood, breathing in the smell of new timber. But the pleasure of it was snatched away by the jaws of the trap into which he had just discovered that he had fallen. He could not understand how it could have happened. Last week he had been free, after years and years. It had taken so long, and now it was gone. If only he had asked Mortensen questions. He shook his head slowly – he wouldn't have known which questions to ask.

He walked on between the packing cases. They were going, these consignments. And he was not, he had to stay shut up in this warehouse. They would be swung out over the canal and lowered into the hold of one of the waiting barges. He had seen it from the bridge at the end of the street where he went on sunny afternoons to stand with the old men and watch the water traffic. He would stare at the barges and the skiffs, absorbed by the dramas of loading and unloading that went on in front of each warehouse: the nets that swung wide, the pulleys that jammed. And then, always at a certain point, his eyes would stray above the canal to the towers and steeples of the city, barely visible between factory chimneys across acres of

grey, slanted roofs. He would try to re-trace the possible
course of his journey, but since he didn't know from which
point in the city he had started he had no idea to which
point he should return. He rubbed a little square in the
dust of one of the long windows and peered out of it at the
dark alley below. He must get back up there. That was
where he had felt that everything was alive, everything
was possible. Mortensen had tricked him into a dead end
job – but he wouldn't stay. Mortensen was always telling
him to lie low. He was cunning. He tried to frighten him.
He devised complicated procedures for Robert to enter
and leave Zak's house so that it should not appear to
anyone watching that he lived there, and busied himself
erecting various barricades inside the house to put off
intruders.

'You can't be too careful. You got to watch all sides,'
Mortensen had whispered. 'There's them round 'ere ain't
got nowhere to doss would give an eye to 'ave this place.
And there's 'ordes of thieves, just millin' about all night.
Then there's your aunt! Varmint like 'er can't never be
trusted. You don't want 'er knowing where you are.'

'But she does.'

'That's my point. If she comes 'ere and the 'ouse looks
all deserted, she'll think you ain't 'ere no more and she'll
go away!'

If Mortensen had his way, mused Robert, rubbing a
larger hole in the grime, he wouldn't go anywhere. He
would spend his days in the silent, dusty house and his
nights patrolling the warehouse while Mortensen slept.

Leaving the loft he ran lightly down the flight of wooden
stairs until he reached the ground floor. He had discovered
by chance one night a side door leading out onto the
landing stage of the warehouse. Now, drawing the bolts
as silently as he could, he let himself out into a world
tinted silver and shadowed black, where the only sound
was the silky lap of water ruffled by mysterious eddies that

rose and died on the surface of the canal. The darkness hid the bobbing chains of refuse and the magic of the night overlaid the smell of decay. From somewhere far off he heard the whistle of a train. He leant against one of the elaborately curled iron pillars that supported an escape ladder at one end of the landing stage, and stared up at the vast, black city which towered above him. Out here he could feel himself part of it. He could hear its rustlings and whisperings, the rush of boots on cobblestones and then the sudden, ominous silence. It drew him and frightened him. He thought of the detachment and curiosity with which he had regarded the endless streets of brick from the windows of the bus. There was no window protecting him now, no bus to carry him on. He had been set down. Here. And, instead of low mazes of brick running away as far as one could see on either side of him, the bricks had all placed themselves one on top of the other, ranging themselves quickly in towers and chimneys till they almost blotted out the sky. He had the feeling of being an ant trapped under a jam-jar. But, despite Mortensen's instructions to lie low, he had scurried round inside his jam-jar. He had marked off his private landmarks and learned to recognise the streets of the neighbourhood. He knew where to find the old woman who pushed an empty pram round the streets, talking loudly to herself, thrusting her pram under everyone's nose and snatching it away again with a laugh. And the thin man who stood always on the same corner of the square, whispering constantly in a hoarse voice at passers-by, begging for money. But they were not what he had come to the city to find. They were not its heart, where life beat. A light breeze rippled the water of the canal and made him shiver. The moon sailed out across the sky and turned each window of the warehouses opposite him white, blinding them quickly one by one. He did not know what he wanted. He did not know what it was, or where it might be found in all these acres of sleeping streets. How could you long for something when you didn't know what it was? He picked at the flaking paint on the iron pillar and watched the reflection of the moon swaying on the water. It was a place, he thought idly, to bring a girl. To sit with her here on the lowest step of the ladder, his arm round her waist. He could almost feel the softness of her cheek against his neck. He could almost turn her face, half-asleep, towards his. And press his mouth against hers.

He woke the next day from tumbled, confused dreams to find that light was already flooding the room. He lay there, staring stupidly at the streaks of grime on the curtain-less window, trying to gauge by the quality of light how far past midday it must already be. It was a pale light that penetrated everywhere, stripping the room naked, reducing it to drabness. It mocked at the failure of his resolution to get up early; he felt it dismissed even his presence in the house. It was like the stare of the women on the corners of the streets through which he walked to the warehouse each evening with Mortensen. Who stood in twos and threes and then, as they approached, drew themselves apart so that one by one they could turn on them this same, mocking, inquisitive stare that flooded deep down inside him, searching, in the split second that their eyes met, in his most secret places. He would feel their eyes like fingers of light probing along his stomach and he would quicken his pace. He shook his head to rid himself of their memory. They added to his ominous sense of being trapped. He felt, obscurely, that the women and Mortensen had some knowledge – whether of himself, or life in general – that he did not. Something that he ought to know in order to move in the world at all. The thrill of living rough, with unwashed sheets on a never-made bed, waking when he pleased, eating when he felt hungry and never changing his shirt, was beginning to pall. The battered label-less tin cans that he had salvaged from the shop had lost their feeling of being a lottery and had all come to taste the same. Eating them cold, straight out of the tin with a spoon, was no longer a daring thing to do, it began to seem to him solitary and miserable.

His curiosity, however, to discover the city was unabated, and he pushed further out into unknown territory beyond the streets with which he was already familiar. He wandered along streets lined with factories, looking up at the slatted ventilation shafts from which came a cacophony of machinery, and at the tiny, barred windows, and was reminded of the prison at home. Here there were streets and streets of prisons. He half-expected to see his father stride towards him, his truncheon swinging lightly from his belt and his boots striking against the cobbles. His father would like it here. In between the streets wound dark, dingy lanes and alleys strewn with wastepaper, trickling with water from broken drains. From time to time he would come upon men unloading long carts, scurrying up ramps with sacks on their heads, hauling huge bales in nets onto loft platforms that projected out over the lane. And he would pause for a moment to watch them and then, dodging across their path, hurry on.

The factories and warehouses soon became fewer and were interspersed with dilapidated houses that all had the same boarded-up look, as though their inhabitants lived complicated lives of subterfuge and distrust. He passed row after row of doors that looked as though they could no longer be opened and windows that had long since ceased to give light. He imagined their owners returning to them only after dusk, sidling in through cracks, sliding between bricks which they pulled to after them, and padding all night round dark, little rooms, watching for dawn. Several times he thought he was approaching the centre of the city. He imagined he could feel the ground rise slightly beneath his feet. Clusters of shops appeared among the houses and there seemed to be a sudden increase of people. But they always faded away again, like a dream he could not sustain. It was always the same, despite the fact that he took what he was sure was a different direction each day; he always ended up in a maze of tiny streets with the light beginning to fade and his fear of Mortensen discovering his absence tugging at him like a chain. It was, he thought, as he retraced his steps, as though the centre of the city only existed as a myth. That he had imagined he had passed through it. And yet he could remember it quite clearly. He stopped. He could recall the exhilaration of it exactly as if it was a sound ringing in his ears. He looked about him at the empty late afternoon streets of the quarter, the blindness of them, the dull rectangularity of them stretching away, already familiar, before him, and disappointment rose slowly, like a mist, through his thoughts. He trudged on. The triumph of his arrival, the wild excitement, had not been sustained. When the novelty of his new surroundings wore off, it had become clear to him that he had done no better for himself than if he had stayed in the small town – except that he was free. This was the city, too, this numbing greyness all around him, the city he had dreamed of for so long, but this had not been a part of his dream. It was, he thought, as if he had had one idea of the city and Fate had had another. They had been like two people talking at cross purposes, each thinking the other saw their own vision. His wish had been granted, but he had not wished for this strange, blank world in which he felt so cut off. He had thought that getting to the city would be an end in itself, that just the achievement of reaching it would assure him of a new life. But it had proved to be only a beginning, and somehow he had taken his first step in the wrong direction.

What he wanted now were friends and advice. But, full though the city was of people, it was a curiously lonely place and he knew no one to talk to. There was only Sol and Lil in the café, and then Mortensen was always there doing all the talking and looking about him with his little eyes to make sure he didn't miss anything. Sol looked quite kindly; well, he looked mournful with his long face, so that you thought he might also be kind. But then he might not. And, even if he was sympathetic, he still might tell Mortensen. Robert had no doubts about Lil. From the very first day she had treated him with disdain. She sat behind the counter on her stool and slapped down change in front of them when they went to pay for their meal. She never looked at Mortensen, though it was his money, only at Robert. 'This money ain't for you,' her eyes said, 'you ain't worth no money. You just get fed scraps, like a dog.' Then one day, while he was waiting for Mortensen at the counter, she had stood up to attend to something and her overall, which had apeared to be bunched up in her lap, fell away to reveal a smooth round bulge, like a saucepan, hidden beneath the cloth. Robert had stared at the bulge unable to believe his eyes. The likelihood of Lil having stuffed a saucepan up her overall seemed to him far more plausible than the fact that she might be pregnant. The idea that somebody had ... had ... He couldn't imagine what might have had to be done to make Lil pregnant. His knowledge of conception was limited to smutty, play-ground jokes, but still he was sure that someone would have had to kiss her. At least. His eyes travelled from the bulge to her face to test out in his imagination how this appalling preliminary might have been achieved but he never got that far. Lil had got there before him and, as he had looked up, her eyes had spat fire at him like a cat's, and like a cornered alley-cat she had hissed with rage at his discovery of her.

One morning as Robert and Mortensen entered the café they found it in chaos, Sol rushing about between the tables while behind the counter, amid a blue haze, sausages blackened unattended and dirty plates overflowed the tiny sink. Of Lil there was no sign.

'She's blowed up!' explained Sol, mopping his forehead.

The next day things were no better in the café and the news was worse.

'She's been took up horstpital.' There were deep lines on Sol's forehead and spots of grease on his white shirt. 'She won't go down.'

'How long they goin' to keep 'er?' Mortensen had asked, shuffling with excitement on his chair.

'Till she go down, they say. But she won't go down.'

'What you goin' to do?'

'I dunno.'

Perhaps, Robert thought, she wanted to blow the child out of her. Or perhaps it was the child, who suddenly had an inkling of what its life to come might be, fighting back. If she exploded, it could escape. If she exploded – the thought suddenly struck him – then I could escape! Her dad wouldn't have no one to help him then and I could have her job. I could leave the warehouse and have money!

Money was becoming an increasing problem to Robert. His stock of tins salvaged from Zak's shop was rapidly diminishing. And, when he complained to Mortensen that the matches had run out and he was down to his last candle, he had turned on him in rage. 'What you lighting lights for in there! You'll give the whole game away, get yourself seen!' But it was more than the hunger and being afraid of the dark. He came to realise that nothing could be done in the city without money. You could not even open a conversation without money in your pocket to lead it on. It would come to money eventually: a smoke, a bottle of beer, or a bag of chips. He would hang round the neighbourhood shops, staring into their empty windows, longing for an apple or a loaf of bread, or just the pretext to go inside to talk to the girl behind the counter and ask for a pennyworth of this or two ounces of that. How much longer, he wondered, did Mortensen think he could keep him without money? But Mortensen appeared to feel entirely secure. He hardly ever left the snug now, but stayed slumped in his chair, little whistling snores issuing from his slack mouth. He thought of the way the old man's eyes stayed shut as he crept out and flickered open without fail the moment he returned. The sleep-cracked whisper that always said the same words, and the crust of dried spittle along his lower lip.

'Everything all right?' And then: 'Put on the water, son. Make us a cuppa.'

And the extra piece of sausage that he found on his breakfast plate, representing his promotion to night-watchman.

Now that a potential solution to his problems had presented itself Robert couldn't wait to get to the café each morning to see if Lil was back or not. Each afternoon he would watch from his bedroom window to see Sol return from the hospital, trying to tell by the droop of his shoulders whether Lil had decided to come down or had blown herself up further. When Lil had been in hospital for five days, Robert judged the time was right to approach Sol. He watched for his return from his afternoon visit and, when he saw him unlock the door of the café and go inside, he ran down to the kitchen. Squinting in the piece of mirror propped over the sink, he slicked back his hair with water and slipped outside. At the door of the café he halted, the room was in shadow. Leaning against the door jamb, so as not to be seen from the inside, he peered into the gloom. At first he thought the café was empty, then he made out a figure hunched over a table in the centre of the room. He was about to draw back, when his foot slipped and his body pitched forward against the door, bursting it open and startling the figure inside who leapt to its feet. It was Sol, sitting like a stranger in his own café, huddled into an overcoat. He stared at Robert still hanging in the doorway smiling foolishly, and sat down again.

'I thought,' began Robert sheepishly, closing the door behind him and coming forward, 'I thought I'd come an' see how Lil was.' Sol's face seemed to lengthen as he looked at it, the folds of skin below his eyes dragged down by some unbearable weight. Beneath the overcoat the whiteness of his shirt seemed to mock at his distress.

'I just been to see her. I just come from there.'

There was a long silence. Robert sat down opposite him.

'She won't eat nothing now. I took her pound of pears. Best pears, in a bag. She wouldn't have none of it. Wouldn't even open the bag.'

'She coming down?'

Sol shook his head slowly and stared into his cup.

'She ain't goin' to come down. There's two of 'em, now. That's what they tell her. Twins. That's a gift from God, I said to her, twins. But she's taking it real hard. Won't speak, won't eat. That's not right. You can have shock.' Sol tapped one finger on the table to emphasise the theological distinction. 'You can have that. But only for one or two days. You ain't allowed to go on, that's setting your face against God. You in for mortal, then! I told her, I said: you have to stop, Lil, else you run the risk of one of them coming out cripple or daft, or something. She ain't a grateful girl, my Lil, but even taking her nature into account she gone too far.'

'Isn't she coming back, then?'

'Don't ask me!' Sol suddenly clapped his hands to his head. 'Don't talk about it! What she have to get took so bad about it for?'

Robert wondered whether this was the moment to press his suit. As he hesitated, Sol's fingers parted.

'I should be being congratulated!' he said thickly. He dragged his fingers slowly down his face, the gold wedding ring on his left hand bumping from plane to plane, and laced them together beneath his chin. 'An' all I have is worry.'

Robert opened his mouth to speak, but Sol went on:

'Worry about her. Worry about this place – you seen what it's like early mornings!' He shut his eyes. 'I can't never get cleared up.'

'Yes,' said Robert loudly. 'Yes.' Sol opened his eyes with a start. Robert rushed on: 'That's why I come. If Lil – I mean, you know – if she isn't allowed back on account of being – well – *ill*. Then I'd like to help you. Do her job,' he added quickly, in case Sol should think it was for free.

They stared at each other.

'I dunno,' said Sol slowly, 'what about the warehouse?'

'I can't afford to stay there. I got to find myself a proper job. With a wage.'

He practised this short speech for the rest of the afternoon and delivered it to Mortensen that night during their first tea-break. He was surprised at the distance, the almost disdain, he felt for Mortensen's venomous spluttering. Mortensen was like a tactician outwitted; winded and gasping, consumed not by the defeat itself, but by the fact that his defences had been breached, that his enemy had been underestimated. He darted glances all round the room, as though he expected further attack, then stared fixedly at Robert as if trying to ferret out what he had overlooked in him before.

'An' 'ow long notice you goin' to give?' he demanded finally.

'Notice?'

'Yeah, notice.'

'What you mean?'

'You 'ave to give notice. You can't just leave a job without givin' time for a replacement to be found. Who's goin' to do your job?'

163

'You didn't have no one before.'

'What about your trainin'? You can't leave 'alf-way.'

'I'm going in the café business. I'm having different training.'

It hadn't struck him before, but it did now. It was an argument that beat Mortensen into grudging silence and then became the line of thought that pacified Sol's concern that perhaps he was poaching from one of his customers.

'Course he's not pleased,' admitted Robert. 'But he was always going on about training himself. Always on about it to me.' Sol stood on the other side of the counter, polishing a small spot on the water urn with the cloth he carried on his arm. Round and round he rubbed, sucking in his lower lip, his eyes glued to the gleaming spot, his mournful face longer than ever. Robert shuffled anxiously behind the counter. Sol's brooding silence began to worry him. What if he'd lost Mortensen only for Sol to change his mind!

'He kept on saying it were the most important thing. So he had to agree, in the end, that if it were better for me to get café training, well then ... ' Robert hoped Sol was convinced. The oval head did lift at that point, it did nod in recognition of the point Robert was trying to make.

'I wouldn't like to offend no one,' said Sol. 'Especially not one of my regulars.'

Having almost set his conscience to rest over Mortensen, it then occurred to him that perhaps it looked as if he was abandoning Lil too quickly for this total stranger.

'Yes, well ... ' He stopped polishing the urn and folded the cloth carefully. 'So long as you realise it's temporary. I don't mind teaching you what you have to know, but this is Lil's place by rights. Minute she wants to come back ... ' His voice tailed away and he looked meaningfully at Robert from under thick, black eyebrows.

By staying awake half the night, Robert managed to be at the café the next morning just after five. He stumbled out into a grey dawn and crossed the street as though he was treading water. The whole city seemed to be still asleep, the houses withdrawn into themselves, the tall factories behind them, silent and no more menacing than cardboard cut-outs. For once there was no pall of cloud overhead, only the slightest haze under which the clear light slipped unnoticed. Sol was waiting for him at a counter stacked with piles of food and crockery. His voice was still husky with sleep, but he was ready for all comers, his sleeves crisply folded back to the elbow, the little, black hairs bouncing along his skin, a rare smile on his face. He wasted no time, but beckoned Robert over to him.

'Take off your jacket, roll up your sleeves.' He thrust a mug of tea into Robert's hands. 'We ain't got much time till they come and I got to get me fries on before that, but I'll take you through it, bit by bit. Give you a general idea of the workings of the place. Now then!' He bustled round to the other side of the counter and pointed with a fish-slice at the various mounds before him: 'You got your milks, your eggs, your breads all cut up, your puddings sliced ready; you got your water boiling. You got your plates all here, your cups all there. You got your tables all laid up. There ain't nothing you haven't got to hand, there ain't nothing you haven't thought of. You're prepared for anything.'

Over the top of his mug Robert glanced blearily round the café while Sol's incomprehensible enthusiasm washed over him. It had always seemed to him when he had come in here before that the place would look all right if only there wasn't such a haze of frying, or so much water trickling down the windows; if there wasn't such a clutter of people and plates. And here it was, scrubbed clean, empty, windows so clear you could even read the menu painted outside across the glass. Yet the sight of it made his heart sink. At its best it was nothing but a dismal room laid out with rows of formica-topped tables, chipped at

165

their edges, its stained cream walls glimmering up to meet a grease and dust-encrusted ceiling.

Robert's real training sessions began when the early morning rush was over, during the long, mid-morning lull when the café was mostly empty and he was allowed to sit down on Lil's stool with some coffee and a slice of bread. He would then struggle with the strange syntax and grammar of this new world and was led stumbling through its rituals feeling as if he would never understand them or see their point. Why did it matter whether you put the salt cellars away on the second rather than the third shelf – indeed, why take them off the tables at all when you were only going to put them back on again next day? And what was the point of turning all the chairs upside down on the tables last thing at night when the first thing you had to do every morning was to put them all back down on the floor again? All this fussing and all these rules and places for this and places for that, when all he was ever allowed to do was washing-up. He almost wished he had stayed with Mortensen, but the thought of money at the end of the week kept him going.

They were having one of these training sessions one morning, when Sol, in the middle of explaining how to get thirty-two slices out of a loaf of bread, suddenly said to Robert:

'You know, my Lil ain't never forgiven herself that one of us didn't go over and pay our last respects to your uncle. She thinks her condition might be on account of your uncle's unappeased spirit.'

Robert stared at him, but Sol went on.

'We didn't never speak that much; he didn't come in the café and we didn't have no cause to go in his shop. But we were neighbours. We were, so to speak, in kindred trades. And we wouldn't like him to think it were any disrespect. Perhaps you could – er– im*part* that to him.'

166

Robert shrugged his shoulders and said, to reassure Sol:
'Oh, I shouldn't worry. He weren't my uncle, anyway.'

Sol's jaw dropped. A frown of extreme anxiety furrowed his brow. The youth who sat before him on his daughter's stool, smiling quietly, turning his empty cup in stubby fingers, was not what he had thought him to be. He was without reference, without relation, without credentials. Sol could feel himself coming out in a cold sweat.

'Ain't you got no parents, either.'

'Course.'

'Are they here?'

Robert shook his head.

'You over there by yourself?'

'Yeah.'

'What you doing in that house if it ain't yours?'

Robert told him his story. By the time he had almost reached the end an old man had come into the café and asked for a cup of coffee. Sol, who had been leaning on the counter all this time, waved his hand weakly at Robert.

'You do it,' he said thickly.

With great care Robert filled the cup from the urn, the old man peering over the counter with little, bright eyes to watch him, sucking his teeth in anticipation. It was only when he put the cup on the saucer that he spilt any of it, but Sol didn't seem to notice.

'Go on,' he said. 'No. Go back to the beginning and start all over again.'

During the second recitation, he interrupted Robert constantly with questions and then appeared to mis-interpret Robert's answers entirely, ending up with a version of the story that made Robert gasp.

'But, I just told you, it weren't like that.'

Sol shook his head mournfully.

'You ain't stopped to think of the anguish of your parents, have you? Of their sorrow, their sacrifice.'

'What sacrifice?' spluttered Robert.

'You tell me, how can you think a man like your dad, a guardian of law and order, an upholder of justice, how can you think any ill of him at all? And your mum, think how she suffered.'

'She did that anyway.'

'She suffered on account of you. They both did. I know that. As a parent.'

'You ain't never sent *Lil* away.'

'To your *aunt*. Your father's sister, that's where you was sent. To family. And prospects. I can't think,' Sol leaned back, shaking his head at Robert as if he was completely incomprehensible, 'how you was so foolish as to run away from them prospects.'

'If you'd met her ... '

'You was her only close relative. You was sitting on a gold mine.'

'She treated me like a slave – she wasn't never going to give me no wages.'

'Lil works alongside of me and she don't get no wage to speak of but she don't complain. She knows it's all for her one day.'

Sol was devastated by Robert's revelations. He lumbered round his café, bemused, going over each point in his mind, glancing up from his abstraction every so often at Robert and wincing, as though the very sight of him sent stabs of pain shooting through his head. First Lil and now this! Sol was well aware of the wickedness of the world, of the insidious, creeping habits of downfall and danger. He had protected his family and his café against both, building around them walls of propriety and order which nothing before had ever breached. They had withstood the death of his wife and the raising of his daughter. They had ensured that he had never had any trouble at the café – he had been careful never to allow any credit, nor any drunks. But now, unwittingly, he had allowed into the heart of that citadel this boy, who seemed to have no

168

idea of what was right and proper. To have run away from home – two homes! Sol shuddered as though he could not bear even to think about it. To pretend to have an uncle that he didn't and to carry on living all by himself in a house that wasn't even his! Sol couldn't make up his mind which was the worst of these crimes and stole another look at Robert, busy refilling salt cellars. And to look so innocent all the while! To be so quiet and helpful. Sol bit his lip. He couldn't deny, the boy was all those things. What had possessed him to take himself up and put himself down in a place without a soul to know him? Hadn't nobody told him the dangers of breaking up the order of his life, like that? He thought of Lil, and crossed himself surreptitiously, he'd never had any problems of that sort with her, never would have. He'd made sure she knew what was what. He'd never had no running away from home, he'd had a hard enough job just getting her to marry. And as for having no one to speak out for her, she had references everywhere – everyone that went in the café knew her, everyone that lived on the street! She could be placed, related, aligned and linked by anyone as had the interest, he thought proudly. Not like that boy. He picked up his cloth and began swabbing down the nearest table. He should never have let him in the place, he should never have let him talk him round like that. Come the end of the week he'd pay him off, tell him he wouldn't do. Best thing. He straightened up the chairs, banging them angrily together. Except that he needed someone here to mind the place when he went to visit Lil, and in the mornings when the rush was on. Necessity seemed to be forcing him into compromising his principles. He stared out of the window at the empty street for some time and then stole another look at Robert. Finally, he struck the back of a chair with his hand – he could stay on condition that he reformed, on condition that he mend relations with his parents, that he settle down to a proper working life and didn't consort with bad types and didn't bring no riff-raff into the café. Sol strode between the tables towards the counter where Robert was working, threw down his cloth and eyed him severely.

'You written home since you been here?'

Robert looked up, surprised.

'No.' He took in at once the gravity of Sol's expression. 'I . . . I wanted to wait till I got a job . . . with money. Tell them about that. I got to send money home, but I haven't been earning anything yet.' He shook his head for emphasis. 'Mortensen didn't give me nothing.' He didn't add that he didn't have a pen, or paper, or money for a stamp, or inclination to spend his precious wages on any of these things. That what he wanted was chips from the chip vendor's trolley and a bottle of soda pop to drink in the sunshine on the towpath of the canal watching the barges glide by. That what he wanted was to put pennies into slot machines and win prizes, and walk around the lamp-lit streets and hear music coming out of doorways with flashing neon lights above them. Instead he grinned at Sol and then turned back to his salt cellars slightly puzzled, as Sol coughed, bent his head, snatched up his cloth and mumbling, 'Yes, well, see you do,' went off to wipe some more tables.

Saturday came and seemed to pass more slowly than any other day Robert could remember. Towards noon it rained, long slow drops. Sol fussed about getting wet on his way to the hospital and Robert fidgeted behind the counter, performing endless calculations as to how much Sol might be going to pay him. The more he thought about it the less he could remember of their original conversation. For some reason, the more it rained, the more convinced he became that there had been some condition on his having any wages at all, and that, probability being what it was, it was likely therefore that he wouldn't get anything. Towards the end of the afternoon the rain stopped, pale yellow streaks suddenly appeared in the grey cloud and then were blotted out by the swift approach of evening.

It was Saturday night. And on Saturday night, when you had money in your pocket, you went out. Robert was going to do that, he had it planned, he'd seen where to go. On a street he'd only discovered the other day were bars and cafés and a place with penny-in-the-slot machines. He waited impatiently for Sol to give him the signal to start cleaning up. At last it came. At last, above the clattering of chairs on tables, he heard the delicate chink of coin against coin and, looking up, saw Sol counting money out onto the counter. Finally, they stood alone together in the semi-darkness of the deserted café.

''Ere,' muttered Sol, pushing a small pile of coins towards him with the tips of his fingers, 'see you Monday.'

Out in the street Robert walked very fast past dimly-lit courts and silent factories, ignoring the tottering advances of the beggars and the stares of women clustered in the shadows. Eventually the road curved away from the monotony of factory walls, narrowed for a time and then branched in two, leaving a kind of buttressed island in its fork. Across this island spread a café with large lighted windows running down each side. Around it huddled other, smaller establishments making a tiny oasis of neon light. This was the place Robert had discovered. But now it was not quite as he recollected it. It was crowded with people. For a moment his footsteps faltered and he thought of turning back, but the people coming on behind him carried him forward with them into the crowd. On a tide of cheap scent and beer and sweat, overlaid by the reek of chip fat from the chip vendor who had set up his trolley just before the island, he found himself drawn along. As doors opened he found himself tumbling towards them in the wake of people going in or coming out, catching sight, across the blare of light and noise and cigarette smoke, of leering faces and wide mouths. When the crowd swirled across to the island, Robert detached himself from the mainstream and stood for a moment beside one of the long windows of the café, looking in. But he found it no less daunting than the others. At the back of the room stretched a long bar behind which a team of waiters worked with a facility and speed that took his breath away. Before them a crowd pushed and swayed. Steadily people peeled off, clutching brimming glasses, and steadily others pressed in to take their place. All down the room were long counters where people stood turned towards their companions, or staring fixedly at the bottles and glasses piled up before them. Next to Robert's window a man swiftly dissected half a roast chicken with a penknife, wiped the blade clean on his bread and began rapidly to stuff morsels of flesh into his mouth, washing them down with gulps of beer from a tankard at his side. Around him, at every counter, was the same feverish consumption. Admittedly some people laughed and some had their arms round each other, but the rest seemed possessed solely of the glum desire to consume. Robert allowed himself to be drawn back into the stream of people on the pavement and carried on past the central door of the café. They crossed to the right-hand fork of the street; but on this side it was just the same. Robert pulled away. There were too many people. He couldn't think with so many people around him. Saturday night along with his courage, was slipping away.

He walked a few yards into the semi-darkness higher up the street and looked back at the cluster of lights. He could not let himself go home until he had been inside one place and had one drink. Then he noticed, across the street, a sign swinging in a lighted passage: Chez Madeleine. He crossed the street and ventured into the archway. All was silent. He pushed open the door onto a flight of stone stairs leading downwards; a smell of damp and disinfectant wafted up. Cautiously, he descended; still there was no noise. At the bottom of the stairs was another door and beside it a lamp with an opaque glass shade in the form of a billowing flame and, drooping from the lamp, a chain of faded paper flowers. Robert stood in the passage looking uneasily from the paper flowers to the door, trying to catch some noise that might tell him what lay beyond it. He was about to put his ear to one of the heavy panels, when he noticed a tiny, round spy-glass set into the wood. He stared sheepishly into the minute glass eye. It stared back at him. But the door did not open. He tapped his knuckles gently against one of its panels and to his surprise it swung lightly ajar.

He found himself in a low room whose occupants looked up, startled, as he entered and then bent their heads again as he walked between the tables to the bar. As he approached, the barman, who had been sitting almost out of sight behind another billowing lamp, rose and slowly folded his evening paper. Robert laid one hand gingerly on the edge of the bar. Under its glass panels it appeared to be covered in pale pink satin, pleated and swagged to hang down the front of the bar in elaborate folds. To the right was a high stool made of the same twisted iron work as the flimsy chairs and tables, its white paint chipped and its seat stained as though someone had spilled a drink over it. Beside it on the bar was a little frilled circle of paper, a small dish of nuts and a china ashtray containing a thin black cylinder which tapered to a kind of mouthpiece, like a whistle, at one end.

'Beer,' whispered Robert to the barman.

'Cold?'

He nodded. He was cold. There was a kind of damp mustiness to the room which the electric fire, fixed high up on the wall above the bar, only seemed to draw out further. The barman took a bottle out of a small, white cupboard and with much display prised off the cap and poured it into a gold-rimmed glass so that it pounded and welled and bubbled up to a head of foam. Robert carried it carefully to one of the rickety tables, sipped abortively at the froth and looked about him.

Behind him the barman's evening paper rustled and at the table next to him a small, dark man turned a page of a pink racing paper spread out in front of him. A nicotined forefinger darted to a word and then moved swiftly from line to line, while the other hand reached out for his glass. Across the rim his eyes left the paper and flickered over Robert, eager, weasel-sharp eyes that assessed and dismissed him in a second. At a table a little way down the left-hand wall, underneath a flickering wall-light, sat a middle-aged couple, facing each other. The man had his back to Robert and his head bent to the table. The woman, however, looked steadfastly in front of her, her features pressed like painted currants into a mass of doughy flesh. A black coat was open to reveal more black beneath and round her neck was draped a strange, spotted fur, worn so thin in places you could see the skin. Her large hands grasped the handle of a big, black handbag resting in her lap. As Robert stared at her, she picked up the small glass of green liquid in front of her and, without seeming to open the painted lips at all, tilted it against her mouth. Above her the wall-light behind its billowing glass flame blinked on and off, like a nervous tic.

Suddenly, over in the far corner, where two old men sat, a concerto of scratching, darting and twisting broke out. It was as if an army of gnats, fleas and mosquitoes attacked them. Robert stared at them eagerly as they writhed and jumped, but could see nothing that might be causing them such distress. No one else seemed to take any notice of them, but their pouncing and scratching went on so long Robert felt he ought to go and help them. Just as he was about to rise, the barman padded slowly past him carrying a bottle with a silver bulb on the end.

To Robert's surprise, he did not spray the insects, or try to swat them, instead he calmly refilled the glasses in front of the old men, slipped a small paper under the tin ashtray on their table, then, with compressed lips and an expressionless face, he walked back to the bar. Mysteriously, the anguish of the old men gradually ceased, until they were able to sit quite still. Robert was amazed. He sat staring at them, taking an occasional sip at the froth on his beer.

The forlorn room settled into a tense silence, disturbed only by the rustle of newspaper pages and an intermittent buzzing from the faulty wall-lamp. Then, as if he could bear it no longer, the husband slammed his fist into the wall. The lamp instantly went out. The old men jerked back into their frenzy of scrabbling and jumping. The racing man started in his seat as if all his creditors at once had burst into the room. And the wife, almost over-balancing on her flimsy chair from the effort, aimed a vicious kick at her husband's shin. He collapsed, head in hands, over his empty beer glass. At this point the door to the street swung open and a young man bounced into the room, hands in pockets, black eyes in a dark face surrounded by a mass of tight corkscrew curls. He almost danced up to the bar, looking round him for someone evidently not there for he seemed not to notice the other occupants, who twitched and sank back into their own reveries like marionettes deprived of life.

'George,' Robert heard him say as he reached the bar, 'my little sister been in tonight?' He clicked his tongue in annoyance. 'Ahh late, late, late.' The words tailed away like the soft chattering of a bird. There was the light chink of coin against glass and a low laugh. He came prancing back among the tables, almost passed Robert and then turned, smiling. He touched the back of the empty chair with long, brown fingers:

'You *mind*?' the vowel drawn out, long and caressing.

Awkwardly Robert shook his head. The boy slid into the chair. He hunched his shoulders, wriggled himself comfortable, leaned back and nodded at Robert.

'You waitin' here for someone?'

Robert shook his head. He felt colourless and drab in the presence of this person. Any words that he might utter would sound flat in comparison with the way that this stranger took up language and poured it out again, giving it the intonation and juxtaposition of his own tongue.

'You been here before?'

'No.'

'No, I ain't seen you here before.' He gave Robert a smile of collusion. 'This ain't no place that I frequent.'

'Them other places . . . ' began Robert hastily.

The stranger waved a hand.

'Them others – they worse! They barns for cattle.'

The pronouncement made, his friend leaned back again.

'I come here for my little sister,' he explained, 'it give pleasure to she. You seen my little sister?' He swivelled round in his chair, squinting at the door. 'She late.' He turned back to Robert, 'You seen her?'

'No, I don't . . . '

'You see her,' he tapped a finger lightly on the table and shook his head, 'you don't forget. She am a *prin*cess!' His voice had climbed higher and higher in its exuberance until it dissolved into high-pitched chuckles, like tiny stones bouncing down a mountain-side. In spite of himself Robert smiled, picked up his glass and drank deeply. The head of froth had gone and in its place ice-cold bubbles burst against his tongue, swept away his breath and erupted into his head, where he felt them split apart like ripe fruit, like brilliant large-petalled flowers, until he felt his skull had swelled to fill the room. He gasped and hiccoughed and felt his head sway heavy and precarious on a neck that had gone strangely stiff.

'You like that stuff?'

'I ain't never had it before.'

'Where I come from beer is for hobos, for back-woodsmen. When you in the city you go for liquor. You been in the city long?'

'Couple of weeks.'

'Couple a weeks?' His companion leaned over the table screwing up his face into an expression of extreme curiosity, the voice twisted into such inquisitiveness that it was like the squeak of a corkscrew trying to draw out Robert's secrets:

'Then how come I ain't seen you around?'

Robert shrugged: 'I ain't seen you, neither.'

His companion laughed, deflected for a moment:

'No one don't see me, 'less I want they should see me.' He bent again to his interrogation. 'You live round here?'

'Down the road, near the canal.'

'You work in one of they factories?'

'No.'

'No, you don't look like all they other poor devils.' He bounced impatiently on his chair, wrinkled his broad nose and grinned as though giving up on a riddle. 'What your game?' he wheedled. 'What you *do*? How come you got shoes on your feet an' a coat on your back an' you sitting in *night* clubs?'

'I'm in the caterin' trade,' said Robert and leant cautiously back on his rickety chair.

'The cat-er-in' trade!' His companion carefully enunciated each syllable, rolling them round, soft and honeyed and perfectly finished on his tongue while he gazed at Robert as though re-appraising him. Suddenly his eyes sparkled:

'An' which bit, exactly, of the caterin' trade are you *in*?' He waved his hands. 'You order the supplies? You dispense the supplies?' He jiggled in his seat. 'Or you empty the trash-can?'

'I ... I work behind the bar.'

'Oh!' His eyebrows shot up. 'Like George.'

'Well, it's more . . . it's not a bar, it's not a club – like this. It's more . . . food.'

'You work in a *rest*aurant! You a chef?'

'Well, I do a bit of food. Sort of easy things, cups of coffee and things. It's not a big place, like a restaurant. It's more a – more . . . '

'Uh ha,' the other nodded, rocking backwards and forwards on the edge of his chair, sucking air through his teeth and smiling very gently.

They fell momentarily silent. Robert chased a drip of condensation that trickled down the side of his beer glass with his forefinger.

Into this silence there was a light click as of a door closing. Robert looked up and saw, advancing between the tables, a young girl, scarcely older than a schoolgirl. Her skin was as dark as his companion's and her black frizzy hair was scraped tightly back and held in place by numerous pins and plastic hair-slides ending in a bunch at the nape of her neck. Her big eyes were fixed on their table, her mouth compressed into primness as though her mother's injunction not to speak to strangers still rang in her ears. She wore a cotton dress, cut without shape of any kind, falling straight from a childishly round collar into a sort of tent that was too big for her, and below which thin brown legs stuck out like those of a delicate bird.

Robert's companion, noticing how he stared, turned round just as she reached their table.

'My little *sister*!' he squeaked, uncurling his legs below the table with a great scraping so that the table shook and the glasses tottered. Without a word the girl slid onto the edge of a vacant chair, crossed her legs demurely at the ankles, settled a small, pink, plastic handbag on her lap holding its handle with both hands and sat stiffly, staring out into the middle distance as though she expected someone to take her photograph. This very act of not

smiling and not looking made Robert stare at her all the
more.

'George! George!'

To Robert's surprise the barman ambled over to their
table. He beamed down at the girl with an almost fatherly
tenderness and she, moving her head a fraction, gave her
mouth a slight twist in acknowledgement.

'Now, George, what you *have* for my little sister?' Her
brother seemed almost to dance in his chair, every part of
him that could move vibrated with excitement. He turned
to the girl. 'You want a brandy flip, Princess? You want a
strawberry menthe?'

A tiny giggle escaped his sister, her shoulders hunched
for a second and shook, but she made no reply. 'I know,
I know!' her brother held up a finger. 'Cham*pagne* for
the Princess!' George beamed. 'You make her up a *pink*
champagne.' George inclined his head and turned away.
'An' mind you don't put too much of that eau de *vie* in!'
he called after him. He turned to his sister and the smile
suddenly evaporated: 'Princess, what you got them socks
on for?'

Her face fell.

'This Saturday night, you big night. What business you
going to do with little girl socks on like that?' He leant
back aggrieved and then said in an emphatic whisper: 'You
have to wear stockings!'

His sister shrugged.

'They got all tore up.'

'Someone been rough with you?'

She screwed up her face and hunched one shoulder:

'Just bit by bit they get tore up.'

Her brother frowned at her and then, remembering
Robert, spread his hands on the table between them.

'Anyway, honey, I'd like you to meet a friend of mine.'
One of the hands gestured towards Robert. 'Say how-do.'

One small, brown hand disengaged itself from the handle

of the handbag and proffered itself stiffly towards Robert. He touched it with his fingers and was startled to feel how cold and rough it was.

'Princess Bel,' announced her brother.

'Robert,' he muttered.

George returned and placed a glass before Bel with a flourish, contemplated it for a second and then hurried away. Its rim was coated in white powder from which a short, paper straw protruded and in the vee of its bowl nestled a cherry from which tiny bubbles seemed to burst upwards through pink liquid.

'*Pink* cham*pagne*,' drawled her brother and leaned back in his chair. His sister burst into delighted giggles and seemed to clutch at her handbag more tightly than ever, looking from Robert to her brother. He waved a hand at Robert's glass.

'You want another of they?'

Robert shook his head.

The boy turned to his sister.

'You goin' to drink that, now you got it?'

Obediently Bel picked up the glass. Across the pink bubbles her eyes shone and with one slurp she half-emptied the glass.

'Whoo-ee!' whistled her brother. 'There ain't no lady can knock her liquor back like my little sister!'

Bel released the straw and put the glass back on the table. Robert stared suspiciously at the pink liquid.

Her brother pushed his chair back and stood up.

'I got to be going.' He tapped a finger on Bel's shoulder.

'I'll come around see you like usual. Mind you be good.'

Turning away, he nodded at Robert and bounced off towards the door.

Without him they felt themselves sink a little in the dullness of the room and struggled, each of them, to resurface. Robert took a long pull at his beer and Bel readjusted her dress over her knees with rapid, darting movements of one hand, still keeping the other round the handle of her handbag. She waggled her head at Robert.

'I ain't seen you here before.'

'No,' he cleared his throat, 'I ain't come.'

'It's nice here, don't you think, nicer than them other places.' She wrinkled her nose. 'There's George. And them lights. An' all that pink satin on the bar, I ain't seen that nowhere else.' Her voice wasn't like her brother's. It was clear and soft like a little girl's voice, but it didn't have the intonation of her brother's, the sudden, unexpected stress on a particular syllable. It was as though someone from the city had taught her the language and she had got so used to speaking it that the memory of any other had faded from her mind.

'You live round here?'

'Nile Street,' he jerked his head, 'down the canal.'

'Oh, I know Nile Street. I live just up from there. Hendrye Place. You know Hendrye Place?'

Robert shook his head. He was beginning to feel increasingly uneasy. He couldn't fit Bel or her brother into any pattern of life that he had so far encountered. He could not understand who they were, what they did, or why they had latched on to him. The attention of Bel's brother had been puzzling enough, but Bel's was even more unfathomable. The departure of her brother seemed to provoke in her the necessity to play hostess. She rolled her eyes at Robert, patted her frizzy curls and attempted to cross one knee over the other. But the bony joints would not stay put and eventually rolled off each other. She tried to engage him in conversation, prattling on in her little-girl voice, but she sounded as though she was repeating some kind of lesson, something learned by rote. Robert had the eerie sensation that her brother lurked behind the closed door, listening with his ear to the crack, to hear her lesson, and that she repeated the clichéd questions not for Robert's benefit, but to please her brother.

181

Robert's one desire was to leave the place, only he could not think how to do it. He tried to drain his glass, and managed no more than a mouthful: the beer seemed to get heavier and heavier, its bubbles bursting like cannon-balls against the roof of his mouth. Bel picked up her champagne, wedged the tiny straw between her large front teeth and simpered at him.

'Isn't your brother coming back for you?' demanded Robert.

'Oh, no,' she smiled, 'he leave me to my own device.'

'Yeah, well,' he stood up hastily, scraping his chair back along the floor and rocking the flimsy table, 'I got to go.'

'You ain't finished your drink.'

'No,' Robert took another slug at it, but it refused to diminish. 'I haven't got time.'

Bel wriggled in her chair.

'See you around then. Now that we neighbours.'

Robert spent the next few days on tenterhooks lest Bel should wander into the café. He wished that he had never let on where he worked, or at least that he had warned her how only men came in, or how severely Sol would view the intrusion of friends into his place of work. And just as frequently he pondered over how it was that he had never seen her out in the street before. He grew more proficient at washing up and making coffee and begged to be allowed to try his hand out-front. But Sol would not be swayed.

'You're doing well enough for a beginner, but you got a lot to learn behind the bar afore you go anywhere else.'

Sol, in his turn, began his suit for Robert's reconciliation with his family in earnest. He harped much, to begin with, on Robert's mother. So that Robert, replying to his constant questions, frequently found memories of the small house in the meadow creeping unbidden into his thoughts. He remembered, as if after a long bout of amnesia, how in the winter the grass was arched and bent

182

in the early morning under the weight of frost; how his breath had blown out before him white in the sparkling air, like the steam in his mother's kitchen. And how, in summer, the grass of the meadow became brown and curled till the earth showed through hard as cardboard except under the trees bordering Langdat's field where it grew luxuriant and cool, almost long enough to lie hidden in. And he wondered what his mother would think of the way he lived in the deserted house – the dark, dusty rooms, the tousled bed which now had the scent and feel of a second skin.

One evening, emerging from the café into the street, Robert collided with a girl hurrying past. In the collision she dropped a package and it fell, soft and heavy to the pavement. Robert dived to pick it up and was surprised to feel it warm through its layers of newspaper.

'My supper!' laughed the girl, noticing how gingerly he held it. He stared at her. It was Bel.

'Oh!' she exclaimed. 'Of course.' She looked beyond him to the lighted windows of the café. 'That's where you work, isn't it. And that's the house you live in, over the road. I come here a couple of times, but I ain't seen no light, so I ain't knocked.'

'Well, I'm not there much, only to sleep. Gets a bit spooky. It hasn't got no lights.'

He was surprised how pleased he was to see her. The rush of feeling confused him and left him standing there awkwardly silent. She smiled shyly, a gawky, gap-toothed smile, clutching her parcel to her chest and shivering a little. She looked different to the last time he'd seen her. He wanted to detain her in conversation but he could find nothing to say until, pushed beyond endurance by the silence and the obvious passage of time, he heard himself invite her over to the house. The moment the words were out he cursed himself. She hesitated, however, rocking backwards and forwards on the heels of her shoes:

'Well, I dunno. If it ain't got no light in there ... '

She was going to walk on. She was going to smile and say goodnight and disappear off round the corner to her brother and her mother, to a house with people in it and chairs and things. And he would just have to wander over the road, like he always did and let himself in to the shadowy house that never felt entirely deserted. He kicked ferociously at a pebble in the gutter and missed.

'Why don't you come round my place? It ain't far. And besides,' she held up the parcel, 'I got something to eat. Hot!'

In Hendrye Place the houses were tightly wedged four or five stories high. They stopped at one of the battered doors and Bel kicked a broken beer bottle out of the way. 'People don't have no respect for property as they don't own,' she complained, searching in her handbag for her key. They passed into a narrow hall from which a flight of stairs led steeply up into the darkness. There was a close smell of cats and linoleum and decayed cabbage. Bel stumbled forward into the gloom.

'There ain't no light,' she whispered, 'but just you follow me right to the top of they stairs.'

Robert had scarcely put one foot on the lowest stair when a door flew open along the hall and an old man shot out.

'You ain't allowed no men in here!' he shrieked.

On the step above Robert, Bel plumped her hands on her hips and clicked her tongue in rage.

'This ain't no *men*,' she sang out, 'this is the friend of my brother, who am invited for *dinner*!'

'Out on yer ear!'

Bel bent forward over the bannisters.

'You just mind you don't skin your eye, peering through my keyhole!'

'I know what I know without having to peer through

your key-hole,' screamed the man and retreated, banging his door shut.

'Some people don't have no shame!' exclaimed Bel and stamped off up the stairs.

Robert followed her up and up into the spiralling darkness. At every landing and half-landing he could make out doors leading off. Some were as dark as the darkness around them, under others a line of light would show, or noise. The low chattering of a radio, or the mournful loneliness of dance music, would lean out to engage his attention, like whispering in his ear, as he hurried past. And from every room, overlaying the close, suffocating smell of the house, came the scent of its inhabitant. He marvelled how so many rooms could hang in the air, at how the stone staircase could continue so high without the weight of it crashing through the floor of the house into the cellars. The proportions of the inside of the house seemed to bear no relation to the outside. It appeared, from the street, as narrow as all its neighbours, but once its front door closed behind you, it billowed up, vast and cavernous into the black recesses of its roof. Here Bel stopped and unlocked a low door. Robert, teetering on the topmost step of the stairs, clutched at the banisters, felt them wobble in their sockets and imagined himself crashing hundreds of feet to the stone floor below. He made a rush for the open door and, as Bel switched on the light, found himself in a strangely shaped room under the eaves, with sloping ceilings at varying angles, as though in some places the roof went up and at other places it went down.

'It's very nice,' he said looking round. At the far end of the room there was a bed and next to it a cardboard screen, round the corner of which Robert could see part of a white china basin. Then came a small table with an upright chair, opposite it a chest of drawers and lastly, near the door, in front of a gas fire, a small armchair by which he stood, running one finger across the ridges of some brightly-striped material draped across its back. Bel grimaced to hide her pleasure and, catching sight of his hand on the cloth, said, 'Oh, that; that come from Martinique, my brother say. He like to remember they things. He got it off a boat come into port here, in the way of some business.' She laid her coat on the bed and began to unwrap the newspaper parcel. 'I get these pasties for he; there's only one place in the city where they spice them right.'

Robert moved towards the table, peering at the pies which were now uncovered, steaming gently and smelling of lard and pepper.

'I don't want ... '

Bel held up her hand and shook her head.

'I buys these every week, but my brother don't hardly never come.' She set the pasties out on plates, shaking her head and smiling to herself. 'I know he won't hardly never come, but I buys these just the same, an' round about now,' she glanced out at the darkness beyond the window, 'I eats mine. An' then tomorrow I eats his. He meet me every Saturday without fail; he always there before me, waitin', an' he never miss a day. An' he say every time he leave me: "See you Thursday, Bel." You heard him. "See you usual," he say. An' I know he don't come an' I know he don't intend to come. Here,' she held out a plate to Robert, 'take this. Sit there, sit there.' She waved towards the armchair. Dragging the upright chair next to him and balancing her plate on her knees she sank her teeth into the pie.

'Ahhh,' she sighed, gazing contentedly round the room, her mouth full, 'I ain't eat all day.' Her eyes met Robert's still hesitating over his pie, and beamed. 'You don't want no knife, do you?'

Robert grinned, picked up his pie and bit into it: warm fat trickled out. Under the steamed crust there seemed to be an unidentifiable mixture of vegetables and meat juice more peppery than anything he had ever tasted, so hot that his one aim was to get it out of his mouth as quickly as possible and then, the sensation having diminished, to taste it again.

They chewed on in slence. The complicit silence of the satiation of hunger, the silent self-absorbed pleasure of feeling one's belly fill and one's body warm. They did not need to look at each other or to talk to know of the other's pleasure. Robert, in between watching his pasty diminish, looked at the stained rug before the fire, at the goose pimples disappearing from Bel's thin brown legs and at the toes of her shoes where the shiny plastic had scuffed away to reveal the upper, the colour of wet cardboard. This was the real Bel, who got as cold and hungry and probably as lonely as he did. Who waited in her attic for visits from a brother who she knew would not come. And who consoled herself playing house, as though the only reality lay within these four walls where she could set out her plates and cups, arrange her furniture into 'rooms' and wait in front of the fire till the right time should come to eat her small portions of food.

She finished first and leaned back in her chair, delicately licking her fingers.

'When my prince come, I ain't going to do nothin' but eat.'

Robert smiled at her.

'When's that?'

'Any day. My brother keep saying, "One day, Bel, your prince is goin' to come. One day, when you least expect it, he's goin' to *be* there." He got it all worked out, my brother. So that's what I'm waitin' for. You want a cup of tea?'

Robert came again that Sunday carrying two small cakes he'd got cheap just as the baker's was closing the evening before. He'd wrapped them carefully overnight in an old newspaper, but they'd gone a bit dry. The plan was that they should walk up to the centre of the city. Bel expressed surprise on hearing that he'd been unable to find his way back up there; she'd been there lots of times, she said. But in the event it rained. By the time he arrived at Bel's house his jacket was soaked through. She was waiting for him in a bright green dress several sizes too small and absurdly flounced at the neck and wrists with wide frills. The effect was like that of a circus dog as she pranced around him, pulling off his jacket and draping it over an orange box to dry, fussing about the wet on the carpet and the rain on his head. From one of the drawers of the chest she brought out a thin, frayed towel with which she insisted he dry his hair, while she made him a cup of tea.

'We won't eat nothing yet,' she said putting the cakes proudly on a plate and covering them with a strange circle of net weighted down with coloured glass beads. 'You just get something hot in you, chase that cold away.'

She brought a cup for herself, too, and sat on the edge of the upright chair sipping at it and smiling at him over the rim with big, shy eyes. He wandered over to the window, nursing his cup in his hands, and stared out at the rain, screwing up his eyes till he could make out each drop.

'It looks lighter; you think it's going to stop?'

'No,' Bel stared placidly out at the low sky. 'It's going to rain all day long.'

'All day!'

'That's real Sunday weather. Only one thing to do with that!' and she plumped round in her chair to face the fire and stretched out her toes.

Robert paced between the two small windows on either wall, checking on the quantity of rain falling in front of each. Finally, he came and perched on the edge of the armchair.

'Well,' he said, 'we could wait. Till it's just drizzling.

That wouldn't get us very wet.'

'What's all the rush? What you want to go chasing after them bright lights so fast? The shops don't have no lights on, Sunday. Anyway, everywhere look just the same in the rain.'

'It's not the bright lights.' He hesitated. 'It's getting back up there ... I just have the feeling that if I can get back to where the bus put me down and start out walking again that this time it'll come out right. I feel like I'm in the wrong place down here. That first day, when I got out of the bus, I just stood on the pavement gasping like I was gulping in new air. And all round me there was this feeling of excitement. Like buzzing in my ears. Like tingling all over me. It wasn't anything specific – the street was crowded full of people and noise and no one was taking any notice of me. It was just something alive in the air. And I knew that at last everything was possible. Everything had come right after all – I could feel it. I'd got free of my aunt, I'd made it to the city.' He paused. 'Only someone had put the wrong message in my pocket. And I was led down here. Away from all that. Into this kind of dead place, where everything's covered over black and everyone acts like they don't expect to have much of a life – like they don't want things to get better, they just expect things to get worse. That's why I have this feeling that if I go back up there, and start again, it'll come out right. It's like I'm here by mistake.' He gazed down into his empty cup and shook his head. 'Perhaps it would have been different if Zak hadn't died.'

'Died!' echoed Bel.

'Day I got there.' He smiled mournfully at her. 'I need never have come. But being down here, and there being no Zak and having no money and everything, I just took what was offered. I was glad of the help.'

'What did you do?'

He told her about the time he had spent in the

189

warehouse, then about his job in the café and then, at her insistent prompting, about life with his aunt. Bel's reaction to his aunt was gratifying; she clicked her tongue and hissed out her breath and shook her head in disapproval.

'So here I am,' he finished. 'I've got to the city, but it isn't what I expected. I don't quite know what I expected, but it isn't this. Perhaps it would be different if I was in another part of the city. Or if I knew what I wanted to do – if you don't know much about the world then you can't tell all the different things there might be in it. But nobody gives you any ideas. They all want you to take the safe thing and do the same as they do so things will always go on as before.' He paused. 'Your brother's not like that, he's not like anyone else round here.'

'Ah, he ... mmm ... ' She stared into the small jiggling flames of the gas fire, half-smiling and slowly nodding her head as though lost in a dream. Then she laughed, as if coming to her senses with a jolt.

'Marcel – he ain't really my brother.' She hugged her knees to her chest, rocking slightly on the edge of her chair. 'Still I can't hardly remember a time when he wasn't there. Before that there's just wet streets. Long, cold, dark, wet streets. And people hurrying like they was frightened, pulling me along. And then no one anymore. Till Marcel come. Marcel maybe ten, eleven. And then there is just Marcel and me. Marcel always holding my hand, finding abandoned rooms, bringing back bits of food and broken cups and cast-off clothes. He take care of me all that long time.' She shook her head in amazement. 'And he always know what to do.' She fell silent for a moment, then smiled. 'Now I'm growed up he say I have to earn my own living. He give this room. This is my boudoir, he say, and I have to make it nice and keep it clean and don't bring no men in it. My brother tell me, right from the beginning: Bel, don't you never bring men home. Don't you never let they know where you live. You safer in the streets

190

and in the alleys where you can holler, than shut away
in you room. And he right. My brother always right.
He saw I have to keep this place for when my prince
come. For when *he* come, then this is where I bring
him.'

'What prince?' asked Robert.

'The one I told you about. The one my brother say is
walking around looking for the time when he'll find me.
That's why I have to keep myself smart,' she patted the
frizzy bunch of hair tied with a green ribbon at the nape
of her neck, 'and mind my manners – he taught me all
them things.'

'That's why he calls you Princess Bel?'

She giggled. 'He do that to be nice. And to remind me
to act like he teach me.'

Robert stared at her. He watched her collect up their
tea-cups and dab with a cloth at a spot of tea she imagined
she saw on the stained hearthrug. He thought of her
brother who was not her brother. And of Bel standing
primly on street corners in her scuffed, plastic shoes. But
the images would not fit, they provoked questions that he
did not have the courage to ask.

It was late when he left. The street, still shiny with rain,
stretched black and deserted. A wind had got up, a warm,
gusting wind that blew wastepaper out of doorways in
tormented circles, whisking it high in the air and dropping
it again in a sudden lull. In one of the gusts a girl seemed
to be blown out of an alley-way and carried off down the
street, head bent against the whirling papers, a dark coat
flapping round her. Under one of the lamps she paused
and looked over her shoulder at Robert, pushing her hair
back from her face and letting her coat fall open, turning
slightly so that he could see the outline of her body
beneath. In the lull of the wind he could hear the regular
tread of his boots drawing him nearer and nearer to her
without his being able to stop them and he felt his cheeks

burn. Under the flare of the lamp her face and neck looked white as paper. Then the wind gusted again, her hair whipped free, blotting out her face, her coat wrapped itself round her body and she turned and hurried on. She stayed, however, always just in sight, a dark shape in the darkened street, buffeted and tossed as though she had no more substance than a ghost. At one point she encountered a man weaving his way along the pavement and went up to him. They appeared to lean together for a moment, blown along by the same wind, and then whirled apart. The man staggered on and the girl continued as before, turning every so often to glance at Robert, who began to feel that he would never escape her. Then, just before Nile Street, she vanished.

The image of her remained with Robert all night long. But in his dreams her face was not paper-white under the lamp and the gusts of wind tugged not at a long curtain of hair, but ripped frizzy, corkscrew curls free from their battery of confining pins and slides. It was, instead, a small anxious face, perplexed and frightened by the violence of the wind. Her coat was not held provocatively open, but, tightly buttoned, battered the thin body like boards. The recognition of the figure suffused Robert with a kind of panic; through layers of sleep he struggled, turning and twisting, to call out to her.

'Go in! Go *in*!'

But she would not hear him. She stood on in the dark, deserted street, clawing desperately at her escaping hair, while the wind tore her to pieces.

The dream did not fade with the coming of day. Its image remained, a dark shape in the corner of Robert's mind from which seeped a distracting uneasiness. He turned over and over in his mind fragments of Bel's story. He pieced words spoken in a clear, sing-song voice to blurred pictures of a prim, little figure. He heard her high-pitched giggle and saw again crumbs stuck to her upper lip, and her thin, bony knees clasped by small, brown hands whose nails were as closely-bitten as a schoolgirl's. He thought of her brother, her imaginary lover and Bel herself out there in the streets of the city. Bel and her prince hunting in vain for each other through streets and alley-ways that grew in his mind into immense, black canyons, and her brother hunting them both. And then, himself, out there too, searching for Bel in streets that had fallen strangely silent except for the echo of his boots and the gusting of the wind.

When the café closed that evening, he set out to look for her. The evenings were lengthening and the drawn-out end to the day had an exhausted softness to it. The unaccustomed lightness dwarfed the streets, reducing the shadows and making the buildings draw back into themselves, grey and dusty. He kicked at the drifts of dust and wastepaper that lay in abandoned doorways. He stared at the women he passed and the dull light faded the colours of their mouths and eyes until he could not tell which were housewives gossiping in doorways and which were not. The light deepened and still there was no sign of Bel. He kept expecting to see her each time he turned a corner, trotting towards him with her peculiar mincing gait. Corner flashed upon corner; streets turned into alleys, passages, cuts between blank brick walls until, when he found himself back at the top end of Nile Street, he gave up and went home. He felt a strange relief not to have found her that was, however, tinged with unsatisfied curiosity as though it was something merely postponed, not settled. He went out again the following evening and the next. And when, at their appointed time and place, he at last caught sight of her standing in a shop doorway eating chips out of a twist of newspaper, the shock was so great that his first instinct was to slink off down the nearest alley-way. But she had seen him. The newspaper was lowered and she beamed at him through tightly-shut lips, grinding the heel of her shoe against the wall behind her in a squirming circle.

'You want some of these?' she asked, holding the paper out towards him, and then, drawing it back again, slid another chip furtively into her mouth. 'We can get some on our way.'

They walked down to the canal, to a place just to the left of one of the bridges that Bel knew, where there was a minute landing stage accessible by a flight of stone steps from the road. Here they sat swinging their legs over the water, watching the light fading behind the warehouses that lined the opposite bank and the trails of debris that swirled downstream. From the nearby bridge some boys were throwing stones at a half-submerged bottle. Out of the corner of his eye Robert glanced at Bel. She was leaning back contentedly against the wall of the embankment, her eyes screwed up against the low evening sunlight. He looked at the rows of hairpins that seemed to grip the back of her head like a metal brace, decorated with an array of plastic hair-slides, and at the way her thin wrists hung awkwardly from the washed-out sleeves of her cardigan. He stared at the profile of her face, so close to his that he could even see grains of salt stuck to her chin, he willed her to become aware of his gaze and to turn her head so that he could say to her ... so that he could ask her ... Abruptly, she tipped up the newspaper to lick out the residue of salt and vinegar, crushed it into a ball and flung it into the canal where immediately it became a new target for the boys on the bridge. They began to pelt it with stones, hitting it once or twice, but it floated soggily on, unfolding on the surface of the water like a bedraggled paper flower. And the words that he was trying to formulate melted away in the artlessness of her gestures.

But he continued to watch her ceaselessly: in her room, out in the street. He almost pushed her with the intensity of his thought into letting fall some sign, into committing some provocation ... It was concern, he told himself; it was friendly, brotherly concern for her welfare, out in those dark streets. That was where he really wanted to find her, out in the streets. He did not go to her house, as one friend might, looking for the other. He went out into the streets, he paused at the shadowed openings of alleys, peering cautiously into their gloom, listening ... He was not sure what to listen for, what sounds of scuffling, what words. Or what he might see. But he wanted to see it. He wanted to see what it was ... how it was ... He could not bring himself to believe that she ... she ... And so he wanted to *see* it. Because it was so ridiculous. The thought that Bel, with her bitten nails and her silly, little clothes and her babyish hair-slides ... They didn't look like that, the real ones he'd seen. Sometimes, as he stalked the streets, he would feel guilt at what he was doing. For, in her innocence, she remained proof against all his suspicions. He had never found her. Embarrassed at his discovery of himself, he tried to justify himself. Instead of slipping from shadow to shadow, of creeping up behind couples to overhear what they said, to see if the woman's face was Bel's, he would move out into the middle of the pavement, stick his hands into his pockets and attempt to saunter nonchalantly, as though taking an evening walk. He would kick at loose pebbles and listen to them clattering over the cobbles. He was only walking around, he said to himself petulantly, walking around for something to do. And if he bumped into Bel, well, so much the better, they could walk around together, or go and watch the lights on the canal, or the cats fighting on the patch of waste ground. That was all. But he knew it was not. There was a slight uneasiness always with him, a small sense of a larger emptiness, a rolling, sliding restlessness that sometimes lay quite still and sometimes propelled him out of doors.

The weather, which had been growing steadily warmer all that week, suddenly changed overnight. A cold, gusting wind sprang up, more reminiscent of April than late May. All day grey clouds were dragged across the sky, massed and then torn apart. In the long empty reaches of the afternoon, Robert found it increasingly difficult to concentrate on anything. To make matters worse, Sol was in exuberantly good spirits; he brought a chair round behind the counter, and, settling himself opposite Robert, talked endlessly of Lil's return from hospital. Robert stared into Sol's animated face, frowning slightly, unable to keep the features from sliding out of focus. Unable quite to make sense of the words which seemed to dissolve into silence before they reached his ears, so that it became difficult for him to tell which was a real silence and which was not. He longed only for it to be evening.

When at last the café was closed, Robert crossed the street to Zak's house. Wading through the accumulated refuse in the yard, unlocking the back door and pausing to listen for sounds of an intruder, he let himself into the scullery. He frequently expected to find that someone else had taken possession of the place, but it remained cold and empty, a stale, boarded-up smell hanging like cobwebs in its dark rooms. He lit a candle and wandered first into the shop, then into the upper rooms. Everything looked just as it always did, but at one remove, lifeless and unwelcoming. He wondered that he had ever thought of it as home, it was nothing but an abandoned shell in which he crouched and slept. He made himself a cup of tea and then, over the same flame, heated a tin of beans until they bubbled. Holding the hot tin carefully in a folded cloth he dug the beans out with a spoon and ate them, standing up as usual, staring blankly through the dark window pane. Abruptly, he left the house without even locking the door.

Outside in the street it was raining lightly, as though it intended to rain for a very long time. Everything was wet, subdued, chilled to the bone. He turned up his coat collar, dug his hands into his pockets and, bearing right out of

Nile Street and then right again, made his way to Hendrye Place. She would not be there, he was sure of it, sinkingly, anxiously sure of it. Across the veil of rain, he glanced covertly into the faces of the women who waited in doorways and alleys, and knew they mocked him for his timidity. At Bel's house the windows were all in darkness and the set of bells beside the front door nameless. He turned away and doubled back on his tracks towards Chez Madeleine.

Pushing open the door at the foot of the stairs, he almost knocked George off a short stepladder. The ladder wobbled violently as the door banged into it and George, a light bulb in one hand, clung first to the ladder and then to the wall-light he was mending.

'Ohh er,' he giggled. 'You nearly had me over there! Just wait a tick, till I get this bulb in.'

'I'm not stopping,' muttered Robert. There seemed little point to his question, he could see for himself that the room was empty. 'I'm looking for Bel.'

'Oh,' George climbed down the ladder. 'Oh, you won't find her here, not in the week, not on a Thursday.' He pursed his lips and surveyed the room from beneath raised eyebrows. 'There's nobody come out on a Thursday. As you can see. I do me housework, Thursday, that's how you caught me. Rainin' outside, is it?'

'Yeah.'

'Well,' he snapped the two halves of the ladder shut, 'she'll be out. Shame, in'it, in this rain. Sure you won't have a drink? Not a quick one?'

Robert shook his head.

'Well, you could try Marcadet Street ... Rose Lane ... Sebastopol Place ... '

She was in none of those places. He soon found himself in unfamiliar territory, but he walked on, never quite stopping, taking care not to appear to falter. The women's faces flickered past him: disembodied pale shapes hanging

197

in the shadows, eyes and mouths swallowed up by the night. None of them Bel.

He had been walking for some time in streets that had grown progressively more deserted, their doorways empty and dripping with rain, when suddenly he turned the corner and found himself, with relief, among people and lights again. His first impression was of a street of lighted windows, of groups of people, of noise and bustle – a tangible, identifiable world. But as he walked down the street he realised that it was almost silent. The women who stood in pairs under the street lamps and the men who lounged round the door of a mission-hall half-way down the street, or strolled down the opposite pavement, gave to the place an underlying current of unease. Some shuffled restlessly, some of them even walked about, but these slight movements did not animate them. There was some other animator that they waited for, some click of hands on a clock face that would set in motion their inter-action, some noise that would unleash all other noises. Robert paused beside a group of men to get his breath and, as he did so, one of them nudged his neighbour and pointed across the street. The other man laughed, but Robert, peering over his shoulder, was transfixed. He stared across the street and then drew quickly back out of sight behind the men.

Circumventing the puddles with fastidious precision, a pink, plastic rainhood spread out over her tight, black curls and tied beneath her chin, her coat buttoned austerely to her neck, her small handbag held primly before her, was Bel. She tip-tapped her way down the pavement, past the women who waited for the men and the men who waited for the women, tearing apart the threads of their tension on the toes of her rain-soaked shoes as if they were cobwebs, unaware of the danger she might provoke. It was difficult to tell whether it was bravery or innocence that propelled her onwards through that shuffling, whispering silence, slowing her pace and lifting her head to each man who walked past her. Suddenly, it appeared to Robert that everything that had gone before had been merely a game: now that he saw her, he could not stand and watch. She reached the end of the street, and, without faltering, trotted on into the darkness. As she disappeared, he quietly detached himself from the group in front of the mission-hall and slipped after her.

Once he had turned the corner he took to his heels, but the crashing echo of his boots frightened the small figure ahead of him in the darkness and she darted off down a side street. He caught up with her near the end and seized her arm.

'Bel!'

The free arm whirled in the air and the handbag came crashing down on his head.

'Bel, it's me. It's Robert.'

But the body went on struggling, pressed back against the wall, her eyes tight shut. He felt the thin bones of the wrist that he held twist and grate against each other. The other arm, confined by the wall at its back, battered his shoulder repeatedly and ineffectually with the hand-bag, but it felt like little more than the lame beating of an injured wing. He let go of her and stepped back, spreading his arms wide to prevent her running away again.

'Bel,' he whispered.

She opened her eyes and hit him once more with her handbag, for good measure.

'What you done that for! Frightenin' me like that!'

'Bel, I've been looking for you all over!'

He touched her shoulder and found it quivering with rage and fright. She shook him off. But his need to touch her, to secure her, was so overwhelming that he could not entirely take his hand away; it hovered tentatively in the space between them.

'You shouldn't be out in these streets – walking round like that.'

'Why not?' she demanded. But she let him close his fingers round her arm. Holding even just her arm gave him courage. He shook his head and stared earnestly through the darkness at her:

'You shouldn't ... walk up and down ...' he stopped; he couldn't think how to explain it to her, he couldn't think how to proceed on the long, jumbled chain of thought that led back past his fear for her to fear for himself. But she broke in angrily.

'Those women won't never let me stand with them, that's why. They say I bad for business.' Her breath hissed between her teeth as if she was vehemently expelling all taint of such infamy. 'What they know!' Robert grasped her arm even more tightly, but she shook herself free again. 'What they know!' She straightened her rainhat, glaring fiercely at Robert.

'Bel, come home.'

Tight-lipped, she jerked down the sleeves of her coat and hung her handbag back on her arm.

'No.' She looked up at him. 'Not now I got this far.' She glanced beyond him to the end of the street, where a dimly-lit space opened out, and prodded with her fingers under the rainhat making sure the rows of hairpins were still in place. The movement reminded him suddenly of the figure of Bel in his dream, and he felt overwhelmed with hopelessness. It was as if she had no recognition of where she was. The rain was something that could be kept out with bits of plastic, the dangers of dark alleys fended off by pretending they didn't exist. He had known all along, but he had not been able to bring himself to believe it.

'You know where we are?' she whispered excitedly.

Robert shook the rain out of his eyes.

'You aren't going *on*?'

'You like plantain?'

Robert stared at her. She nodded towards the light space at the end of the street.

'Down there's the docks. Where they bring 'em in sometimes. They always droppin' stuff down on the docks. All you have to do is pick it up. You comin'?'

She pulled at his hand, felt his resistance, slipped her grasp and ran on alone.

Where the street opened into a wide, cobbled space lit by arc-lights from the quays on the far side and the dim street lamps set along the curving line of low houses behind him, Robert caught up with her. As he stretched out his hand to detain her, she darted forward, running awkwardly across the cobbles, her heels splayed out sideways. Robert held his breath, but on she went towards the dark tarpaulin-shrouded shapes and towering cranes, on and on till she had almost merged with them. Then he found himself running, out over the immense space terrifyingly exposed under the lights, the fear of it so sharp, so explosive that he felt like screaming, but the only sound in his ears was the sob of his breath and the crashing of his boots against the wet cobblestones. He felt as if he was running over a stage watched by hidden spectators, but however fast he ran the safety of the wings always eluded him. He remembered suddenly the men escaping from prison, the shots that had crackled out like breaking twigs and the turning, falling figures. It was going to happen to him any minute – the sharp clatter of gunfire and then the wet road coming up to meet him. His legs moved, but the earth was spun round beneath him so that he seemed to be running always on the same spot. Suddenly a huge, black shape loomed before him, he put up his hands to save himself, felt them slide down wet tarpaulin and found himself in darkness between stacks of cargo. He slipped behind them and came up against a wire fence beyond which were the black silhouettes of ships and machinery and the oily glimmer of water. He peered back across the deserted cobbles, mistrusting the silence.

'Come on,' whispered Bel, tugging at his sleeve. 'We got to get in the fence.'

They darted from stack to stack. Every time they reached a post in the fence Bel bent down to examine it. At last she found what she was looking for and began to tug at the wire netting. A long section came loose from the ground which she held as high as she could.

'Go on and then hold it for me.'

She jerked her head at the gap to indicate that Robert should roll underneath.

Inside the dockyard Robert felt safer. It had a strange, oily, stagnant smell, a mixture of marine oil and rotting refuse. A variety of small ships and boats were tied to quays cut back from the main stream of the canal, most of them already dark, their crews ashore or asleep. There was an occasional thump and squeak as a boat grated against its moorings, or a far-off burst of noise from one of the bars on the street opposite.

'Keep your eye on the ground and stay close.'

Ahead of him Bel crept from shadow to shadow, from customs shed to loading derrick, stooping quickly to pick things up and drop them again. Robert followed. Rain veiled the moon and in the misty darkness he felt that the shadows were moving, dark angles of sheds and bales shortening, then lengthening, following them; the wheels and pistons and huge, drooping nets turning slowly to watch them as they passed. The silence seemed almost to be breathing as it waited, vast sleeping breaths, waiting for them to stumble. Into this silence came a kind of rooting, snuffling noise, then a low, growling sound followed by intermittent grunts. Robert froze. He flung out an arm to grab Bel, but she pottered on beyond his reach, head bent. He found he couldn't move, nor could he call out to her. He opened his mouth but only soundless whispers came out. He stared wildly round at the darkness. It was silent again. Then there was a sudden grating sound close by and a high-pitched cry followed by a low, indecipherable moaning. Sweat poured down Robert's back. He saw Bel stop. She came back to him and tugged at his arm. The movement broke speech out of him and he began babbling in a hoarse whisper at her, so that he heard almost nothing of what she whispered to him till she put her hand over his mouth and dragged him with her towards a stack of bales.

'Ssh, listen. Hortense!'

The shuffling noise began again, and then the growling, low and rhythmical, a singing, swaying sound that grew and lengthened into words slurring and rumbling into each other. Astonished, he moved his head towards the end of the stack and whatever it was on the other side seemed to move closer to him for the next line was so soft he could hardly pick it up and yet he heard it distinctly.

' . . . singin' the stop house blues. Woa . . . ' there was a crump and a slide and a tinkling noise as if something very heavy had fallen:

' . . . k up this mornin' . . . '

He peered round the bale. On the ground between the two stacks was a pile of rags, and attached in some way to the rags was a glass bottle that glinted and wavered in the air.

'dreamin' a dream of you.'

The bundle wheezed and hummed and struggled with the bottle.

'Woke up in the mornin '. . . '

There was a loud 'pop' as of a cork and a light, splashing, guzzling sound and then a harsher louder growl that made the hairs rise on the back of his neck:

'Got them bars afore my eyes . . . '

The paralysis suddenly gave way to panic and he struggled to be free of Bel's grasping fingers.

'They say them bars is gonna *be* there ... ' rippled the voice, 'until the daaay I dies.'

Robert took to his heels.

Throughout the endless journey back across silent streets they spoke to each other only by means of monosyllabic noises: small expressions of breath, hissing retorts magnified by the stillness bounced back at them by the curtain of rain, till the air about them resounded with compressed rage. Robert deliberately walked as fast as he could with long strides, so that Bel was forced to keep up a sort of limping run, squelching in wet, disintegrating shoes. However, because Robert did not know the way, he was forced to halt at every crossroads for her guidance. Sometimes she would push past him irritably, at other times she would deliberately slow her pace, so that his pride pushed him into making his own decision, when she would dart from behind him down quite another street, forcing him to turn back. Robert was sure that she took him on purpose down the least used, worst lit streets and passages. He could not recognise any of his surroundings, none of it seemed like the way he had come and so he had the feeling not that he was returning to safety, but that he was being led on into more uncertainty. When they arrived at Bel's house, he felt no pleasure or relief. Instead he looked about him distrustfully as though the image of the familiar street had been superimposed mirage-like upon an alien place. But the key turned as smoothly as it ever did in the lock, the dark, suffocating staleness still hung about the hall and the arrangements of Bel's room, as she slowly pushed open the door, seemed not to have moved at all since he had seen them last, they merely looked more lifeless and drained of colour.

He dropped into the armchair and lay there, head thrown back, letting minute rivulets of water collect on points of hair and trickle down his face. Behind him he could hear Bel making small, covert movements. Finally, she came and perched on the edge of the other chair, her face set into a kind of hooded rage, slightly turned away from him. She had changed her clothes and was dabbing at her wet hair with a cloth. On her feet were large, fluffy slippers, torn and stained, the nylon fur discoloured. She shuffled them about, pointing them this way and that, looking down at them as if scrutinising them to best advantage. Then, with attempted languorousness, sliding down slightly in her chair, she stretched out one foot to turn on the fire. A jet of gas was released, but the muffled foot could not flip the switch hard enough to ignite it. The gas continued to pour out into the room. She dabbed with her toe at the switch. The smell of gas became stronger, an acid, warning sharpness, but, as though she refused to acknowledge it, she did not alter her position, or try to exert more force on the gas tap, she just went on kicking delicately at it. Robert remained inert, feeling the rain trickle down his face and slide under his collar, determined not to move. Suddenly, with a roar and a billowing out of flame, the fire ignited. They both jumped and in doing so turned instinctively to each other:

'What you have to spoil everythin' for?' burst out Bel. 'What you have to go runnin' off for when we ain't found nothin' yet?'

'What you making such a fuss about a couple of old bananas for?'

'They ain't *any* old bananas,' she hissed, 'you don't know what you're talkin' about.'

'They're not worth going into a place like that for. They're not worth wandering around in the dark for, risking getting knifed or done for stealing. You go in them places late at night for a couple of old bananas then you're mad!'

'I ain't!'

Robert sat up suddenly, fists on knees:

'Then what are you walking round in them streets for all dressed up?'

She pouted.

'I ... '

'You're not going to find a prince.'

'Yes, I am.'

'No, you're not,' he sank back, his voice scarcely audible, 'anymore than I'm going to get a decent job and a nice place to live.' He closed his eyes.

'You got a place to live, you got that house.'

He stared at her fiercely:

'I'm living there like a tramp! I haven't got nothing: no light, no heat. I come here to be something, not a rat in a hole.'

Bel put one hand lightly on his knee. With a fingertip he traced round each finger and across the small, bitten nails.

'I always had this idea,' he began, 'I always had this thing in my mind of how it would be. And it kept me going all the time I was at my aunt's. It was like I was lost in dark caves, but I knew there had to be an outside, however much everybody else told me there was no such thing. And now – I don't know. I've got to where I thought the outside would be, but it turns out to be just another cave, bigger and lighter, but still just another cave.'

He turned to her:

'I was sure, I was sure when I got out of the bus that I'd found it. It was so exciting; it was like I was on the edge of something. But when I got down here, it's as though nothing's changed, no one's any different. Now I just feel as if I'll never find that other life. The longer I stay here, the less sure I feel of it. It's as though if I don't have some proof that it's real – I always thought of it as "real life" and whatever I was living in as something temporary – or that it *could* happen, I'll gradually stop believing in it.' His voice tailed away. She looked up at him, her face blank in a kind of attentive puzzlement, as though he had gone beyond the scope of her imagination. Suddenly she brightened.

'I'll take you up to where the centre of the city is. First thing, Sunday, we'll go up there. First thing!'

They did go. She led him triumphantly from street to street and the ground did feel eventually as if it was rising slightly, the houses did grow taller and, massing closer together, did give way to shop fronts and office parlours. Finally, she stopped, half-way down a street.

'Here we are!'

Robert stared about him. In the Sunday silence everything looked different. In the absence of bustle and traffic everything appeared strangely abandoned. Now and then a person would scurry past them, head bent, or from an adjacent street would come the intermittent sound of a car. And then the silence would stretch out again. Robert turned to Bel:

'Are you sure?'

'This is the centre, this is where I come. All down here they have a market, Thursdays.'

Robert shook his head:

'This isn't it.'

They wandered on, an aimless, crestfallen silence growing between them, until the disappointment and pointlessness of it brought them to a halt.

'It doesn't seem the same – without people.'

'We have to come back another day, then.'

'How can we. I got to work in the café all the other days.'

Well then,' said Bel firmly, 'we have to get you another job.'

Back again in Zak's house Robert felt himself adrift, without thought or purpose. He wandered from room to room unsurprised by the logical progression from one to the other, but feeling it unrelated to himself. Ending up in the bedroom, he stood at the window staring out at the houses opposite, all sense numbed by the slowly-forming thought that perhaps he should leave. He pictured himself packing. He saw the suitcase drawn out from under the bed, his hands folding his spare shirt and vest. He saw it clearly, as though it was preparation for an action that he was just about to carry out; in his mind he moved towards it, he could almost feel his shoulder turn. It stayed there like an image hanging just behind him, as though he could turn round quickly and catch sight of himself busy at the other side of the room. But he did not move from the window. Before him the line of chimney pots and beyond that the stepped bulk of distant buildings clarified and sharpened in the fading light. Then, as the light deepened, they began to dissolve until, with a blink of his eyes, he lost them in the darkness.

What if I were to leave, he thought, set off again to find another place; and wondered where he should go and how and what to? But each of these questions only left his mind blanker than before. And then, like a shadow on that emptiness, hovered the thought that leaving would be like running away. There must, he said to himself, pushing at the emptiness with the blindness of his dreams, in this vast city, be something better than this. There *must* be. He saw in his mind's eye the maze of streets spreading out, acre after acre. There must be *something*! But instead of an answer to these questions there came only bafflement, creeping out from the corners of his mind, tinged with fear.

The following evening he found Bel waiting for him at a discreet distance from the café. She seized his arm.

'Come on! We goin' to find you a new job. Remember?'

He shrugged his shoulders.

'What difference does it make?'

She dragged him almost at a run from factory to factory to peer at the notices which hung like hymn boards at the

Works entrances, announcing on slotted cards what hands they were short of. Most of the boards had no cards in them. From those that did Bel would read out the announcement in a loud, suspicious voice.

'Truckle loader. Hmm! That don't sound like any improvement on what you got. Sweeper. Greaser. Slurry dredger.'

Her head would shake itself angrily and her tongue click itself against her teeth. 'What they *think* ...! Come on.'

Her determination pushed him through the rest of the week until the urge to leave had dulled itself into a vague anxiety of something mislaid. Something, he couldn't precisely say what, lost, dropped in a confusion and remembered only afterwards when it was too late to go back and pick it up. He regarded it as having been a weakness, a temporary loss of faith, and was glad he had said nothing about it to Bel. But it was something which clearly had crossed her mind too, for as they sat one evening on the parapet of one of the bridges over the canal after another unsuccessful tour of the factory notice boards, she turned to him.

'Them places is no good, them factories. My brother right – they eat your soul. All them jobs we saw, hangin' on them boards day after day, they must be the worst jobs of all. Or else they been taken already and just no one bothered to take out the cards. There ain't nothin' there for you, nothin' that's right. What you want is somethin' different, somethin' with a bit of life, where you ain't cooped up all day.'

Listening to her he watched the dark water of the canal glimmer and sparkle as it eddied against the piers of the bridge. As the light sank lower, the dusty streets seemed for a moment to be lightly powdered with gold. Only for a short time at dawn and then again at dusk was the light low enough to slip under the pall of cloud that hung eternally over the city. A little wind shivered down the canal, making a dark zig-zag down the central channel. Robert jumped down from the bridge.

'I can't believe something won't turn up. I can't believe there's nothing here. Look,' he swept his arm out over the city, still glowing in the last of the sun's rays, 'at all that! Where is it hiding? Where?' He grabbed the iron parapet of the bridge and tried to shake it, dislodging nothing but flaking paint under his slipping fingers.

Bel shook her head at him.

'You make the bridge fall down, you ain't goin' to find nothin' but a cold river.'

They wandered back across the bridge, Robert banging his fist on the parapet in time with his footsteps. It gave back a dull, slightly hollow sound each time he hit it, as though it was as baffled about life as he.

'Sol was on at me again today about sending money home. He keeps saying have I written to them yet. He doesn't like it that I'm here on my own. He doesn't think it's right, it gets him all worked up like he was frightened.' He turned to her. 'I can't understand it.'

Bel clicked her tongue.

'People always so fond of other people's business. You think they'd have enough to do with their own. He certainly got a pile on *his* plate with that little-minx daughter you tell me about.'

'I don't know how I can send anything home,' mused Robert as they dropped down into the familiar alleys that interlaced the bank of the canal. 'You know all those tins I took out of Zak's shop? Well, I only got two left now. What am I going to do?' Bel's eyes gleamed.

'Ah,' she said, 'you have to practise economies. That's what you have to do.'

'Economies?' The word lurched unfamiliarly off Robert's tongue. Bel's face crinkled with delight, economies were her favourite pastime.

'You have to start cooking.'

'I never done no cooking!'

'You better start learning then, and in between you can give me some money and I'll cook for you one or two nights. But then,' she held up a finger, 'you have to learn the back way into my place because none of them bells in the front don't work and besides we don't want the landlord should see you too often.' They halted on the edge of the square near the café.

'I won't show you now, it's getting too dark. We'll do it tomorrow. And in the meantime I'll ask my brother about jobs.'

When they met the next day, Bel led him through an alley at the back of Hendrye Place and stopped at the back of the neighbouring house to hers.

'We go up here,' she whispered.

Robert grabbed her arm. 'Where?'

'Up over the roof.'

'I'm not doing that!'

'Come on, there's nothing to it! Just up the ladder on this house, along the roof and in through the door to my fire escape. Besides, there ain't no other way.'

Robert held fast to her. 'Why can't we go up your fire escape?'

'Because it start outside the landlord's window.' She hissed and, wrenching free her arm, she began to climb. Left alone in the back yard of the unknown house Robert had no option but to follow her. The iron ladder clung insecurely to the side of the house with rusted iron bolts, but he climbed doggedly just below Bel's heels until the increasing shuddering of the iron frame made it impossible for him to put one foot in front of the other. His hands clung to the rusted handrails as if welded to them and his feet felt weighted with lead.

'You have to tiptoe!' growled Bel. 'Your boots is clanging too much. Everyone will think you is a thief.'

At the top of the fire escape he had to climb over a

parapet to reach the wide gutter where the roof flattened out to meet the parapet wall. From here on it was easy, Bel assured him, just a short walk. But for some reason he could not take his hands from the handrails of the fire escape. He felt himself lured towards the softness of the air and felt his body lean obediently out into space. To move one of his hands would be to fling himself out into that beckoning space, to end this fearful journey dropping like a feather, whirling round and round. At that moment his wrists were seized and hauled upwards and with infinite slowness he felt himself dragged, like a cork out of a bottle, out of his paralysis, emerging in a rush, in a scramble of arms and legs, with a kicking, flailing desire to live, behind the parapet wall.

In time he came to love walking along the roof; instead of apprehension he felt a tingling exhilaration that was both fear and the excitement of confronting fear. There was nothing but other roofs spread out below him tilted at all kinds of angles, slanted one against the other, overshadowing each other and diminishing away into the distance, punctuated by chimney pots. It was a world lifted above the everyday world, in which he seemed to be the only adventurer and in which he felt suddenly free of the oppression of the enclosed streets. He would stand on the flat space that was surprisingly wide, running between the parapet and the slope of the roof, and feel silence all around him with only the faintest impinging of muffled sounds floating up from the street below. It was like an intermediate stage of being. Above him the impenetrable sky, below him the busy world to which he knew he had to return, and in between this warm, silent interval, this unsuspected place. It was like another city built upon the first, as yet uncolonised. There were gardens, sudden sproutings of purple and rose-coloured stems and falls of creeper tipped with brushes of tiny white stars. And arches, flat spaces, sloping planes, clusters of chimney stacks over which roofs could have been thrown, tents could have been stretched and a whole other race of city dwellers could have lived. Instead, there were only occasional visits from sparrows and pigeons and once a rat, taking the same highway as himself, who, upon seeing Robert, was so alarmed that it rushed away over the roof, its claws slipping and scrabbling on the tiles. This was how he would leave when the time came, he said to himself, stepping lightly over the whole city from rooftop to rooftop, the tiles warm beneath his feet. Rows of blank windows stared down at him from taller buildings, but it never occurred to him that anyone might look out of them; such small dusty squares of darkness could only give onto shadowy rooms and factories deserted for the night. Yet one could not be quite sure that, when he stood with his hands on the warm stone of the parapet gazing about him, watching the shreds of cloud turn aquamarine, rose and gold in the setting sun, there might not be eyes staring back at him from the top rooms of the houses opposite.

It became his custom, before he let himself in through the fire escape door on Bel's top landing, to worm his way round to her attic window set low down in the roof and knock on it twice. This was their signal for her to open her door. They had decided that for him to knock at her door once inside the house would make too much noise. It might arouse suspicions among her neighbours; worse, the sound of it might echo down the silent staircase and be heard by her landlord. It gave their meetings an intimacy that was lacking in all his other dealings with the city. The privacy that he had to himself in Zak's house was merely that of loneliness. Their secret signals, the clambering over roofs, the silent entry into Bel's house, these were the privacies of friendship; they turned it all into a game, with its own rules and secret procedures, to which they alone were privy. Frequently, he would find Bel hiding behind the door, her finger to her lips, shaking with laughter. Or he would push open the door and see her across the room, leaning against the bed doubled up, giggling helplessly. Smiling, he would close the door behind him and then start to laugh. And with the closing of the door he entered each time into a world in which he found himself, at last, the centre.

They slipped very quickly into an easy familiarity. Bel was not in fact a very good cook and, once the initial excitement of having someone to play house for had passed, her moods of solicitude would fluctuate wildly. He noticed that they waxed and waned with the quality of the food. It became clear to him as the days passed that at times she was not able to match his contributions to the kitty and they were reduced to eating strange stews that consisted mainly of potato in spiced gravy, or unidentifiable vegetables fried together in a gluey mass. But as though to make up for it he would find the table neatly laid, the room scrupulously tidy and Bel bubbling with housewifely fussiness, a clean cloth pinned at her waist for an apron.

Then there would be whole days together when he would discover her in the grip of a lassitude, an overwhelming laziness in which all she wanted to do was to lie back in the armchair, winding one of her tight curls round her finger, talking inconsequentially and giggling. There might be pie and chips in rapidly cooling newspaper on the table, or there might not. But there would be in the room a subtle undercurrent of something foreign and new, something that unnerved him and made him want to leave almost as soon as he had come.

His own efforts at cooking were generally unsuccessful. Bel tried to teach him the arts of economy. Economy fascinated her; it was a word she rolled round with awe and pleasure on her tongue, her eyes almost glazed at the thought of its infinite possibilities. Woven into a web of sufficient complexity it could take the place of life itself.

She tried to instil into him the virtues of partially rotted fruit, limp carrots, ends of bacon and day-old bread.

'You got one advantage,' she pointed out to him, 'you always going shopping in the *evening*. It sometimes difficult to get they to sell you stuff cheap in the afternoon.'

But shopping seemed to Robert even harder than cooking. Shops were always on the point of closing when he got to them and, far from being glad to unload their perishables onto him, shopkeepers would angrily turn him away. He would be able to see through the door the bored shopgirl cleaning her nails with the point of a pickle fork, waiting till the exact time came for her release. He would see on a chipped enamel tray ends of sausage, lumps of brawn, red, curled saveloys, while beside him the proprietor, fitting shutters into place, sending screws home through boards with a single flick of thumb and forefinger, would growl threateningly at him till he moved on.

There was only one place that was always open. It was the smallest of all and had somehow sunk below the level of the road, for there were two steps leading down into it. Descending, Robert had the feeling that all the dust of the street collected here. His feet would scuffle against tiny, pointed stones, minute scraps of paper and scarcely perceptible drifts of grey powder. Sheets of newspaper were spread across the counter on which were laid small piles of vegetables: shrivelled carrots, onions with long, green sprouts growing out of them, a saucer of cooked beetroot. Sometimes there was a plate of saveloys, ends of bacon and, under a glass cover, a corner of ham. Behind this dome the old proprietress, fine-boned as a bird, would station herself, obscured in the dark interior by the optical distortion of the ground glass. There she would hide, watching her customers till she saw they had discovered her, when she would dart out nodding her head at them and at her wares, sidling with great speed up and down behind the counter. Robert could never think what to buy. He would shuffle in the dust, fingering the money in his pocket, his head full of roast beef and chicken legs. He would look up at the row of drearily familiar tins on the shelves behind her head and then down at the food on the counter and try to think what didn't need cooking.

'Come on,' the old woman would cajole, 'what you going to have?' Then, as though her patience had given out, her bony hand would dart from pile to pile, plucking out a wizened carrot and dropping it next to three or four fragments of bacon, scooping them up with surprising dexterity, singing out a price; then, in Robert's prolonged silence, she would fling them back onto the counter and dart to another combination of items. This would go on until Robert, in confusion, would acquiesce to one of her bargains and would find himself outside in the road clutching a piece of hard cheese and half a stale loaf, or a pickled egg turned green with age and a soggy handful of cooked beetroot wrapped in newspaper. Disconsolately, he would wander home and drop the food onto the kitchen table and stare blankly at it and wish that it was one of the nights that Bel was cooking for him.

The next time he went round to Hendrye Place, Bel was perched on the arm of the easy chair evidently waiting for him for, as soon as he opened the door, she swept up a small pile of books from the seat of the chair and jumped to her feet.

'Come on,' she said, 'we're goin' to the library.'

He looked round the room, disgruntled. There was no sign of any supper.

'Library? What for?'

She pushed him gently before her out onto the landing, clucking her tongue and shaking her head.

'I don't know why I never think of it before. They got newspapers there that you can look at, free. For jobs.'

Robert had never noticed the library before. It stood at the back of a school and possibly once had been either the schoolmaster's house or the caretaker's lodge. It was approached from a narrow lane winding between a high wall on one side and the school wall on the other in which there was a gate that had a wooden notice tacked to it with the library opening hours. Bel pushed open the gate:

'See, they open late Mondays and Thursdays.'

She hurried him up the asphalt path, patting at her hair, pulling at the collar of her coat to make it lie more squarely on her shoulders. 'You'll find the papers laid out in the reading section. But you ain't got to talk in there. It's silence. All the time.' She shifted the pile of books to her other arm and grasped her handbag possessively. The expression on her face looked to Robert all squeezed up; squashed into tight lines of superiority, as though she was preparing to enter some holy place. He let her push past him into the building. The swing door swung energetically behind her emitting at every swing a puff of stale air, air that seemed to come out of a tomb, from beyond memory. In small bursts, like recognition, it wafted out to him, the scent of school corridors, of disinfectant, wet boots and the languid, stifled smell of paper worn thin by the constant turning of pages and overprinted by the grubby finger-prints of generations of schoolchildren. The scents that it blew at him seemed like teasing invitations, like whispered warnings of what he might find inside. He looked into the darkness where Bel had vanished. The swinging of the door was now reduced to a hair's breadth, to a self-absorbed, rocking motion that seemed to mock him. He shoved against it with his shoulder and it gave instantly before him, beating wildly back and forth as he strode through it and into the room beyond.

His eyes were at first drawn upwards to long, barred windows set high in dark schoolroom walls. Down the length of the room rose huge, shadowy bookstacks, dark caverns in which dim figures moved. Pieces of cardboard with the word SILENCE printed on them were stuck haphazardly around the walls or propped in frames on ledges. Silence appeared to have cowed all the inhabitants of the room into shamefaced tiptoeing shadows, and seemed to have swallowed Bel entirely. Robert hovered uncertainly on the doormat. As his eyes grew accustomed to the gloom, he saw that in the centre of the floor was a vast mahogany desk behind which a young girl moved with calculated indifference. With no regard for the demands of silence, she picked up a pile of books and appeared to hurl them one by one onto a book trolley behind her. She then turned to a dark figure waiting to be attended to in front of the desk and, seizing that person's books, flipped each of them open so loudly that his heart jumped as though she had fired a pistol into the room. Marooned on his doormat he began to feel absurdly conspicuous, but he could not move without drawing the girl's attention to himself. As she turned away to flick through a tray of index cards he sidled quickly across the open space to the farthest end of the desk and immersed himself in reading the library notices displayed there. He could not see the table of newspapers – only the girl. He discovered that, by keeping his eyelids lowered and his head lifted just sufficiently to see over the top of the rack of membership forms, he could continue to watch her. He could watch how the curls at the back of her head bounced and swayed as she turned, how they rolled softly together and then swung apart, gleaming as they moved, until he could almost feel the strands unrolling between his finger and thumb. It was a hypnotic game of imaginary pleasure that he wanted to continue for hours but which was interrupted by his attention being drawn to the little ripples of colour and shade that flushed her cheeks. They seemed to him like thoughts, which, fluttering across her mind, were simultaneously mirrored in her face for him to read. But the curling of her lower lip, the almost petulant droop of her small mouth, the sharpness of her chin and even the very angle at which she held her head made it clear that she did not intend it to be so. She picked three cards out of the tray and slapped them onto the polished mahogany counter. Robert, as though rebuked, blushed and looked down at the details of the mobile library service for old-age pensioners. When, cautiously, he raised his head again, she was standing alone at the desk staring vacantly before her. He did not notice Bel march off to be lost among the bookstacks, his eyes were riveted to the girl's face. Imagining himself undetected, he let them move as with the slow sensuality of fingertips across the smooth brow, over the unbelievably delicate tip-tilted nose; he let them fall onto the softness of her mouth and slide languorously over the petulant curve of her lower lip to pause for a moment before sinking, half-dazed, into the milky shadows of her neck. She turned her shoulders slightly and, above the starched collar of her blouse just visible over her library overall, he glimpsed the fine, white teeth of lace against her skin. He bent his head quickly to study The Rules of the Library, but he found he could not read the words. 'Lace!' he whispered to himself, then again: 'Lace!' and it sounded in his ears like the passport to vast, unknown territories. His hands gripping the edge of the desk slipped sweatily from their grasp, the lobes of his ears seemed to be burning and his stomach had turned to water. To confuse matters further, light drifts of cachou-like scent appeared to be overlaying the musty smell of the library, clouding his brain. The Rules of the Library in their large photograph frame were suddenly jerked out of his view and their position rearranged on the counter. In their place the face of the library clerk stared unsmilingly at him.

'Yes?' she demanded.

He marvelled at the way her perfectly drawn features

were exactly placed in the oval face and how, when she opened her mouth, sounds came out of it. No sounds came out of Robert's mouth. He didn't want to talk to her, he just wanted to look at her. The rose-coloured mouth flattened itself into a surprisingly hard line:

'You returning, or taking out?'

Robert shook his head. He cleared his throat:

'I want . . . to join,' he said.

He told Sol that he had become a member of the library.

'Oh!' Sol had said. 'Books.' And then, somewhat at a loss, had gone off to straighten tables and chairs, flicking the end of his dishcloth over the formica surfaces as though to imply that there were other skills in the world apart from reading. He did not tell Bel that the newspapers had been entirely swept out of his mind and that, instead, he had joined the library. It was not exactly that he forgot to, for the image of the library floated frequently into his mind, non-sequential images and sound: the darkness of the bookstacks, the white skin of the girl behind the desk, the pistol-like sounds with which she had made his heart jump, the lending tickets he had fingered in his pocket all the way home, while Bel had held forth.

'Little Miss Cat's Whiskers!' she had spluttered. 'Little Miss Know All! I ain't never seen her smile – you notice that? Smile might crack her doll face. An' if she bend her head to the same level as other folks keep theirs, all them little primpsy curls of hers might fall out of their place! I ain't going there nights no more. I ain't interested in being looked at down nobody's nose. They always put her on late nights – maybe that what make her so sour.'

Maybe, thought Robert standing in the café drying a tea-cup slowly round and round in his cloth. Maybe. And he abandoned himself again to the contemplation of the startlingly beautiful image of the clerk which, ever since their meeting, seemed to hover in the back of his mind, ready to float out and smother everything else. He felt he could never tire of looking at her, nor did the surprise of seeing her diminish. It was, he decided, something to do with the very cleanness of her. Her white blouse, the glimpse of lace, the way her hair shone; it made her stand out among all the dingy, shabby people who inhabited that part of the city. He recalled the slightly sweet, powdery scent of her and looking down caught sight of the dirt under his fingernails and the grease stains round the cuffs of his rarely washed shirt. She was unlike anyone else he had ever seen. She looked like someone from another place entirely, not real; set down here without having wanted to come – like himself. All at once he felt a desperate urgency to see her again, to prove to himself that she did exist. He had a sense of his body as a huge empty reservoir of memory of her that he had drained dry, and the sense of urgency became as real and anguished as that of a man wandering without water in a desert. He licked his lips, as if they were already cracked and dry, and looked across the room at Sol, who was standing talking to one of his customers. He'd ask him for some time off. It wasn't fair that he never got a break from the café. Sol went out for a couple of hours every afternoon to see Lil. He didn't even get ten minutes. He stared fixedly at Sol as he came up to the counter. He'd do it, he'd say it, minute Sol got close enough...

'Couple of beers, son,' said Sol.

Robert went on staring at him, feeling sweat prickling on his skin until, his cheeks blushing, he managed to jerk his head downwards and, snatching two bottles, prise off their caps. This went on till lunch, by which time Robert felt almost wild with fear that he might never see the library clerk again and Sol had begun to wonder whether the boy wasn't sickening for something.

'You all right, son?' he asked finally.

Robert seized his chance.

'I'm – I'm terribly hot,' he replied in a weak voice, 'I couldn't have a breather of ten minutes or so, could I? To fit in with when you goes off for the afternoon, of course.'

Sol looked at him sharply.

'Well, I don't know.

He began to stack plates, crashing them one on top of the other. Another customer came in and he turned abruptly away to serve him. When he came back, he smiled mournfully at Robert.

'Tell you what, I'll let you take Lil her lunch today.'

Robert gaped at him.

'You ain't seen her for ages. How about that? Nice little walk. I want to be sure I'm here when the delivery man comes, anyway; see about that overcharging.'

Early afternoon was the most deserted time of day. There seemed to be no shade, just heat beating down through a copper-coloured gauze of smoke from factory chimneys. Sol had given him Lil's lunch on a tin plate, slapped a metal ring on it and tied a sheet of newspaper over the top. Heat from the tin plate was now beginning to come through the newspaper onto his hand. He thought of leaving it in a doorway, tipping the greasy, slithering mess into the dust. He couldn't think why Sol had sent him to see her, he and Lil had never got on. Robert didn't care if he never saw Lil again, but he was curious about her husband. He didn't believe, for a start, that he really existed. He couldn't imagine anyone, *anyone*, marrying Lil. They would have to be out of their mind. They would have to be deaf, or blind. And he didn't believe about the garage that this husband was supposed to have. Sometimes Sol called it just a workshop, but either way it didn't make much sense. No one could afford to have a car down here, you hardly ever even saw a car passing through, there were only lorries and vans. If there weren't any cars, what was the point of a garage. He turned right and then left, and found himself in Lil's street. It was wider than an alley-way, but hardly a street, and it ended in the high, win-dowless wall of a factory.

'Right at the end you'll see it,' Sol had informed him, 'made of wood.'

It was unmistakeable. A narrow, shack-like building propped at the foot of the wall. The bottom half of it was a shed whose door was wedged open to reveal a dark, cave-like interior, and, on top, a sort of hutch. It looked like a child's drawing, with windows and a door on the side, up to which led a ladder-like staircase. Each plank looked different, as though they had all been scavenged, as though none of them fitted and, if anyone commanded, they could collapse neatly, one falling after the other like shuffled cards in two packs, to restore the street to normality. Robert tried to feel pleased as he approached the narrow shack, to make a glow of superiority overlay the cold, creeping fingers of fear that trembled up and down his back. But he could not. The plate began to burn his hand and he shifted it to the other. His mouth began to feel dry, so he licked his lips. He thought of giving the plate to the man he could see crouched on the floor of the shack bent over a piece of twisted metal and telling him ... But the blow torch the man held in his hand drowned out words and in the darkness of the cavern around him, hung with loops of tubing, tools, charts, tyres suspended from the rafters and calendars of undressed women, Robert's shadow did not penetrate. He went round the side to the stairs and climbed them slowly, on tiptoe. Each one of them creaked, each felt as if it was going to give way beneath his boot. When he got to the platform at the top he put down the plate and listened; timidly he knocked on the door, scarcely a slither of knuckles. The blow torch hissed at him from its cave; everything else was silent. He knocked again. Instantly there was a thump from inside the hutch and a heavy creaking sound that came closer and closer, swaying the frail edifice. Robert clutched tightly at the handrail. The door flew open. A vast, grey balloon tethered inside a flowered overall, whose strings could scarcely meet across the huge, protruding belly bobbed and swayed towards him. In the gape of the overall the sagging breasts were half-covered by a grimy cardigan. Hair hung in long, greasy strands around a bloated face in which tiny, rage-bright eyes struggled to keep from being entirely submerged by flesh.

'Oh,' said Lil sulkily, 'it's you.'

Robert stared at her. The eyes glared defiantly back at him. Hastily he bent down, picked up the plate and thrust it at her.

'Dad not well?' she snapped.

'Delivery man,' whispered Robert.

She shuffled back into the room and poked among the litter that covered a table in its centre. Robert stared at her blue, mottled legs and then peered into the murky depths of the room. Behind the table he could make out a sink, to the far right a large, rumpled bed. There was a stove in one corner, a wardrobe in another and everywhere trailing clothes, stacked newspapers, dirty dishes. At the table Lil pulled off the newspaper, found a dish and tipped the half-congealed contents of the tin plate into it. But to Robert's imperfect view she appeared simply to tip the food over the pile of debris already littering the table. Waddling back to him with the empty plate, she caught his astonished stare.

'Seen enough, 'ave yer?' she spat, shoved the plate into his hands and slammed the door.

As though released from the mesmeric spell that the darkened room in all its clutter and filth, its smell of suffocating flesh and unwashed clothes, had cast over him, Robert turned and clattered swiftly down the stairs.

He didn't slow down till he found himself close to the lane leading up to the library. Looking in a shop window, he smoothed his hair down as best he could and, pausing at the gateway to the library to hide the greasy tin plate, he went inside.

It was like going into a room that had been stored away in his memory which had preserved all the details of it exactly, right down to the figures of himself and the library clerk. She was there; her head bent to a filing tray. He could not bring himself to look at the newspapers; only tramps did that. Stiffly he propelled himself towards the bookstacks, his chest muscles so tight, he thought his ribs would crack. He passed deliberately close to the desk, gazing shyly at her, willing her to look up. Obediently she lifted her head and glanced at him, briefly, with an expression of veiled disgust. Startled, he slid quickly behind the protective cover of the bookshelves. From there he watched her covertly, moving from line to line of the book stacks, taking books out of their shelves, opening them and staring across their printed surfaces at the figure behind the desk. It was all very puzzling. It was as if she drew your attention and then despised you for having looked at her.

Sol was reading a newspaper in the café when he burst in. He lowered it just sufficiently to stare in surprise at Robert's dishevelled appearance.

'I . . .' panted Robert. 'I lost my way!'

Sol pursed his lips. 'How's my Lil?' he asked. 'She well?'

'All right,' gasped Robert, gulping water.

'She ask where I was?'

Robert lifted his face from his cup for a second, paused as if searching his memory, then shook his head.

'I don't know what you have to run for. In this heat.'

Nevertheless, from then on Sol gave him quarter of an hour's break every day. The next afternoon he was back at the library. Staying in the shelves that stood close to the desk, he inched his way along them, his hands running blindly over the dusty heads of the books, staring out through the space between one shelf and the next. At the counter the girl stood vacant and bored, moving her weight from one foot to the other. Picking a book at random, Robert took it over and laid it down on the desk. Turning her head very slightly so that she could not see him, the girl went on gazing out into space. An older woman marking off a pile of books near Robert paused and looked up.

'Miss Grund,' she called in a low voice, 'would you come here?'

'Miss Grund!' whispered Robert. 'Miss Grund...'

Miss Grund banged a date stamp onto his book.

'What?'

Robert gripped the sides of the book with ice-cold hands – she had heard him.

'Good afternoon,' he brought out slowly.

Miss Grund arched her eyebrows and with a swish of petticoats flounced off to the far side of the desk.

'Afternoon!' she flung inaudibly over her shoulder.

'Afternoon,' he whispered to himself as he raced back to Nile Street. 'Afternoon!' he yelled as he hurled the book into the kitchen of Zak's house. 'Afternoon,' he breathed at the water urn, clouding its surface, as he waited restlessly behind the counter of the café for the afternoon to be over.

There was not much more they could say to each other in the library, thought Robert, not with all those notices for SILENCE up and with that old woman around. She probably didn't like being talked to in there anyway. Not at her place of work. But tonight, when they stayed open late, he could wait outside in the lane. He could go up to her and say... He paused; he couldn't think what best to say. He tried to picture his reception by Miss Grund and his boldness began to subside. She might stare at him coldly as she had done today in the library; she might

226

flounce off. She might tell him never to come near her again. He picked uncertainly at a spot of grease on the counter. That wasn't what was supposed to happen. He thought of the submissive Miss Grund who flooded his dreams. She was the one that he could picture smiling as he came forward to meet her, her mouth trembling a little with shyness, inaudibly accepting his offer to walk her home. But what if he encountered the other Miss Grund?

When the café closed he stationed himself outside the entrance to the library lane, and then, feeling that he was too obviously close, retreated back over the road where he kept watch from an empty doorway. He stared into the grey, swirling street until it blurred before his eyes with the effort of concentration. The two Miss Grunds jangled in his head till the thought of either of them became so unbearable that he felt entirely unnerved and was just about to hurl himself from his doorway when the library clerk emerged from the exit of the lane. Her appearance on the street so startled him that he was struck speechless. He gazed at her: she was real, she had legs and could walk on them like other mortals. In those precious seconds that he struggled for movement, breath and thought, she snatched her woolly cardigan across her chest, turned sharply left and trotted off up the street, her full petticoats swinging against her legs. She did not dawdle, Miss Grund, in fact she could walk very fast in spite of the remarkably high heels on her shoes. By the time Robert's legs had recovered the power of movement, she was already far up the street. Keeping to his side of the road, he ran after her. But even as he ran, impelled by the fear of losing sight of her, doubt pulled him back. It was the determined force of her step, the fact that she never once looked back, that made him realise that he was not in her thoughts at all. She was not aware that he was there, nor did she show any signs of having hoped that he might have come to meet her. And so, having come almost level with

227

her, he dropped back. All confidence gone, he became furtive. He could not confront her, he told himself, until he could think of something to say; until then he could only follow her. They passed on through the drab streets, she hurrying ahead, he tiptoeing breathlessly a safe distance behind her, hoping that the heavy tread of his boots would not give him away. For her to turn and see him following her would be unbearable; it would be the end of everything. Every sort of opening line passed through his mind and was rejected. Sometimes his fantasies overlaid his caution and he lost sight of her ahead of him to the more enticing vision of her stopping, turning and smiling, a light, at last, of recognition in her eyes. In the more frequented parts of the neighbourhood, where there were bars or shops open late, or where the vast courts and tenements gave onto the street and people lounged in groups on the pavement, he would creep close to her. In other streets, empty but for a single, shuffling tramp, a straggle of children, or an old woman at her door, he would drop far behind.

As the factory quarter began to give way to acres of identical, small brick houses with red-leaded doorsteps and narrow, blank windows, each street indistinguishable from the next, he finally slowed and stopped. This was Miss Grund's home, he knew that without even having to follow her to her door; this place of carbolic soap and disinfectant and laundry blue and starch, of red lead and black lead, this place of neighbours' eyes behind lace curtains, and tight-shut front doors. From the shadows of the last tenement, he watched her disappear between the brick walls of this maze and stood for a long time afterwards listening to the squeak and echo of the heels of her shoes growing fainter. As she receded into the void, he felt the first, restless pricklings of recrimination. The light, dipping lower, suddenly cast the end of the street into shadow and the wall against which he lounged became sharp-edged, lumps of mortice and unevenly set bricks digging into his back. Why had he not overtaken her earlier, when they were still within territory she might not think it strange to encounter him in, and spoken to her? Said – anything? Anything to break the silence that hung between them thick as a fog through which she did not seem to see him. Plunged into doubt, he lurched from the wall at his back and returned the way he had come, striding quickly, pushing forward with a blind intensity against an impenetrable skin of understanding through which he could not break. The streets he ran down were reduced to planes of grey in the dusk, through which he was vaguely aware of sightless lines of windows and doors wedged into black recesses.

'I love you,' the words formed in his head savagely, sounding like a snarl of defeat.

He came into wider, more familiar streets, closer to home, and among people slowed his step, his fierce concentration dissipated by the distraction of noise and light. But still the questions beat on in his brain.

He decided to force her to notice him by becoming the library's most voracious reader. Every time he went, he decided, he would take out his full quota of three books, the three most difficult-looking books he could find, so that to anyone observing him, and the library had so few patrons that he could not help but be noticed, he would appear as a remarkable young scholar. He would become their best customer, their fastest reader. Like that she wouldn't be able to help being impressed. He sought Sol's advice.

'They have colleges here?' he asked.

'Colleges?' Sol pronounced the word slowly as if it was a strange dish he was expected to cook. 'I dunno. Up in the city, I expect they have them.'

'What kinds?'

'Well . . .' He cut a slice of bread very carefully into four.

'This an' that.'

Robert marched off to the library to put his plan into action. He pushed open the swing door, strode across the empty polished floor and, as he neared the desk, faltered. All conviction that Miss Grund might reciprocate his feelings drained away. It was again as if he was looking at a different person. There was the beloved face, but the rose-coloured mouth was pressed into a hard line of impatience and the eyes that seemed to stare right through him were entirely blank. It made his heart jump with fright as though he had committed an impropriety towards a person of mistaken identity, and he slunk away to the bookshelves to stand in their gloom and pick at the bindings of the books, puzzling at the discrepancy between his vision and reality. And yet, when he took her his books to be stamped, for a moment she did look at him, directly from under lowered eyelids. A look that for a moment reached out and drew him into her, before her eyes glazed again into indifference and she turned listlessly away.

It became the pattern of his visits. With these glances of rejection and invitation it was as if she wove silken tethers through his skin, which she then wound around her wrist. He felt the pain, a pain more subtle and full of sharp-edged delight than anything he could have imagined. He saw the silken threads and was proud of his chains. He embroidered them with meaning and coloured them with fantasy. He became proficient at summoning her to him wherever he happened to be. Standing behind the counter in Sol's café, staring out at the steamy room through a haze of burning fat, he could feel filaments of her slide across his mind. He could even conjure up the sweet, cachou-like scent of her, a private smell of soap against skin. Delving for greasy plates in the sink, he could imagine her bare arms glimmering through clear water, her white blouse unbuttoned. Walking through the grey streets, he became able to draw her from wherever she was

230

to walk at his side. She came, on these occasions, secretly, leaving her body behind so that no one there should suspect her departure, nor anyone out in the street see her materialise beside Robert. Sometimes she came instantly to his summons, at other times it would take longer and require a concentration so intense that every muscle in his body tightened to such paralysis that he could hardly put one foot in front of the other. And then, suddenly, she would be there. He would feel a displacement of air beside him, a filling up of space, and an ease would spread throughout his own body. He never turned to see her beside him; that was an inherent part of the pact. He was not to demand proof, if he did then she would vanish. If he trusted her then she would come to him always. And she did.

'It must mean . . .' he whispered hesitantly to himself, 'it must mean *something*.' And the enormity of the 'something' that he was convinced it had to mean stopped him in his tracks. It couldn't just be him on his own, if it was he would have experienced the phenomenon before. It must be her too. She must think of him at precisely the same moment that he thought of her. The vision of worlds governed entirely by imagination opened up in front of him and he felt himself draw back before the prospect of their infinity, clutching at the safe, tight parameters of the world in which he had been taught to live. He looked across the counter at the dull-eyed faces who stared vacantly back at him, sitting out the minutes of their lives in a kind of bored perplexity. He turned his head and saw shadows pass in front of the steamy plate glass window, the same ambling figures passing the café at the same time of day, trudging mechanically as though following tram-lines, small circuits of existence. Against that, the limitlessness of his dreams beckoned, a drift of scent fleetingly overlaid the warm, stale smell of the café, and he was struck once again by the miraculousness of this secret communion. He

231

glanced quickly round the café, but not an eye had flickered into life. Sol still lounged in the same position against the till, slowly twisting his wedding ring round and round on his finger. No one had noticed. How could such a thing happen without the most detailed prearrangement, without his having warned Miss Grund that he would think very hard of her at such and such a time and that she must do the same? And yet they had not said a word. They had never spoken. They had never spoken, but he felt that she was the person closest to him in the world. He could draw her to him at any moment of the day and at night he followed her patiently, ceaselessly down the endless corridors of his dreams, never managing to take her in his arms, or break the spell that froze her heart, but feeling more and more convinced that that was what she wanted him to do.

'You find anything?' Bel asked him as they strolled through the streets one evening.

Robert looked blank. His head had been full of stiff petticoats and high-heeled shoes and rose-coloured lips that were aligning themselves, coalescing into a form that he could feel rather than see taking shape beside him on the pavement. In one second more there would have been three of them walking side by side up the street. Bel, himself – and Miss Grund.

'What?' he said irritably as the vision faded.

'Anything in the *papers*! Ain't you been looking?'

'Oh. No, nothing much. Nothing that's an improvement on what I got.'

'Nothing?' Bel persisted. 'After all this time?'

'Well, I can't look *every* day.' They fell silent. He hadn't looked at all. He'd never even been over to the side of the library where the newspaper table was. He couldn't bring himself to, not under the scrutiny of Miss Grund. Well, the *possible* scrutiny of Miss Grund. She might look up and see him just as he opened one of the newspapers and

232

then he would have fallen immediately in her eyes, he was sure of that. From then on she would only ever look at him in the despising way she had. And he wanted only to impress her. He wanted her to see him as a romantic figure who read books all day: handsome, mysterious and learned. The newspapers were irrelevant now, anyway. He didn't want another job. He didn't want anything to change – except the susceptibility of Miss Grund towards him. He had at last discovered the hidden thing that was waiting for him in the city, and felt from then on as if he was living in something as fragile as an eggshell. Any violent change, any violent movement, would shatter all his hopes. He couldn't even tell anyone about Miss Grund until he was sure of her. Not even Bel. Perhaps most of all not Bel. As if she sensed him think of her, she looked across at him.

'I ask my brother about jobs and he say he'll think. I tell him only thing for you, really, is leavin' an' he say he don't think you long for this place first day he met you. We turn right here.'

Economy, Bel had decided, had to be the guiding factor of their entertainment, too. It meant that they were limited almost entirely to walking about.

'I told George in Chez Madeleine he won't be seeing you for a while,' Bel had informed him, and then, to cheer him up, had added, 'I'll take you to see the cinema next time you come round.' That was where they were going now. It was in a neighbouring district, though the demarcation line between one quarter and the next was scarcely visible. If anything the buildings were slightly lower and the streets marginally wider, but there were still the same dilapidated houses and drifts of dust and newspaper at street corners and a worn-out feel to the end of the day. Against the lingering daylight the lighted windows of bars and cafés had a feeble, half-hearted look, as though they

233

did not believe either in their pretended gaiety. The cinema, when they found it, was little more than a barricaded kiosk at the entrance to a shadowed hallway, piled up with posters and smelling of urine. Robert stared avidly at the poster pasted up in the passageway. It was of a man whose craggy features were sharply outlined against a desert scene, one arm encircled a woman with a mane of hair the identical blonde to Miss Grund's and a prominent bosom, and the man's gun was pointed at a far-off cactus.

'Can't we go in?' he wheedled.

'They closed today,' replied Bel smugly. 'That's why I brought you. We can't afford none of them things now.'

Summer coming suddenly to the city made Bel's task easier. All day the sun beat down through the copper-coloured pall of smoke squeezing the last breath of air from the dusty streets, which took on an exhausted look. The houses seemed to reel back against one another, their bricks swollen and reverberating with heat. They appeared to be as overcome as the old women who, with the dulling of the light, brought their chairs out onto the pavements and sat, legs splayed, their faded dresses pulled up to their thighs, the palms of their hands planted upon their knees, fanning themselves with handkerchiefs and complaining to each other how they had never known such heat so early in the year. It was impossible to stay inside. Bel and Robert would wander from bridge to bridge seeking an illusion of coolness in the waters of the canal. In their excursions they found abandoned jetties where Robert poked at the bumping trails of flotsam with long sticks, releasing pent-up odours of decay, and hoped, so he told Bel, to uncover a dead body. But there was only one body that he longed for, and he continued to pursue it relentlessly, silently and faithfully, without ever appearing to have any success. His wanderings with Bel were the anxious filling in of time, the prodding on of hours till he could see Miss Grund again, and he frequently was silent and abstracted.

He took advantage of every chance to visit the library. He followed Miss Grund home night after night, but could never pluck up enough courage to speak to her, though he was sure she knew he was there. His failure began to be compounded by a vague fear that either his passion would subside, or Miss Grund would be carried off before his very eyes, while he still stood there inarticulate with love. He had the overwhelming sense of time slipping irrevocably away, and knew that nothing could arrest the mechanism. He could not move it to pity by his own inability to act, it would not slow its seconds for him to gather courage, nor would it hasten the inevitability of their meeting to assuage his longing. Time was not concerned with the affairs of men. It took its beat from the turning of other worlds and measured its pace by infinity. Fearing that time might deny Miss Grund to him forever, he became possessed by a prowling restlessness. The drudgery of the café became unbearable and when he tried to escape into his fantasies he could scarcely summon the image of Miss Grund at all. Frequently when she came he felt he loathed her. He chided her for her tardiness, denounced her as unfeeling and then, staring into her blank face, was overcome with love for her and crushed her, doll-like and unresponsive, to him, her arms dangling outside his embrace, her flesh squashed like soft rubber against his own.

In the café the heat was so unbearable that they kept the door propped open all day. Sol didn't like it because it let in the dust and the flies, but his small, grease-encrusted ventilator turned so lethargically in the breathless air that there was no help for it. He worried, too, about Lil. He would fidget to be gone on his afternoon visit to her, and returned looking more anguished than ever.

'I hope she's all right,' he kept saying, 'weather like this could bring her on and she ain't got no woman with her. Only that husband. I should never have let her marry

235

him,' he would mutter, huddling back onto the stool behind the counter. 'Like an oven that place is. She don't know what to do with herself, my poor girl. She'd go and lie down in the street, get a bit of air, except she don't trust herself on them stairs.'

But, as swiftly as the heatwave came, it went. By the end of the week clouds massed up from the east and that night thunder prowled over the city in ever widening circles, rain fell and in the morning life was back to normal again.

He went, as usual, on the next late opening night of the library to wait for Miss Grund, determined this time to speak to her. It had rained all day, slow rain that had left everything gleaming and slippery as though covered with a film of oil. He stood in a doorway, his coat collar turned up, peering through trickles of water that ran down from his soaked hair, idly watching through almost closed eyes two men loading a cart with barrels; half watching the cart, half watching the lane to the library. It seemed a very small cart to take the stack of barrels piled up beside it on the pavement even if, as he supposed from the easy way the men swung them up through the air, they were empty. They went on piling them up on the cart and he went on watching for Miss Grund, wondering what it was that she did that took her so long, staring in between at the passers-by. He jiggled anxiously from one foot to the other. She would be here any second. He moved out of the doorway. The mountain of barrels had grown so high on the cart across the road that they almost obscured the exit of the lane. They were doing it deliberately so that he would fail. He moved further out. Across the road the carters began yelling at the pony between the shafts of the cart, urging it forward, slapping its rump with the palms of their hands. Robert, beside his doorway, danced in rage at his blocked view. And the hooves of the pony clattered in echo, slithering and stumbling, trying to get a purchase on the wet road. One of the men pulled off his leather belt and sent it whistling through the air onto the pony's flank. Robert jumped. The pony fell. And slowly, as though caught in a web of suspended time, the topmost barrel began to roll. Looking as light as a feather it bounced from step to step of the mound of barrels. The pony struggled to its feet lurching and whinnying, straining to break free of its harness. But the traces held, and behind it the cartload of barrels lurched and swayed with it. As the topmost barrel landed on the pony's back there was a splintering crash. The hindquarters dropped instantly. The forelegs scrabbled on the road, as though to drag itself away, then fell, too. Time was suddenly released. Above the screams of the pony, the shouts of the men and the shrieks of bystanding women came the relentless pounding of barrel after barrel. The pony lay among the splintered shafts of the cart, its flanks heaving, its head rearing and falling, its mouth dragged open by the taut bit, from which dripped foam, flecked with blood. A great, dark pool spread out around the animal which widened at each convulsive movement. And still the barrels cascaded down. One crashed into the gutter beside Robert, jerking him out of his paralysed horror. Miss Grund! He raced across the road between the rolling barrels behind the cart towards the lane. The noise from the pony had sunk to a terrible, bubbling moaning sound interspersed with long, shuddering breaths. Halfway up the lane he saw Miss Grund come through the library gate. He flung his arms wide and ran towards her.

'No! No! Not down there!'

Miss Grund flattened herself against the wall.

'Mr Rinoul!' she screamed.

Robert halted in front of her and pointed down the lane to the crowd in the street and shook his head, gasping for breath:

'You mustn't go down there. You wouldn't like it. It's a horse ... it's had an accident ...'

Miss Grund gave another scream. A middle-aged man turned from locking the library door and hurried down the path.

'What's all this!' he demanded, glaring at Robert.

'It's a horse, had an accident, right outside the lane. I don't think Miss er ... should see it; it's, it's ...'

Above the noise, out on the road, there was a high-pitched whinnying scream, a creaking, scraping rush of noise against the cobbles. A gasp from the crowd. A shot. And then, suddenly, silence. Miss Grund clamped her hands to her ears and screwed her eyes shut. Mr Rinoul, his hands not quite touching her shoulders, hurried her away up the lane and Robert followed.

'Oh!' whimpered Miss Grund against Mr Rinoul's lapel. 'Oh!' Mr Rinoul tried to push her away a little, his impatient glance flickering from Miss Grund to Robert to the crowd at the end of the lane and back to his clerk who, deprived of his coat lapel, was swaying slightly, her eyes still shut, one hand over her mouth from which issued curious gulping, sobbing sounds, as though she was preparing to have hysterics.

'I can't go down there!' wailed Miss Grund, screwing her eyes even more tightly shut. 'I can't, I can't!' she wrapped her arms round her body and began to sway from side to side.

'Look,' said Mr Rinoul rapidly, 'I got to go!'

He shot his wrist out of his coat sleeve and tried to peer at the dial of his watch in the gloom. He held it out towards Robert and shook it. 'My sister!' he explained urgently and shook his head. 'I can't be late.'

'I could escort the young lady!' burst in Robert. 'I know a way round that cuts out most of that street. She wouldn't have to see nothing.'

'Oh!' The librarian backed a little way further up the

lane, buttoning up his macintosh. 'Oh, well, then. If you're sure . . .' And his face in the twilight appeared to be drawn into a grimace of relief.

Miss Grund, realising that she was going to be abandoned, tottered after him.

'Miss Grund! I live right the other *way* from you. I'm very sorry, but . . .' his voice quavered and broke.

Miss Grund had stopped swaying backwards and forwards. She had opened her eyes very wide.

'I'm not being sent off down no short cuts with no stranger!'

'Miss Grund!' The librarian was almost beside himself, his head seemed to roll in despair on his neck. 'I just *told* you. Besides,' he came back down to where she stood and whispered through clenched teeth. 'This,' he jerked his head towards Robert, 'isn't a stranger. It's that boy who's always coming in the library.' Miss Grund stared sulkily at him from beneath lowered lashes.

'I'm Robert,' he said hesitantly.

'There!' exclaimed the librarian. 'Well, goodnight, Robert. Goodnight, Miss Grund.' And he hastened off up the darkening lane.

There was a pause during which they both listened to the rapidly departing footsteps fade into silence. Robert cleared his throat.

'The lane's just up here.' His voice sounded to him no more audible than a whisper. He turned towards Miss Grund to engage her attention, but found he could not bring himself to look at her. So he began to move, in a sideways, crab-like fashion, towards a black smudge of an opening ahead in the wall. Miss Grund sniffed; she brushed some imaginary dust from the sleeve of her cardigan and, eyes deliberately averted from his, followed him.

It was very dark in the alley. It had almost stopped raining, but above them the sky lowered and thickened, as though night had fallen prematurely. Down the high walls of the tenements on either side of them water trickled incessantly, slithering over blackened bricks. In places it fell in single, unbroken streams out of blocked pipes and broken guttering, crashing like tiny waterfalls onto the cobbles of the alley, collecting in dark pools and running in thin streams alongside the uneven path. They stumbled against broken bottles and past soggy heaps of rubbish. There seemed only to be the rain and the sound of rain and the disconcerting echo of their footsteps. And, with the passing of every second, the slipping away of his chance. Each brick seemed like a marker to what might have been, he saw them gleam dimly in the half-light and then they were gone. Was it there that he should have turned and seized her in his arms, was it here that he should have kissed her, and here ... and here? But they were gone, these moments, these seconds of time reserved for him, marked out for a particular action, even as he hesitated. He lowered his head and marched on until the unbearable thought of his loss made him want to turn round, to go back, feeling with his hands along the wet, dark wall of the alley till he found the place in time where he could have kissed her. But he knew instinctively that he could not go back. There was one chance, only one, and if you did not take it, did not imprint experience on it, then its significance faded and crumbled, slipped sideways and coalesced with other lost opportunities into a smudge of regret.

They reached the point where the alley divided, one arm curving back to rejoin the main street. It was almost over and still he could not bring himself to speak. Miss Grund had surrounded herself with spikes of indignation and contempt forming a kind of protective cage which moved with her. He could hear her slither and gasp behind him and the metal tips to her heels squeak against the wet cobbles with a raw, grating sound, like that of a thumbnail on a slate. Perhaps one of her heels would be wrenched off and he could mend it – perhaps she would slip on the mud and he could pick her up? There was a sudden splash. He stopped and turned and Miss Grund cannoned into him. He felt the soft impress of her against his back.

'You all right?'

She pushed him angrily away from her.

'Why don't you look where you're going!'

'I thought you'd slipped.'

'Aren't we there yet?'

Robert stood unwillingly aside.

'Almost. Look down there, that speck of light – that's Henage Street.' As though at the end of a long tunnel, a small triangle of slightly lighter gloom could be seen. They resumed their journey, and the triangle grew slowly larger, blotted out now and then by dark figures which crossed and re-crossed it. Miss Grund hurried eagerly at his shoulder. The triangle of light grew larger until it dwarfed the blackness of the alley, in another moment they would be shot out into the glare of the street. Robert thought desperately of making one last attempt to enfold Miss Grund in his arms, he had almost slowed and half-turned when she shot past him into the light and stood there shaking out the folds of her skirt, tottering first on one foot and then on the other to examine the state of her shoes. He followed her slowly, watching her as though from a distance, hovering uncertainly on the pavement like a dog who has slunk along after his master so far and now knows he is about to be sent home. He wondered if, for the sake of his own pride, he shouldn't dismiss himself, before she had a chance to do so.

They had come out among a string of small shops. Opposite them was a café, whose blurred window provided most of the illumination for this part of the street, and, on one corner of the alley, a bar from which a gust of light and noise blew out with the opening and closing of a door, leaving behind on the pavement three men. They took in immediately the picture of Miss Grund balanced on one leg, displaying the other, as it were, for their delectation, and cunning, clumsy smiles spread across their faces. Clustering unsteadily, shoulder to shoulder, they advanced upon her. Robert moved forward, one hand stretched out to take her elbow, but she saw them too, and, pulling her cardigan round her, swerved to the right to avoid them. Robert a pace behind her, his hand an inch from her elbow, swerved too. A chorus of wolf whistles broke out and as she passed them the man nearest her suddenly turned, hopping in front of her, swinging the other heavy-booted leg towards her, as though trying to hook it round her own.

'Have pity on me leg, miss!' he pleaded. 'Just a little touch. Have pity on me leg.'

Behind him his companions seemed to collapse, entwining themselves round each other's necks, snorting and bellowing with laughter. Miss Grund stepped out onto the road, Robert at her heels. As he passed him the man's eyes glistened in the lamplight, gleaming with delight.

'Wouldn't you take pity then, sir, on me leg?'

His words were almost drowned by shrieks from his companions as, slumped on each other's necks, they tried to draw breath, sobbing with laughter. Miss Grund bounced back onto the pavement, snatching her arm free of Robert's tentative fingers. Even in relative safety higher up the street, guffaws still reached them as the man repeated the performance for his friends.

They turned a bend in the road and found themselves in a darker stretch of tenements and tall rooming houses. Now and then there were couples in the shadowed doorways, or a single figure drawn back out of the light watching the passers-by intently without moving so that frequently it was not seen, one merely sensed a presence, a tangibility to the shadows. Robert glanced sideways at

Miss Grund. Her face looked paler than ever, the eyes hooded, her mouth sullen and shadowed. Her hands plucked at her clothes with sharp gestures as though trying to restore propriety and dignity, to brush off outrage as though it was unsightly dust. He struggled for something comforting to say to her, to let her know how much he felt and understood. Miss Grund's was a constant struggle against insult and ugliness; she felt it keenly, bitterly. Her nature was so delicate she could sense it where others might not see it, and defended herself constantly against its invasion. It was her lot to endure life among people she clearly despised, to have her white collars and cuffs constantly besmirched by the very air around her. Robert opened his mouth to tell her all this. But, as if she heard his intake of breath, she turned suddenly to him:

'What d'you come to the library all the time for?'

Robert felt his face burn, but it seemed not to be composed of flesh anymore. It had become a huge, bony cavern devoid of thought, being or personality. He scrabbled frantically in its recesses, searching for words, and heard himself say:

'I'm studying.'

'What *for*?'

'Law.' It fell out of his mouth with such ease it surprised him as much as it surprised her.

'Law?'

'Yes.'

'But those books you take out are all sorts.'

So she had noticed. He felt the blush leave his cheeks and the blood pump faster through his veins, warm, heady.

'That's preparatory,' he said. 'You have to do that, read all you can, all different subjects. You got to know,' he paused, feeling lines of attention being drawn and tightened between them like the first filaments of a spider's web, 'about everything; every kind of life. If you want to be a judge that is.'

243

At the beginning of her street she stopped, burrowing her arms into the sleeves of her cardigan, and nodded her head at a house half-way down the road:

'That's where I live. But you don't need to come any further.'

'Can I walk you home again? Sometime?'

She arched her eyebrows:

'Maybe.'

And swiftly crossed the road away from him.

He stood rooted to the square of pavement, watching her to her door. Then the door closed on her and he ran as fast as he could out of the red-leaded maze, away from the zig-zagging identical streets. Finally, he arrived, breathless, among the dark tenements and warehouse buildings. They rose suddenly above him like cathedral arches and he ran singing under the arches and raced with his blood down crooked streets. Reckless with love, feeling no fear could touch him, he tore down dark alleys and through cut-throat passages making towards the canal, wanting to swing from the lines of grey washing that hung in the drab courts, and run with his shadow before him over the cobblestones all night long. He found himself at last not far from home, in a lane between back-to-back houses so narrow he could stretch out and touch either side with his fingertips. And thus he ran, arms wide, blistering his fingertips against the bricks just for the hell of it: the faster he ran the more his skin burned and his elation soared so that he wanted to shout out loud. Till the shadow of a shadow moved in a corner, close to where he was, stopping him dead.

'Back, back, back,' said a low voice, sounding in the silence like a pebble over cobbles. 'There's things about to happen here you don't want no part of.' Long, brown fingers fluttered briefly in a patch of light, like the shadow of leaves stirred by a night wind, waving him away. 'Out.' The sound was barely audible, the final 't' like the soft click of a door closing somewhere. Robert glanced fearfully over his shoulder. In every corner of the alley he seemed to see shadows moving. Without being aware that he, too, had begun to move, he found himself running, breath gasping in his ear, and the clattering of his heels echoing down narrow streets. He did not stop till he reached Zak's house.

Alone in its empty rooms the feeling of fear subsided and the exhilaration of triumph returned. Up in the bedroom he flung himself on the bed and lay there smiling into the wall, smiling into her face that materialised among the plaster cracks, each contour of it perfectly remembered. Her own, slow, waking smile. In the stillness of the room he began to talk to her, his lips moving silently, his brain unaware of what they said. Beyond the dust-streaked window pane the real world seemed entirely removed. The house held them within its warm, empty rooms, safe from all intrusion. He talked and shyly she replied from her plaster wall; then, at a certain point, he opened his arms and she floated into them. Close to his cheek was the unbelievable softness of her cheek, the scent of her hair. He could feel her body pressed against him and watch her eyelashes demurely lower as he bent his head towards the small, rose-coloured mouth. It was the sense of her yielding: the warm skin beneath the white, starched blouse, the slight parting of the unsmiling mouth, the rumpling of her hair, which, messed about by his caresses, would then have to be washed and set all over again. It was the fact that she would endure all these things for his sake that made him swell with pride. And when, sometime later, he uncurled his arms from the soft airiness, rolled over on his back and stared at the bars of moonlight across the floor, her presence still lingered, like a warmth or a scent, around him. He could feel something curled about his neck, like the impress of arms, as he padded downstairs to the kitchen. And, as he stood alone in the bare shop feeling the magic drain away and the house return to its shadows, he was sure he could still hear her, breathing.

He consulted Sol next morning about how to become a law student. Sol looked mournfully at him across the splutter of frying eggs. He raised his eyebrows and stuck out his fleshy lower lip.

'You on about them colleges again?'

Robert grinned. 'How d'you get taken on?'

Sol steered the eggs slowly round the pan, making a kind of whistling noise through his teeth.

'You got to have exams.'

'Exams?'

'Yeah.' Sol nodded, 'exams.'

Robert still looked blank.

'You went to school, didn't you?'

'Course I did, everyone's got to go to school.'

'Well, then, you got exams, or not?'

Robert looked down at his hands. 'Exams' sounded like some childhood disease such as measles that might show in red splotches on his skin.

'I don't think so?' he said.

He worried vaguely about exams all the rest of the day. He didn't think he'd ever had them, but perhaps he could pretend he had. Or perhaps Sol was wrong. What would Sol know, anyway, about such things? But Miss Grund might, she might ask him all sorts of questions.

Miss Grund, however, didn't appear very anxious to talk to him at all. The atmosphere in the library seemed altered. It felt charged with knowledge, with some kind of awareness, so that when he entered it and Miss Grund came forward to take his books, everyone in the room, not only the elderly librarian, immediately looked up to watch them. What was even more surprising though was that Miss Grund pretended to hardly know him. She answered his murmured greeting, but when he asked her if she could take five minutes off she seemed to instantly take offence and shook her head. And when, the next day, he suggested she meet him behind one of the bookstacks, she picked up his books and went off without a word. He waited among the bookshelves, but she never came. Puzzling over it later, remembering the looks that passed between Miss Grund and her colleagues, it came to him, all of a sudden, that she must be acting under orders. Somewhere it had been decided that there was a certain way that librarians had to act and anyone who went to work in a library had to be trained to it. They had to learn how to pout and sigh and click their tongues with exasperation, they had to practise stretching their patience to breaking point and then learn to switch to an alternative state of vacant boredom, until it became second nature to them. You weren't meant to enjoy yourself in a library the way you were in a café, so that was why they had different rules. Also – and this struck Robert as very significant – it was free. That meant you could have anyone walking in – people who didn't even have the price of a cup of tea, who might not know how to behave, or read the signs saying SILENCE! So librarians were no doubt instructed to maintain a dignified distance from their customers. Robert stopped suddenly in his tracks, overwhelmed by a desire to rush back to the library and tell Miss Grund that he had guessed the secret of the discrepancy between her beautiful face and her disdainful manner. To reassure her that he knew it wasn't really her true nature, that it was something she was compelled to do for the library. He even started back a couple of steps and then halted. She wouldn't want him to expose her in front of all the others.

Out in the street he expected her to be released back into herself. And so she was. So deeply into herself that she might have been walking alone. She kept disconcertingly far apart from him, drawing her cardigan tightly round her as if to exclude him further, gazing at her reflection in shop windows as she walked as if that was the companion she desired. He had to beg for her attention, plead for her to turn her head, but never did she allow any hint to pass that she might feel anything for him. Finally, he plucked up courage to ask her out.

'I thought,' he began, too low for her quite to hear him.

'What?'

'I thought – you might like to come out for a walk – on Sunday.' She stopped and looked at him, as though appraising him for the first time.

'*Did* you?' She turned away again and walked on.

'Yes. Wouldn't you like ...'

'My mum wants to see *you*.'

'What for?' His mouth went dry and the guilt of his desires rushed on him as though they had been discovered. Miss Grund smirked as if she had not only found them out, but told them to her mother.

'When?'

She shrugged. 'You might as well come now.'

When they reached Miss Grund's house she did not take out her key, she knocked at the door, like a stranger. There was silence, then a shuffling noise, then the door was pulled open by a large woman who balanced on the sill in boat-like fluffy slippers. Caught within the strong frame, imprisoned behind spreading flesh, was another Miss Grund. Against the blurring effects of age and the weight of double chins it was obviously difficult to maintain the superciliousness of her daughter's sharp profile, but the remnants were still there in the drag of the flesh and the deep-etched lines of the skin. The same cold, dismissive eyes swept blankly across Robert's face to rest on that of her daughter where they softened, gazing with pleasure at the reflection of herself. Without a word she turned and shuffled back down the passage, closely followed by Miss Grund, who moved forward as though pulled by an invisible string, without a gesture or sideways glance at Robert, who was left alone on the doorstep. He stepped hesitantly across the threshold and politely scraped the soles of his boots against a woven fibre mat that lay just inside the door. Ahead of him the women had already disappeared down the passage into a back room. To his right a thin ladder of stairs led up into darkness and, as he turned to close the door behind him, he glimpsed a box-room of a parlour to his left. Expecting that one of them would come to call him in and not liking to follow them uninvited, he waited in the hallway, watching for a figure to appear in the oblong of light at the end of the passage. Standing there in the half-darkness he felt himself caught between tightly-pressing walls that were squeezing the breath out of him. The impulse to fill his lungs with air became overpowering, but he was afraid that if he did the walls might split and crack with the expansion of his chest and the lifting of his shoulders. He tilted back his head to snatch air from the low space above him and became aware that he was not in fact being suffocated by the closing-in of the walls but by a strange odour that hung about the hall and which seemed to have transformed all the particles of oxygen into dust. He gulped for breath and his nostrils were instantly choked by the dry, biting sharpness of ammonia and carbolic. The air seemed to have been turned into scrubbing powder, slimily overlaid with linoleum polish and nauseously sweetened with gardenia and freesia and lily of the valley. The thought that his lungs might burst drove him finally down the passage towards the inner room.

In the kitchen the women were murmuring to each other, caressingly, the first greetings of the evening. Sensing Robert's presence in the doorway they looked up, unwillingly, and ceased their conversation, fragments of words tailing off regretfully into the air. Miss Grund sank onto a stool, drawn up beside a formica-topped table

249

folded against one wall, and began unbuttoning her coat. Her mother pulled a kettle onto the stove and lit the gas under it. To the stifling airlessness of the room was added the piercing smell of gas. Underneath the electric light bulb in the centre of the ceiling a brightly-coloured cardboard cut-out of a bunch of roses began to revolve on its string as the heat rose.

'Get the cups out, Sylvie!'

Miss Grund stood up. Sylvie! Robert stared at her. It was as if her mother had removed a layer of her clothing so that he could see her more intimately. But she showed no sign of embarrassment at the revelation of her private name.

'Sylvie!' he whispered wonderingly in his head, but she did not even look at him.

She slid open the glass door of a cupboard fixed to the wall, her face set in its habitual expression of lifeless perfection, and took out the three cups with painted flowers and silver rims which waited ostentatiously in a row.

The tea was poured but only Sylvie made any attempt to drink it. She immersed herself in the drinking of it as though there was nothing else of any interest to do in the room. Mrs Grund pushed hers away along the draining board. And Robert, weak-kneed and limp-palmed, could not trust himself to pick his up. Mrs Grund folded her arms across her chest and fixed her eyes suspiciously on Robert:

'My daughter, Sylvene, told me all about you bringing her home that night they had the accident outside the library.'

Robert shuffled dismissively in the doorway.

'That was fortunate,' Mrs Grund moved her weight heavily from one foot to the other like a boxer limbering up, 'that you were there. Just passing, were you? Or you live round there?' Robert nodded. Mrs Grund went on

250

staring at him and as the silence grew he realised that there had been two questions.

'Passing!' he blurted out. 'Just passing. And also,' he added quickly, 'I do live quite near. Down by the canal. Nile Street.'

'Ohh. Really. I didn't know there was no houses left down there. I thought that was all factories. You know there was houses down there, Sylvie?'

Sylvie looked up blankly. 'I've never been there, Mum.'

'No,' Mrs Grund leant back against the stove and shook her head and the double chins waggled in corroboration on her neck, 'we don't never go down that area. Your parents live down there?'

'No.'

'Ohhh.' More could be inferred from the tone of Mrs Grund's exclamations than any of her words. 'You don't *live* with your parents, then?'

'No.'

'You in one of them hostels?'

'No, I got a house.'

'House!'

'Well, it's not much.'

'They dead?'

For a second Robert toyed with the simplicity of killing them off, but things seemed to be moving too fast, Mrs Grund's eyes were boring into him, making him trip over his own thoughts.

'No, only Zak. Only this friend of my uncle's. Day I got there he died, so I just stayed on.'

'Alone?'

Robert nodded.

'Man of property!' She glanced swiftly sideways at her daughter and then back to Robert before he had time to contradict her.

'Your parents in another part of the city?'

'They live in the country,' replied Robert firmly.

Mrs Grund curled a plump finger through the handle of her teacup and lifted it to her lips: 'I could tell you was a country boy.' There was a pause while she drank. 'Farm?'

'No.'

'One of them little towns?'

'It's more ... more ... like a very small village.'

'Oh, I don't think I'd like *that*! Isolated. Would you, Sylvie? On the land are they?'

'Law.'

'Oooh.' The breath seemed knocked out of her for a second, but she recovered swiftly. 'Sylvie's father was Senior Clerical. On the railways. Chief Booking Clerk at Hatchett Road. Just before he passed away they offered him Hatchett Road Station House. That was the proudest moment of his life. But I put my foot down. I wasn't having my Sylvie brought up in an area like Hatchett Road. Not after here. You following your father's footsteps, then?' Robert stared at her blankly. She bent towards him as if he was either deaf or stupid:

'My daughter Sylvene tells me you're studying law.' Mrs Grund gave special emphasis to the word 'law', even bestowing an extra syllable onto the end of it.

'Oh, well, not exactly ...'

'My daughter Sylvene said you *was*!'

'Well, not quite yet. I'm just ...'

'We was under the distinct impression you was already learning!' Something akin to lightning flashed between mother and daughter and the air became charged with the rage of betrayal. A noise like static crackled in Robert's ears so that he couldn't exactly hear the rush of words that poured from Mrs Grund, or his own feeble answers. They were off and running in some kind of maze. But every time Robert managed to escape out of one alley and into another Mrs Grund would suddenly appear before him to head him off. While at the exit of the maze Miss Grund, the prize, sat patiently on her small kitchen chair, her vacuous

252

gaze unruffled by the crashing sounds within. Her head was bent to her tea-cup which rested in her lap and she was staring at the pattern of tea-leaves in its bowl. Now and then her lips moved as though, leaf by leaf, she was reading off her fortune. The tip of one of her fingers appeared on the rim of the cup and crept down inside. There it halted for a moment and then, with deliberation, it detached a tea-leaf from one group and moved it towards another. Her tongue slid indelicately between her lips and her brow wrinkled into a frown. The fingertip moved towards a second tea-leaf and then a third and then, gathering speed with a sudden greediness, swiftly completed the process of rearranging her fate. Still imprisoned within his maze, Robert found that however he turned and twisted it seemed endless. It had long ago burst the confines of the kitchen, sprawling out over the city. But over its centre still hung the brightly-coloured cardboard roses, turning and twitching on their string, following his every change of direction like a tracking radar beam. It struck his dazed mind that the maze was perhaps not something laid out before him into which he was driven, but was of his own making, springing up from his own words, and that if he stopped it too would halt. But if he stopped Mrs Grund would catch him and it would all be over. All of a sudden and without the least warning he burst out into the warmth and silence where Miss Grund sat. She leapt up, and a small tea-cup fell from the folds of her dress and rolled away. She looked round for her mother, but all crashing sounds within the maze had ceased. Then she turned back to Robert and gazed up at him through lowered eyelashes. The prize at last was his!

He came, however, to wonder what the prize really was. He had gone after one prize – it had been fixed in his mind – so obvious he would have thought there could be no mistake. But they had seemed to have quite another prize in mind. It was difficult to define, this prize. At his most baffled and confused he even thought it must be Mrs Grund, for Sylvene seemed further away than ever. She had taken to wearing cotton gloves and had had her hair permed into stiff, corrugated paper waves. The cardigan was one day replaced by a shapeless linen coat and eventually a satin scarf appeared, knotted in a fussy bow at her throat. The Miss Grund with whom he had fallen in love seemed to have been buried, the girl who had materialised beside him in crowded streets and filled the silence of his dreams had been left behind somewhere in time. This new Miss Grund did not seem to share any of his desire; it was with the utmost difficulty that he could get her to let him hold her hand. She would permit him only one kiss each night at her mother's doorstep and when, fumblingly, he would try to grasp a second, she would turn her face abruptly away. When they sat in a café over empty coffee cups, he would sometimes stretch out his fingers to touch hers where they lay inert on the table, but she would instantly arch her eyebrows, compress her mouth and slap at his hand with a look of mock offence. Yet at other times, in a dark part of the street, she would press herself against him and then, as she felt him flame up, dart away with a little shriek, running with short, flapping steps so that he could easily overtake her and pull her to him. But when he did she would struggle furiously, lashing out at him, and he would have to let her go.

As he walked home from these meetings alone, the women standing together on corners and in archways would fall silent at his approach. They would read in the tenseness of his body and the wild, shuttered look in his lowered glance the biting longing that beset him and they would move out of the shadows one by one, turning themselves to him. But he pushed on past them, stepping hastily aside to avoid contact with them. He watched men approach women with sour, unsmiling faces. And women

254

laugh at love itself. He saw men and women come together without a word and dissolve together into shadows. What was it? What? There were words and there were no words – but there was always something each saw and recognised and understood.

He became increasingly aware of the summer sliding away. As the tide of light turned and the days began to shorten imperceptibly so he felt the certainty of his journey receding from him and the clarity of his purpose obscure. Every day that he delayed he sensed the walls of the city closing in on him further. The money that he had begun to save was long since gone on small packets of chocolate, cups of tea and occasional bus rides on Sundays out to where grime-encrusted fields clung limply to the outskirts of the city. Here, in company with other couples, they would walk around the soot-blackened, dust-whitened perimeters staring at the paper bags that floated on a stagnant pond and at the deep cracks in the lifeless earth. His lack of money was discussed constantly by Sylvie and her mother over his head. They set this appalling state of affairs, which deprived Sylvie of the treats she should be having, against the potential status of his becoming a student – and a law student at that. Together they talked with an animation that they did not display to anyone else. Listening to them while he ate, Robert could hardly distinguish one from the other. They would discuss the possibility of his finding a better-paid job in a restaurant. He could study days and work nights. Robert would look up from his plate. When, he would point out, would he ever see Sylvie if he did that? And the two women would stare at him and then at each other as though he was an imbecile. They talked, too, of letting Zak's house. So nice, Mrs Grund would say, to have a man about the place again, and pour him another cup of tea.

Robert was constantly hungry. He took to stealing food when Sol was out of the café. He would cut minute ends

255

off the dry slabs of cake that stood in the glass case, or a thin slice from a loaf of bread, and cram them quickly into his mouth before anyone could come in and catch him. He came to think that he went to the Grunds' house only for food. He was hungry for Sylvie, but every time he stretched out a hand towards her food seemed to be put into it instead. He was kept at arm's length by titbits; like a baby, his cries were stoppered instantly by sweetened dummies, or sugared biscuits. Mrs Grund would slide cups of tea in front of him, or her daughter would fetch shrivelled chops and dried cabbage out of the oven for him. And, having successfully deflected him, would fluff out her skirts, smooth her primly curled hair and, turning her back on him, take up her conversation again with her mother.

He saw very little of Bel now, but increasingly he thought of her, of the time when, but for her, he would have given up all hope. He had never talked to her about Sylvene, there had simply been a kind of mute understanding that for some reason he now had less and less time to spend with her. Her teasing waned as she perceived an increasingly hunted look in his eyes. As the weeks passed, first her faith in his dreams was shaken and then, by extension, her own. He saw the change in her: a quickening of uncertainty and then the slow drawing down of her vitality, and knew that in some way it was his fault. And all the time he scrabbled to hold onto the vision which had brought him to the city, but it eluded his grasp, like water. He reached back into his mind to where he thought his conviction had been and found the place numb. He tried to re-evoke the unwavering determination that had propelled his escape from his aunt's house, and stared forlornly at the bright-eyed child who looked mutely back at him.

Lil's twins were born. Sol, elevated to the position of

grandfather, spent all his mornings telling anyone who would listen about the new family and spent almost all his afternoons at Lil's house. When he ran out of customers to regale he would tell Robert, repeating over and over again the details of the birth and subsequent life of his grandchildren. But Robert, beset by anxiety, was an unsatisfactory listener. He stood one day behind the counter staring aimlessly at the steam running down the windows of the café and there came into his mind a picture of the city as a huge, amorphous creature over which people swarmed and which was ever-watchful for those who could not keep their footing, or who lagged behind. Such people the city consumed, their disappearance unnoticed by the others who scrambled onwards. What was this consumption, he wondered. How did it happen? Could you see it before it happened, or was it instantaneous – one minute you were there, the next minute you were gone, dissolved into nothingness. Robert blinked. Everything looked out of focus. Between the tables, Sol seemed to wander, slow as in a dream, wiping each table with a cloth, setting the salts and peppers straight. He thought of the streets outside Zak's house and they took on a dullness, an emptiness and meaninglessness, and he felt himself suddenly lost, wandering in an alien and deserted place. Perhaps this was how it happened. First everything lost colour and purpose, then the walls little by little would move in on him, rooms would get smaller, the house become a matchbox, the streets narrow to pathways, the café dwindle to insignificance.

September came and with it the first hints of cold.

'You got to leave that house,' Sylvie and Mrs Grund told him, 'it hasn't got no heat nor no light. Think what it's going to be like in the winter!' They peered at him from their positions of logical superiority, drawing their cardigans across their bosoms. But Robert kept his head obstinately bent to his plate.

'You could come here,' said Mrs Grund, looking archly over the top of his head at her daughter, 'Sylvie could come in with me. For the time being...'

Sylvie would simper at him from her kitchen chair and he would lift his head and look at her, distrustful, yet overwhelmed by a hunger that blotted everything else out with a longing to be satiated with kisses and warmed by the soft sliding of her fingertips. He had almost ceased to believe that it would ever happen, but he could not let go of it. He was without argument against their logic, but the whole of him squirmed and writhed and refused to submit.

'I'll think about it,' he muttered.

They took him upstairs to show him the room; up the hideously spick and span stairs. They opened the door and stood back to let him in. He breathed in the scent of Sylvie. He imagined his head on her pillow and himself between sheets that had wound themselves round her body. He looked at the painted glass ornaments on the dressing table.

'End of the month?' they said.

Walking back alone to Nile Street he thought of being with Sylvie every day, of leaving Zak's house and quitting Sol's. But, beside the possible pleasure that the thought of her gave him, he was unnerved by a small patch of darkness which grew in his mind: a kind of tear in the skin of the world through which he could make out hunger and cold and then, beyond that, nothingness. It was a very small patch of darkness compared to the image of Miss Grund, but it seeped through the other, destroying the joy of it. It persisted all the way to Zak's house. He lit a candle, heated a tin of beans and carried them upstairs to eat in bed, hunched around by bedclothes. But still it remained, only now the tear in the skin of the world had grown larger and through it he could see himself, so minute he only knew by intuition that it was himself, falling, turning and twisting, dropping through the skin of the world.

He waited each day for his direction to be restored. It was like another sense, this sense of life; a sense more important than all the others. Without it he was powerless and inert, blind and deaf and dumb all together. He would have given any one of his other senses to have had it restored. To feel again its humming energy, its clear-sightedness, its directness and its intuitive guidance. He paced the streets of the city, stood behind the counter of the café and sat in Mrs Grund's kitchen. Waiting, till the days ran out.

He stood for the last time in the bedroom of Zak's house, his case packed and locked on the floor behind him, still waiting. Standing in the silence he listened for the slightest sound, the minutest beating against the air of movement, the soft clicking into place of thought. But the room was as empty, as powerless to help him, as his mind. In utter silence motes of dust drifted, eddied and bumped gently against one another, like stray, half-formed thoughts. He moved to the window and leaned his head on the glass, watching the chimney pots on the roofs opposite become black silhouettes against the fading sky, while he turned over and over in his head what he should say to Bel. How could he explain to her about little Miss Cat's Whiskers whose doll face had so ensnared him? How could he tell her that he was leaving Zak's house to go and live with her and her mother? That he had come to say goodbye. The outlines of the chimneys slowly dissolved into darkness and he knew that in the Grunds' house supper would long since have been cleared away. Perhaps he need say none of that to Bel. Perhaps all he need do was go to Hendrye Place, now, with his suitcase – just calling in, as a person might who was setting out on a long journey, to take leave of a friend – drop his suitcase heavily in front of her, stick out his hand and say, 'Goodbye.' Let her think whatever it was she wanted to think. Whatever would restore her dreams to her. His dreams might all have dissolved, but if he let her think that he had not given up, that he was setting out again on another stage of his journey, she might take heart once more. The moon rose and sailed slowly across the window pane, turning the city to stone. As it disappeared beyond the farthest roof, he moved away from the window, picked up the suitcase and left the house.

The streets were unusually empty and silent, unlit save for the white light of the moon. When he came to the narrow alley at the back of Bel's house it looked as dark as a cave, its close brick walls still warm with a reverberation of heat, like breathing. He began to climb the fire escape, his case clutched to his chest, the weight of it unbalancing him, slowing his heavy steps on the iron rungs, until at last he came out on the roof. As far as he could see roofs stretched away silver, etched with black crevasses. And he realised, suddenly, that he could indeed leave, now, like this, slipping away over the rooftops without excuses or goodbyes; just as he had always wanted to. The possibility – the reality of it – had been a secret kept even from himself, it was only now that he was here that he was free to go. To run without hindrance all along these roofs. Then leap to the next. And the next. On and on . . . He shivered, as if daunted by such freedom opening out before him. He would, nevertheless, go and say goodbye to Bel. Just to tell her. He tiptoed along the parapet of the roof. Her skylight looked as dark as the street below. If she was asleep he would not wake her. As he pushed open the door to the top landing, his case stuck in the narrow doorway, almost tripping him up, barring his way. He propped it up against a nearby chimney stack and went inside.

The house gave out its usual odour of cabbage and cats, and a silence so heavy that the whole building seemed cast

260

under a spell of sleep. There was no sound from Bel's room. He tried the door, expecting it to be locked, but at his touch it swung lightly open. The room was strangely lit with moon and shadows. Inside, he turned for the light switch and as he turned one of the shadows moved. It detached himself from the wall. Moonlight flickered on a mask of flint planes. A hand fell upon his shoulder, gripping it so hard that the muscles were paralysed. In the sudden familiarity of the pain all fear vanished. In the close smell of thick serge, the conviction that it must be his father beat away the fear that suffocated him. He gasped, dry-mouthed at speech.

'Come back for this have yer, son?'

Another shadow moved from the head of the bed. Delicately, from finger and thumb, he held a knife. Its handle gleamed silver in the moonlight but along the blade it was stained black and from the tip, as Robert watched, black drops gathered, swelled, and fell to the floor.

From then on, it seemed to Robert, life slid silently away from him and with it, slipping backwards and sideways into the past, went everybody he had ever known, until there were no people left, and he was alone. The police and court officials patiently shook their heads each time he tried to tell them who he was and what had really happened. Did he think, they asked him, that his young head was cleverer than all their accrued wisdom? They knew perfectly well who he was. They had sent their men to wait for him to return to the scene of his crime, for return such criminals always did, and he had walked straight into their hands. He had crept in over the roof – a criminal action in itself. His suitcase, packed for flight, had been found leaning against a chimney stack by one of their officers. He did not deny it was his suitcase, did he? Or that he had been an associate of the murdered girl? They regarded him sternly and sorrowfully, as though he was an obstinate child who would not admit he was lying, and sent him back to be locked up in his cell again. At last, bemused and exhausted, Robert fell silent. He stood mutely behind a carved wooden balustrade in a large, heavy-panelled room and watched while men in black presented first evidence of a victim and then, like a lost piece out of a jigsaw, evidence of a suspect to an old man in long white hair who listened intently, nodding all the while. The crime, he said, when everyone had fallen silent, was appalling; the criminal brilliantly apprehended. He only wished all crimes could be solved so efficiently. He would propose medals for the policemen. And in a mood of jubilation everyone went home.

They sent Robert home, too. He knew it was home by the way the sky looked between the bars and by over-hearing the guards talking in the passage outside at night. It felt like coming home. The rest of the world was com-pletely suspended, gone as if it had never existed. He lived deep inside himself in a kind of floating consciousness with the reverberation of the slow beating of his blood through the channels of his body often the only sound he heard for hours at a time. He felt himself finally at peace. Nothing was expected of him anymore; there were no decisions to make, no desires, no dreams. He lived at last a life of unthinking obedience: only this grey room and the closing of his eyes for sleep and the opening of them for wake-fulness.

They roused him one morning at dawn and hurried him downstairs between four warders. His unaccustomed, immobile feet slipped and stumbled on the concrete steps, he caught sight of their chips and stains like ragged frag-ments of the real world rushing past him. And then they were out in a courtyard. A courtyard filled with a light so new, so clear and bright that it dazzled him; it burst with such force upon him that it stifled all the dimness of the world in which he had been living. He could feel himself gasp at the clear air, taking breath after breath. The guards fell back and another man in uniform led him over to the wall of the courtyard. Even in the chill of early morning he could feel the sun's rays striking the stone and saw in the crevices tiny, curling green leaves. The man was speaking to him, reading from a paper that shook in his hands, but he could not hear him. The man fell silent, bent towards Robert and spoke again, repeating his last sentence. With difficulty Robert deciphered his meaning. 'Open the gates,' he heard himself say, 'and let me see the meadow again.'

The man looked doubtful, then signalled to one of the warders. They manacled his wrists and ankles and the man turned him away from the others in the courtyard to watch one side of the double gates slowly pulled back. And there it was before him, just as he had always remembered it: the short grass stiff with frost, the birch trees like grey smoke along one border of the meadow, and the bare elms down the other. And climbing up in front of him the railway embankment and above that the translucence of the sky, hanging like water. A sky so newly dawned it looked like the beginning of the world, and Robert, seeing it all, flung up his wrists with a croaking shout of joy. Instantly the brilliance exploded into darkness and he felt himself falling; falling through the skin of the world.